THE
LAST MOPHREY

THE
LAST MOPHREY

L. G. J. Layberry

SPELLMOUNT

This story is dedicated to
the memory of
my wife
Whose selfless devotion to our children and to me
Brought her to an early rest
In a Kentish churchyard
And
To my young friend Clare
Whose smile brightens the Sunday morning.

First published in 1986 by
Spellmount Ltd
12 Dene Way, Speldhurst
Tunbridge Wells, Kent TN3 0NX

©L. G. J. Layberry 1986

ISBN 0-946771-90-1

British Library Cataloguing in Publication Data

Layberry, L. G. J.
    The last Mophrey. – (Oakleigh Farm series)
    I. Title II. Series
    823'.914[F] PR6062.A95

Printed and bound in Great Britain by
Robert Hartnoll (1985) Limited
Bodmin, Cornwall

Chapter One

Robert Felton flicked a few straggling thorn twigs into the centre of the hot white ashes. They flared immediately, giving out a heat which caused him to stand back as if in surprise. He dug his fork into the ground at an oblique angle, crossed his elbows on top of it and leaned on them, allowing his thoughts to run in and out of his mind as they chose. Thorn-burning was a grand job for that exercise, especially so when the hedge trimmings had been there since the autumn, each heap drying out and settling into a compact mass. There was little to do, for the thorns ignited easily and burnt readily. The flames, fanned by a gentle March wind, flicked out their tongues in all directions, reaching the next brittle branch and feeding on it until all merged into a central holocaust that roared skyward, so high and fierce that one's face was scorched before there was time to stand aside. The faint smoke had an earthy tang and an ability to create a deep thirst and a healthy appetite. Also, one could conjure pictures out of the leaping flames, recapturing the distant past.

He walked down to the next fire and scraped in the circle of unburnt twigs, throwing them in a tiny heap into the middle of the hot charcoal. The flames flared and crackled for a few seconds, then died for want of sustenance. He continued down the line of fires, replenishing each one. As his boots scuffed the hitherto untouched furrows he noted automatically how friable the soil had become – slightly dusty on top and damp an inch or two down. One or two passes with the heavy harrows and the field would be ready for sowing. He would send Gerald with a pair of horses to harrow it tomorrow and Bill Marshall could drill the oats the following day. Bob Felton always planned as he worked and his plans generally worked out. He knew every inch of the farm for it had been his home for twenty years except for his absence at the war. He had come here as a runaway lad of sixteen in 1911 and now, in 1931, he was the boss. He owned the land – double the acreage now – in partnership with his father-in-law, but Arnold Ratcliffe at seventy was not half or even a quarter the man he had been in pre-war days. He suffered badly from asthma and was unable to get about at times, when his breathlessness was painful to see. However, his mind was still active and he had a tremendous flair for stock management, so he spent most of his time around the farmyard, seldom venturing out in the fields on foot. He would only attempt a longer tour when he could get one of the men to put the mare in the float so that he could ride round the field and breathe comfortably at the same time.

A dear old man, thought Felton, although a little testy at times. The most recent bee in his bonnet was that his grandson Arthur should become an auctioneer. Perhaps it was understandable, though. His own son Arthur was to have entered that profession had he not died in a tragic accident at an early age. Nearly eighteen years ago now, Felton recalled. He had been present in the last minutes of the boy's life. Recalling it filled him with a sweet melancholy, for the cheerful, lovable boy had been very dear to him. Two years later, Felton was at the Front when his own son had been born and he had not quarrelled with the decision of his wife to name the child after her dead brother. Her parents had been delighted, of course. Bob sometimes wondered if Mr Ratcliffe, as he got older, confused the personality of his dead son Arthur with that of his grandson Arthur, who was very much alive.

Felton remembered that the first Arthur had not wanted to be an auctioneer at all. Farming was all in all to him and the second Arthur had similar ideas. Robert had nothing against the Land Agency profession, and he would not have minded if his son had elected to join them. Membership of such a body did not necessarily rule out farming. A well-to-do agent could be a farmer as well, and often was. But he had no intention of forcing his son into something about which he was lukewarm. If Arthur wanted to concentrate on farming, then farming it should be, but he should go into it properly – college and a degree in Agriculture, at least. Cirencester would be the place – the Royal Agricultural College, they called it. He understood they taught practical, honest-to-goodness farming there. During the war he had met the son of the college farm manager – a man named Goodworth. Bob wondered if the same manager was still there, for he had been impressed by the man's record, character and ability. That was the sort of man to teach Arthur the finer points of farming and that was the place to learn them.

He went along the row of fires again, pushing in the unbent ends of the remaining twigs. He had a tidy mind and did not wish to leave sticks of varying lengths to be dragged all over the field by the harrows. He looked at his pocket watch. Just after four o'clock. Time to get back to the farm and help with the milking. He did not have to do this, for he employed eight men and lads as well as old

Ernie, the pensioner who pottered about on odd jobs. He had been employed on the farm since the turn of the century and the cottage in the stackyard which he had occupied for so long had been made over to him and his wife for the rest of their lives. It was Meg's idea originally, and neither her husband nor her father had dreamed of opposing her. The old chap was now seventy-three and amused himself with a bit of hedge-brushing, hoeing, and thistle-cutting when the weather was fair. Bob liked to see Ernie around for he provided a tangible link with the happy days of 1911 when Ernie, Mr Ratcliffe, the older son Sam and Bob himelf comprised the whole staff of the much smaller Oakleigh Farm of that time. They had worked hard and long in those days, but now with double the staff it was no longer necessary. However, Robert had become so used to the milking routine that he felt out of place when he did not take part. Moreover, his presence helped to keep the men up to scratch. They could not be allowed to slack these days for farming suffered from the slump as much as the rest of the country.

Walking slowly over the Derbyshire soil he breathed deeply, relishing the unmistakable tang of spring. Although the sun had gone in behind the clouds the afternoon light had a durable quality about it – a sense of endeavour as if it were trying to stretch itself as far into the evening as it could. Every year he felt like this and he always looked forward to it. There was no feeling so exhilarating as the awakening of Nature. The insects emerged sleepily, there was movement and noise among the birds and the whitethorn hedges opened their bright green buds – 'bread and cheese', the local children called them as they pinched off a few and ate them on their way to school.

He strode out over the furrows, delighting in the friable quality of the drying soil as his heavy boots broke through the fragile crust. He could just hear the beat of the tractor-engine in Upland Flat where Dick was cultivating deeply for potatoes and he struck off in that direction. Arriving there his feet sank in the deep tilth to his ankles and he decided that to walk across to Dick would be too exhausting. He contented himself with waving a greeting to the driver who acknowledged it, keeping his eye on the boss in case some new instruction should be signalled. But the farmer continued down the extreme edge of the potato-ground into Bramble Close where the anaemic green of the winter turf was assuming a brighter tinge in patches. This pleased him for this pasture was set aside for an early turn-out of young cattle. The next two fields were hay-meadows where Charlie, the lad who drove the third pair of horses, was chain-harrowing to break up last year's dung-pats and this year's molehills. There was sufficient length of grass for the harrows to produce the familiar striped effect of two shades of green. As one looked up the field, the strip of grass leaning towards the viewer was much darker than the adjacent strip on which one saw the lighter back of the flattened blades. It was another undeniable piece of evidence to support the arrival of spring.

Charlie was a willing lad and the farmer paused to say a few words for he was always anxious to stimulate keenness. With the enthusiasm of youth, Charlie was proud of his team, ludicrously so really, for they were the two oldest and least valuable horses on the place. Felton soon walked on and two pairs of horses came into view on the brow of the next field – the Leg of Mutton – where Bill Marshall and Gerald Green were drilling oats. As they had obviously seen him talking to Charlie he would have to do the same by them, for petty jealousies run deep in a small community, as he well knew.

Bill Marshall, the head waggoner, had been at Oakleigh for fourteen years. He was nearly sixty now but still upright, active and strong, capable of driving a pair of horses for nine hours a day in the roughest conditions. His ploughing was still clean-cut, his drilling as accurate as ever, his output undiminished. He was drilling with a pair of black geldings, both born on the farm, for horse-breeding – introduced as an emergency measure during the war – had been continued on a limited scale.

Gerald the second waggoner was newly married and a recent arrival at Oakleigh. He occupied the cottage at Lower Sucklings and was proving himself a diligent workman, pressing hard to learn as much as he could from Bill so that he would be able to follow in the older man's shoes.

Mr Felton stood and watched from the headland as the two powerful blacks, each with a white blaze, nodded their heads up and down as they pulled the outfit with swift strides. The disc coulters of the machine curved up litle sprays of earth as they revolved, partially covering the adjacent row of seed, indicating just how perfect were the soil conditions. Gerald drove his harrows close behind the drill, overlapping half its width. A cloud of dust accompanied him and the faint ruckling sound of the harrows as the tines penetrated the loose soil was yet another of those welcome sounds of spring which so pleased Robert Felton. The drill horses pulled right up to the hedge, paused, snorted, then gently sidled round so that the inner wheel of the turn screwed round without moving its position.

'Whoa!' said the waggoner and turned to his employer, awaiting comment.

'The job's just about perfection, Bill,' the farmer said, beaming with pleasure. The warm sweaty tang of the horses, the dust of the seed-bed, the appetising flavour of the clean, bold grain, and the fresh smell of the newly-moved earth made an aura of such satisfaction as to be almost intoxicating.

'Ar, it is, Gaffer. You wunna get corn sowed much better than this.'

'You'll finish the field?' Mr Felton said, eyeing with some misgiving the wide strip remaining.

'Oo, ar. We'll none come in till the job's done. An hour late mebbe, but the 'osses'll stand it. They're i' good fettle.'

'I'd like to see it finished, that's certain. Don't like little bits left overnight. Breaks up the pattern of the next day's work, and if it rains the sowing might be delayed for days.'

'It'll none rain toneight, Gaffer!'

'I think you're right, Bill, and if it's a fine morning I want you to put the cambridge roll over this tomorrow. Gerald can harrow Twentylands – I've just burnt the thorns – with the drag harrows and Charley can put the super on behind him. If we're lucky, we might get it drilled the day after.' He waved the drill-horses on and watched closely while Gerald gingerly turned his team round, slowly and carefully, to avoid tangling the harrows.

Felton came to the farm through the rickyard pasture. The cowman Ned, and his lad Tommy were tying up the cows after their pre-milking drink at the tank in the yard. They seemed only half willing to leave the open March daylight for the semi-gloom of the sheds. Perhaps they too sensed that spring was on the way. Perhaps they even dreamed of grass-day, hopefully only six weeks away. Bob grinned to himself; these were not the thoughts of a farmer.

There was no need for him to go into the cowshed yet; Frank and Len would be in from the fields in a few minutes to help with the milking. Plenty of time for the boss to have a cup of tea.

He walked through the cooling-shed where the maid, with a great deal of clamour, was preparing the utensils to receive the milk, through the scullery and into the great kitchen. Meg immediately moved one of the murmuring kettles to the centre of the range where it boiled in less than a minute. There were always kettles – polished copper and shining black – on the hob at Oakleigh for Meg followed her mother's tradition of instant hospitality.

'You've had a long afternoon, Bob,' she said. 'Sit down and have a cup of tea in comfort.'

Her husband kissed her as he always did when entering or leaving the house. His love for this comely woman with her full figure, pink cheeks and hair of bold gold had increased rather than diminished in the twenty years which had elapsed since he first set eyes on her in that same kitchen.

'I stopped and finished the burning,' he replied, 'to clear the field for Gerald to harrow there tomorrow. Besides, it was a grand afternoon to be out there – pleasant job, perfect conditions, why should I leave it?'

'I could have come and given you a hand,' interposed his father-in-law who was already seated at the table. 'There was nowt much for me to do round the yard here.'

'You don't want to walk as far as that, Dad,' Bob told him. 'It's too strenuous for your asthma.'

'I haven't got asthma today!'

'Not now, perhaps, but the exertion might have brought it on and you wouldn't have been able to walk back. I'd have had to leave the job to fetch the float for you. You're better to stay near the yard unless you're prepared to put the hoss in and ride wherever you want to go.'

'I'm not *quite* old enough for that yet,' remonstrated the old farmer. 'I'm only *just* seventy, you know.'

'Get outside this tea, you two, now I've made it,' Meg said shortly.

Bob sipped at his cup. His tea was dark and strong, scalding hot, with a good dash of rich milk and plenty of sugar. He let it roll over his tongue and swallowed slowly.

'My, you make a delicious cup of tea, Meg,' he said, not for the first time.

'Well, I ought to – I've had enough experience. Would you like some shortbreads? I made them this afternoon. Edith, take your head out of that *Rainbow* and get the dish of biscuits from the second shelf of the larder.'

'Can't you get them yourself?' grumbled the girl, but nevertheless left her seat at once to forestall her mother's rebuke. She was ten, big for her age as became her mother's daughter, and her features seemed an exact blend of both her parents. Her hair was slightly darker than Meg's and her eyes had the deep thoughtful expression of her father, her chin the same rock-like outline. She fetched a dish filled with the golden-brown shortbread, placed it on the table, seized a handful and continued reading her comic.

They all regarded her fondly, for this wayward but lovable little girl was the favourite of the household. She was oblivious of their admiration, or pretended to be for she knew that her mother would quickly correct any tendency to conceit. She was still attending the village school and eagerly looked forward to the time when she would start at the High School at Burton and travel with her brother on the school train morning and evening. She had been promised a new bicycle for the ride to Willington station.

Bob was enjoying his second cup of tea when his son Arthur skidded by the kitchen window. They heard his cycle bump to rest against the wall and in a few seconds he rushed in breathlessly, swung off his satchel, hung it on the back of a windsor chair and made for the stairs door.

'Have a cup of tea, Arthur,' said his mother. 'It's all ready.'

'No thanks, Mum,' he shouted. 'I want to get changed and out milking,' and he hurried on upstairs.

'No need for all that rush,' grumbled his grandfather. 'We've enough men on this place to milk the cows without the son of the house rushing out as soon as he comes home from school. We're not exactly smallholders! He ought to pay more attention to his studying if he's going into the auctioneering and land agency business.'

'Leave him alone, Dad,' Meg said reprovingly. 'He's only young once! Let him do what he wants to do. We ought to be pleased to think that he's keen on the farm work. Plenty of lads nowadays seem to want to get away from it. Get on their motorbikes and rip away to the town. Anyway, we're not sure that we want him to be an auctioneer. There'd be several years of dreary paperwork before he could take his exams and I'm sure he wouldn't like that, although I've no doubt he can pass anything he wants to. He's in the middle of one now – matriculation, isn't it Bob – and he's taking it in his stride. At least, he never mentions it.'

'Arthur can do anything,' Edith said proudly, throwing aside her *Rainbow*.

'I did think you two would see eye to eye with me on this,' grumbled the old man. 'You know I've always wanted an auctioneer in the family. I'd set my heart on your brother Arthur taking it up, but Fate decided otherwise.' He sighed heavily.

'I'm not going to force the lad into a job he's no liking for, Dad, that's quite definite. Later on he may take to this idea of yours – there's time enough. But if he chooses farming I'll see that he

11

learns it properly. He'll go to an agricultural college and take a degree course. I've been thinking it over this afternoon. If he wants to stick to farming, and frankly I hope he does, he'll do a three-year course at Cirencester Agricultural College.'

'College? A farmer attending college! What a daft idea! Farmers don't need college training. The job can only be learned by practical experience as you should well know. And Cirencester of all places! It sticks in my mind that it's on the hills – poor, thin, stony soil, mostly arable. Nothing like what we've got here. How will that help him?'

'It must be a good thing to learn something of other farming practices. It broadens the mind and makes it more receptive to new ideas. I know you and I got by without it but farming's changing, Dad – getting more scientific. Milk recording, balanced rationing, selective breeding, Grade A milk production, fertilising according to the requirements of the soil as well as the crop. We've been doing it successfully by rule of thumb for years, but that won't do much longer. Another thing – with this depression creeping on us and bringing falling prices we may have to change our policy and reorganise things so that we can manage with less labour. Those are the sort of things Arthur'd learn at college.'

'Well, if Arthur's going to college to learn how to sack some of our men, I'm dead against it,' Meg broke in swiftly. 'They're all old friends – most of 'em, and I'd like to see them all stay here until they're too old to work – like old Ernie Wagstaff.'

'Trust you to over-simplify things and take a sentimental view, Meg. Arthur's coming downstairs now. We'll go out and milk a few cows if they haven't done 'em all. We can talk this over another time. There's no hurry.'

Chapter Two

The Feltons were well pleased with their family. Arthur was clever mentally, skilful with his hands, keen overall and he loved the farm on which he had been born. Edith was bright, pretty, gentle and argumentative. She would have been utterly spoiled, certainly by the menfolk, had not her mother laid down strict rules against it. Meg had been spoiled herself to some degree but she was convinced that she had not and was determined that her daughter should benefit from similar firm treatment.

Bob was delighted that his son took pains with everything he attempted – milking, working horses, riding – for he and Edith each had a pony – and of course tractor-driving. There was only one tractor at Oakleigh and Arthur was delighted to drive it at mealtimes to relieve Dick Marshall, the regular driver who also, from choice, looked after the riding horses. Dick did not mind the boss' son taking over the tractor in his absence for he sensed the lad had a natural aptitude for the job. Moreover Dick was fond of all the Feltons and the Ratcliffe family as well, for he had come to Oakleigh as a boy of fourteen when Meg's elder brother Sam had been the principal man on the farm and Bob Felton had been at the War. Sam had enlisted at the end of the 1917 harvest, declaring that the arrival of Bill Marshall and his son Dick made his own continued presence unnecessary. Sam had been killed early the next year. Dick remembered him well and liked what he remembered. Sam's mother, the mistress of the farm, had never got over the loss of her only surviving son and had died a couple of years later, on the day following little Edith's birth. Dick remembered that too, and Bob's sister Betty who had lived on the farm during those years. She had been instrumental in saving him from drowning, for on his very first day driving a pair of horses he had ambitiously driven his mowing-machine too close to the river bank. A huge chunk of earth had given way causing him, his horses and machine to plunge backwards into a deep part of the Trent and he was trapped under his machine in the swift current. Even now, thirteen years later, Dick always breathed a prayer of gratitude when he thought about it. Fortunately for him, his father had been in the same field and, rushing over, had held his son's head out of the water. Betty appeared, too, and, inexperienced as she then was, had contrived to hitch the other pair of horses in front of Major and Ginger and pull the whole outfit up the steep bank on to firm ground.

Dick had worshipped Betty after that, of course, and when she became interested in riding he had volunteered to look after the riding horses. Sadly, a few years later she had married the rich Edwin Salt who had been a pupil at the farm and they had taken a place down south – Oxford or Buckingham, he wasn't quite sure which.

Dick's feelings towards Meg had always been slightly different, for as a boy he had been afraid of her. She had been the boss when the Marshalls arrived, managing the farm while her parents were grieving over Sam's death. When Mr Ratcliffe recovered he had been a kind, if exacting, employer and Meg's husband Bob, who took over when he returned from the War, had been generous and understanding but something of a slave-driver, wanting a lot done every day. Still, when Dick had asked Mavis, the farmhouse maid, to marry him, the Feltons had built him a new cottage on land nearer in to the village. Not many farmers would have done it, he told himself, and he thought he had every reason to be friendly to the Felton children. The other men on the farm, and their families, felt the same way. Arthur and Edith were favourites with everybody.

When Bob Felton had bought his first tractor in 1922 he had driven it himself for the first season. The extra two hundred acres purchased at the sale of the Hartnall Hall estate made a great deal more work for the tractor at busy times and Bob found that he could not abdicate his responsibility for the general management of the farm to stick to the tractor seat. So he had trained Dick who was then eighteen and the lad had remained the designated tractor-driver ever since. The tractor had been renewed twice in the ensuing nine years and sometimes Bob had thought of buying a second one, but since mechanical power was only needed for ploughing and deep cultivating, he had always stuck to his original assessment of the farm's power requirements – one tractor, three pairs of horses for field work plus a fast trotting horse for running the milk to the station and other odd jobs with the float.

The four hundred acres of the enlarged Oakleigh Farm was nearly half arable and this included about forty acres of potatoes. For this crop, Bob insisted on deep and thorough cultivations before the ridges were drawn and this kept Dick and the tractor busy throughout the second half of March and the first half of April. The work was still going on when Arthur and Edith started their school holidays and Arthur lost no time in laying claim to an hour's driving each day while Dick went home to dinner.

Plainly, Farmer Felton had no objection to this, nor had Arthur's mother and she willingly put aside his dinner to keep hot until he returned an hour later. Edith, who adored her brother, frequently absented herself as well, often to be near him at his work if the weather was fine. Sometimes she watched from the edge of the field but more often sat on the tractor's wide mudguard, her long legs dangling in the well.

On Easter Monday, which although designated as a Bank Holiday by the general public was certainly not a farm holiday, Dick was cultivating for the third time over a distant fifteen-acre field known as Park Hill – old grassland broken up for the first time during the War. There were still a few trees of the old parkland here and there. Half-a-dozen oaks stood in line on top of a short steep bank, roughly in the middle of the field's length and about a quarter of the way in from the other direction.

Arthur took over just as Dick had reached this point and the boy's second trip across the field took him under the trees on the edge of the bank. Edith was not in sight when he started his run. At that moment she was wandering along the lane which approached the field from the other direction when she met Dick on his bicycle. As they met she called and asked him where her brother was.

'Scuffling for taters in Park 'Ill,' he shouted back over his shoulder as he spun down the slope on his way home.

The girl hurried on and entered the field gate. Arthur was at the far end, running a short way along the headland before turning in for the return trip. She waved vigorously but he did not see her, concentrating as he was on his steering, the wheeled cultivator, locally called a 'scuffle', bucking from side to side on its draw-pin. Arthur straightened up his machine, gripping the steering wheel tightly with both hands as the front wheels jarred and twisted when striking the huge clods which littered the field from the first two scufflings. He kept his eyes fixed straight ahead as he guided the tractor along the very edge of the bank.

Edith set off across the field at an angle to meet him, walking with difficulty on the rough surface, still waving as she stumbled along. Arthur spotted his young sister at last, took his right hand from its steering and waved a brotherly greeting. He was fond of Edith and welcomed her presence on his lonely tractor-driving sessions, for among other things it enabled him to display his prowess. As he released his hold the nearside front wheel of the machine struck a large, solid clod, bucked violently, twisted sideways and as the desperate youth tried to correct the steering the offside front wheel scraped heavily over the edge of the bank.

It hovered in mid-air for a short second then dropped; the offside hind wheel spewed clay and grass as it groped its way over the edge, and as Edith glanced across she saw the nearside hind wheel raise itself grotesquely in mid-air. She screamed in terror as the roaring tractor turned a somersault over the edge out of her sight. As it passed out of her view she saw the cultivator, released from its place by the dropping out of the draw-pin when the coupling was upside down, bounce over and over further down the slope. Her heart thumping with fright the girl tried to run over the hundred yards or so of rough ground which separated her from the tractor but she could make only slow progress for there were so many clods strewn over the deep crumbly soil. Smaller particles fell into the tops of her heavy school shoes making running even more painful.

She reached the scene at last. It had seemed a very long time but was scarcely more than a minute. At first she thought Arthur was dead for he lay on his back, his face was white and twisted and his legs pinned to the ground by one of the huge iron wheels. The engine was still running, but through its roar she fancied she could hear her brother's moans. One wheel was poised in mid-air revolving meaninglessly for the engine had remained in gear.

Edith bent down low to Arthur's face and sobbed with relief when she saw his lips move. His eyes were closed in pain but when she touched him he opened them and recognised her.

'Ede – thank God!' he tried hard to shout loud enough to pierce the beat of the engine. 'Turn off the juice! It might set alight! The little tap under the tank marked G and K. Set it halfway between the letters. Then screw down the tank caps if they're leaking. Run and get help. I can't stand much of this! All the weight . . .'

She jumped away from him, ran round the overturned machine and stood in close to the gently-oscillating front wheel. She knew that if one of the lugs of the revolving rear wheel struck her it would push her to the ground with broken bones. Reaching out with both her hands she gripped the little tap and with difficulty straightened it to an upright position between the two letters – K for kerosene and G for gasoline – the American names for paraffin and petrol, as Arthur had often told her. She knew the engine would run until the little box below the tap was empty of fuel – one or two minutes. She had seen it many times. She had also seen Arthur and Dick open a little T-screw beneath the box to let out the fuel and stop the engine more quickly. She reached over again and loosened the screw several turns; the warm fuel trickled out and the engine spluttered, coughed and died.

In the tingling silence she could hear Arthur's low moans.

'Good old Sis,' he gasped. 'Now get help. Run!'

The little girl kept her head and thought rapidly. To cross the rough field and then run over four others and along the lane to the farm might take twenty minutes. The men would be at dinner and so would the horses. To bring them out and collect the necessary tackle and get to the spot might take half-an-hour. Of course Dad could come out with the car but he might not be at home at that moment and no one else could bring the car, for Mummy had never learned to drive. Edith felt she could not leave her brother in that terrible pain for nearly an hour. She must try and help him herself. But what could she do? She was only ten-and-a-half and, although big and strong for her age as became a farmer's daughter, she obviously could not lift the ton weight of the tractor or even lever the wheel up. That would take several men. She knelt down by Arthur again.

'Please, Ede – hurry,' he moaned.

He lay on his back with his left leg crossed slightly over his right, with the knee slightly bent. The iron rim lay on top of his legs, just below the knee. His limbs were taking the whole weight of the machine, for on each side of his trapped legs the rim did not touch the ground. An idea came to her. If she could not lift the wheel perhaps she could scrape away the soft earth beneath his legs and by lowering them relieve the crushing effect. But the wheels would have to be wedged up so they did not sink as well.

Edith looked about her wildly. Almost directly above her, on the top of the bank stood the end oak tree of the line. A few short ends of broken branches were leaning up against the trunk, placed there out of the way of the cultivations. She scrambled up the bank, stumbled to the tree and grabbed the two thickest of the logs and rolled them down the bank in front of her. Retrieving one, she tried to slide it underneath the edge of the tractor wheel but there was not enough clearance. She knelt down in her black stockings and scraped away the hard knobs of loose surface soil with both hands. Then she took up the log again and pushed it hard in the groove she had made until it was well wedged under the iron rim. Arthur seemed to have fainted for he was making no sound. She ran round his head, took up the other branch and repeated the process but it required more effort and more scraping for the wood was thicker... Momentarily, she laid her grubby hand on

17

Arthur's forehead. He opened his eyes, moaned weakly and muttered 'Get help, Ede, get help. You can't do owt!'

'I'll get your legs out Art,' she said valiantly and knelt down again on her sore knees, scraping and tearing at the loose but brick-hard fragments of clay. Her fingernails filled with dirt, sharp particles of grit scratched her skin. Soon there was a great heap of soil round her knees and a shallow trough beside Arthur's leg. She had removed the earth to the full depth of the cultivator's working but her brother's legs were still trapped. She knew she had not quite reached the full depth of the winter's ploughing but the remaining layer was too hard for her small fingers.

Remembering that Dick usually carried on the tractor an old hoe with a short handle for cleaning his plough in muddy conditions or for scraping the tractor wheels before going on the road, she raised herself, kicked away the heap of soil round her legs and peered over the edge of the mudguard. Yes, the hoe was there, pinched tightly between the axle and the front windshield. Unable to reach it from where she stood, she stepped over Arthur, went round to the back of the tractor and snatched the tool from its place. It was a slightly curved dutch hoe, admirable for her purpose and she lay on her front beside her brother and, using the hoe as a tiny spade, dug away at the firm damp earth beside and partly under Arthur's leg. Every minute or so she put down the hoe and scraped the loose soil behind her with her hands. If only she had her little garden spade! The time was passing and she was troubled by the thought that perhaps she should have run for help after all.

Arthur was taking more interest now and encouraged her efforts, having grasped their import.

'Good old Ede,' he said weakly. 'You're doing grand!'

Thus stimulated, the girl dug, gouged and scraped away vigorously, reaching Arthur's foot with difficulty, for it was near the centre of the wheel and there was not much room. She removed the full depth of the ploughing and got down to the subsoil. It was firm and clayey and she could make little impression. But she had excavated a shallow trench three inches or so deep, parallel with Arthur's right leg which was poised on the brink of the depression.

'Can you move your leg now, Arthur?'

The boy tried, whimpered and shook his head. 'It hurts too much.'

'Try again when I pull your trousers.'

Edith knelt down, reached under the wheel and gripped the

loose denim in her finger and thumb, then jerked suddenly. Arthur gave a little shriek but his leg slumped into the groove she had made. It was free of any pressure for the wheel remained poised on the wood Edith had placed in position and Arthur gave a gentle sob of relief. The right leg had been partly trapped under the left, which still remained wedged, but not so firmly. Edith knelt again by her brother's left side and scratched and scraped vigorously with her burning fingers. No need to use the hoe this time. She kicked away the heap of loose soil from Arthur's body, then gave a little tug to his left leg which sank an inch or more away from the pressing iron band.

'Good old Ede,' Arthur said again. 'By gum, these legs do hurt,' he added as the circulation returned. He raised himself on his hips, placed his knuckles on the ground and levered himself backwards inch by inch. Edith ran round to help him, putting her hands under his armpits. Then his boots would not quite clear the wheel and she ran back and held them flat and sideways, one at a time until Arthur was right clear of the overturned machine.

'What are we going to do now?' Edith asked, quite prepared to leave the organising to her brother now that he was free.

'I'll try and stand up,' he began, then looked at his pocket watch. 'It's still going! Half past twelve. Dick won't be back for half-an-hour at least.'

They heard a horrified shout and looked up to see Dick stumbling across the field with great bouncing strides. On reaching home he had started his dinner, but gradually the danger of leaving a young driver to operate on top of that steep bank had dawned on him and he bolted the rest of the meal and raced back to the field.

'Good God! What's all this?' he panted as he arrived at the scene and took everything in with one swift glance.

'By gum, thee's had a rare escape, lad. You might 'a bin killed! What's the Gaffer gunna say about this, Ah'd like to know?' He looked at Edith, then down again at the tractor and the broken mounds of disturbed soil. 'Thee's a rare lass, Edith, and no mistake! Dug your brother out all on your own! My, you're a reight 'un. Just like your Auntie Betty who pulled me out o' th' Trent twelve or thirteen year ago when I were drownin'.'

He helped Arthur struggle to his feet. 'It's no good waiting 'ere. Canst walk to my bike if I 'elp thee? Ah'll run you down to th' Doctor's on me crossbar. You'd best get 'ome, Edith, and tell 'em about it. Oh – you can tell Gaffer there's nowt wrong wi' tractor as far as Ah can see. Ah think Ah can get it back on its wheels.

There's a fencing strainer i' the barn at Clayfields. Ah'll get it and strain from the oak tree and pull her back on her feet wi'out trouble. Get off now, lass. Come on, Arthur, lean on me as much as you can.'

They limped away across the kibbly ground while Edith hurried home, feeling dirty and dishevelled. Even her hair was full of earthy dust. The family had just finished their second course when she entered the kitchen and the maid Gladys was pouring out the after-dinner cups of tea. Edith went in quietly but her mother was already looking in her direction. She put down her cup so violently that the tea spilled, and she jumped to her feet.

'Good gracious me, girl! What ever have you been up to? Just look at your clothes!'

'Oh Mum, I had to . . .'

'Don't make excuses,' said her mother crossly. 'You've been up to some of your tomboy tricks with Arthur, I've no doubt.' She snatched at Edith's pleated skirt. 'Goodness, the state of your knickers and stockings! You look as if you've been dragged feet first by a runaway horse.' Meg was working herself up into a peak of temper and rebuke. 'You'd better get up those stairs to bed, my girl, and stay there without any dinner or tea. Get those filthy clothes off and have a bath!'

'But Mum, I want to tell you . . .'

'Don't argue with me, Edith. Go to bed at once! If you don't go up this instant, I'll follow you up there and tan your bare bottom.' She gave the girl a not very gentle slap on the shoulder and pushed her towards the hall door. Edith dropped her head, sniffled a little, and went out, closing the door behind her slowly and gently, fearful of exacerbating her mother's temper.

Bob and Mr Ratcliffe looked at each other in faint embarrassment. They were not at all pleased with Meg's exhibition of petulant authority.

'You're a bit hard on her, Meg,' Bob said mildly. 'Why didn't you let the kid explain? Could have been accidental!'

'There's nothing to explain. Edith knows perfectly well she shouldn't come home in that state. I just won't have it! She must learn to be lady-like.'

'I don't remember that you were so very lady-like at ten,' grumbled her father. 'I don't like to see my Edith bullied. I'm very fond of her and so is Bob'.

'You men! Always taking the part of a pretty girl, no matter what she's done. She's my daughter and I love her too, but I'm not going to spoil her or let you two spoil her either. I'm going to be

20

strict with her and not let her go wild. It won't do her any harm to go to bed or to have a clout or two for that matter. Anyway,' she added as they heard the sudden gushing of the water, 'she had to go up for a bath. Oh well, if you're so concerned she can come down at tea-time, but she'll go without her dinner!'

The men, having gained a point, sat for a few minutes gazing out at the empty yard, but a little less glumly than previously. They heard the faint beat of a motor engine and in a few minutes a newish Morris Major purred up to the window and pulled up with a slight jerk. Gladys recognised it first.

'Why, it's Doctor Whittaker in his new car,' she exclaimed, 'and Arthur with him!'

As they gazed in astonishment, the doctor ran round the front of the car and helped Arthur, white and limping, out of the passenger seat. Meg and Bob rushed out through the scullery, the cooling shed and out on to the yard. The excitement caused Mr Ratcliffe to breathe heavily with his asthma and he could not follow them.

'It's all right, Mum,' Arthur said, smiling weakly. 'I'm not hurt too bad. And the tractor's not damaged either, Dad – at least, not much.'

'Tractor – damage – what's all this about? What the devil's happened?' demanded his father in consternation.

'She turned over on the bank and trapped me,' Arthur explained, 'and Ede scraped the soil away and got me out from underneath. Didn't she tell you? I told her to. The silly madam, what got into her? I'll give her a good talking to. Where is she?'

'She's having a bath,' said her mother hurriedly. 'Came home in such a state.' Then she realised she had not greeted the doctor who was supporting Arthur by his shoulders. 'Sorry, Doctor. Do come in. What's the verdict? So good of you to bring Arthur home.'

They all went into the house, Bob taking Arthur out of the doctor's hands.

'Arthur's had a lucky escape, Mrs Felton,' Doctor Whittaker said as he sat down easily in the Windsor armchair. He had known this farmhouse all his life, having taken over his father's practice. 'No bones broken, thank goodness. Only extensive bruising and some lacerations. But he's suffering from shock and will have to stay in bed for a week at least.'

'I can't do that,' Arthur interrupted anxiously. 'There's all that potato ground to get ready!'

'No more tractor-driving for you this holiday, young man,' said

21

the doctor firmly, 'and unless I'm quite satisfied, you won't go back to school either. And you can thank your lucky stars that your plucky young sister prevented you from lying under that wheel for a very long time.'

'Oh yes, I must go up and see Edith about that,' Meg said, reddening slightly. 'Will you excuse me, Doctor?'

'I'm just going, Mrs Felton. I dropped Arthur in on my way to my Repton calls. Be sure he gets to bed before the reaction sets in. He might as well have his lunch first I suppose.' He took his departure and Meg set off upstairs leaving Gladys to put out Arthur's dinner.

Edith finished her bath and came sorrowfully out of the bathroom in her nightdress. She heard her mother's foot on the lower stairs and, still fearing Meg's temper, she hurried up the second flight to her own room, hoping to be in bed before her mother arrived and accused her of loitering. Edith lay with her back towards the door, a few tears of hurtful misunderstanding still welling in her eyes. To her great surprise, instead of further scolding, her mother pulled her over in the bed, gathered her up, hugged and kissed her.

'Oh Edith, my dear, I'm so sorry I was cruel to you. My temper again, and jumping to conclusions too, accusing you of being careless with your clothes when all the time you'd been rescuing your brother. Don't cry now, silly girl,' – for the tears were running fast and free – 'you're crying more now than when I scolded you. Now get dressed. I'll get you some clothes out of the airing cupboard and you can come down and have your dinner and tell us all about it.'

She waited while the child dressed and they went down together.

'I feel so ashamed,' Meg said contritely as they all sat round watching Arthur and Edith attack their belated meal, for the boy's terrifying experience had not affected his appetite. 'This is history repeating itself with a vengeance. In 1918 I sent Betty off to bed in similar fashion when she came home bedraggled. I thought she had been stupid and careless when in fact she had been pulling young Dick out of the Trent.'

'All right, Meg, we all forgive you,' her father said benignly. 'Now we want to hear from these two exactly what happened out there.'

For once Bob and Meg allowed their son and daughter to speak at the meal table and even with their mouths full. The story lost nothing in the telling as the two youngsters overlapped each other, prompted, contradicted and argued. Edith, in particular, enjoyed the attention and Arthur, to do him justice, would not deny her her moment of triumph.

'What I can't understand,' said their grandfather when the last chapter had been told, 'is how a girl of ten . . .'

'I'm ten-and-a-half, Grandad,' she corrected him.

'. . . could possibly think out such a plan and put it into effect. Why, I reckon it would have taken me an hour to think of it! How did you do it, my love?'

Now that the excitement was over, Edith was nonchalant about her part in it.

'I saw something like it at the pictures,' she said casually. 'Last year, I think it was. It came into my mind straightaway.'

'Well, thank the Lord for your memory, then. I'm sure Arthur will. And while this is fresh in our minds, I'd like to point out to all of you that this sort of thing might not have happened if Arthur had been studying for auctioneering instead of planning to be a farmer!'

Bob sighed resignedly but Arthur said cheerfully, 'Don't you worry so much, Grandad. Tell you what, when I leave school I'll study at home for the Land Agent's exams, whatever they are.'

'I'll hold you to that, young feller,' said his grandfather.

Chapter Three

Arthur accepted his enforced stay in bed very badly. He had never been kept in bed for more than day at a time since he had passed out of the phase of normal childish ailments and to be imprisoned there day after day of bright spring weather was outrageous. It was a chastening experience for the boy to be told that the field work was going ahead almost as usual and that his assistance was not greatly missed.

Edith of course was her brother's slave, fetching and carrying for him incessantly, taking him news of the farm and the men, the cows, the horses and the progress in the field work. She suffered him to read aloud to her some of his favourite books, and then returned the compliment by reading him her own, which he tolerated for rather shorter periods. They played draughts and cards – 'Strip Jack Naked' – for hours, and Edith carried up the portable gramophone and a box of their favourite records, mostly the songs of Ted Gammon whom they remembered so well.

In spite of Arthur's natural disgust at being confined, the attic bedroom, which had been occupied by their father when he had first arrived at the farm, and later on by his sister, Auntie Betty, when she came, was bright, warm and cheerfully untidy. In the chill April evenings ash logs burned freely in the old open grate. Edith spent the whole of each evening tending to her brother's wants and only withdrew to her own room next door at the latest possible moment and then only at her mother's insistence.

In the absence of the children, Bob, Meg and her father were able to discuss their problems freely as they enjoyed their own log fire in the huge overcrowded parlour.

'We've got to reward young Edith in some way or other for making such a brave showing to help Arthur,' Mr Ratcliffe said pointedly on the first evening they were alone. 'What are you going to do about it?'

'We've been thinking about it, Dad,' Meg replied. 'The only thing we can think of so far is to buy her the new bike already promised and to send her to the High School a term earlier than she expects – immediately after Easter, in fact. This means she'll have at least one term travelling to Burton with Arthur. He can watch her on the bike and take care of her on the train as well, and that will please her and reassure us.'

'Can you get her in at such short notice?'

'I hope so, Dad. They still take fee-paying pupils, you know. I'll go and see Mr Greening first though. Don't want to offend our local school teachers unnecessarily. I'll call and see him at the Schoolhouse tomorrow morning.'

At dinnertime the next day Meg was bursting with news.

'Mr Greening was very helpful,' she told them. 'He telephoned the Headmistress at her home in Bretby and explained the position. She agreed at once to see me and I'm to go to her house tomorrow. Nice of her to deal with it in the holiday week, isn't it? Mr Greening said he was sorry to lose his brightest pupil, but he knew she'd be going when she was eleven, anyway. There's a nice compliment for you, Edith.'

'I don't know what you're talking about, Mum. What *is* all this? It's something to do with me and I don't know anything about it. It's not fair!'

'It means this, Edie,' said her father, beaming on her. 'Instead of you going back to Hartnall School, we're going to get you into the Burton High School. It looks as if I'll have to drive you and your mother to Bretby tomorrow. Tell you what, we'll come back through Burton and buy your new bike which we promised you for your birthday. And we're doing all this because we're pleased with the way you helped Arthur out from under the tractor.'

The girl's eyes shone.

'Oh, good egg! New bike, new school, new clothes!' Then her face fell again. 'But I shan't see my friends at Hartnall school again to say good-bye.'

'Heavens above!' said her mother. 'The things kids say these days! Your friends are not hundreds of miles away, child. If you so desperately want to say goodbye to them you'd better invite them to a party here. That is, if the bank can stand it after paying for the bike, the school and the uniform. How about it, Bob?'

'Well,' said her husband cautiously. 'Things are certainly tight this year and getting tighter with all this foreign food being dumped into the country, but there's enough in the kitty for Edith's tea party, I think.' Then he added, 'Particularly as most of it will come out o' the housekeeping and it'll be your problem anyway.'

On the following Monday morning Edith set off proudly in her new uniform, carrying her new satchel, on her new bicycle to her new school. Arthur, happily recovered and consequently good-tempered, was no less proud to have his smart little sister in his charge. He rode carefully on her offside the four miles to

Willington station, showed her where to store her machine, how to buy her season-ticket. There were other High School girls joining the train but Arthur insisted that Edith should ride in his carriage, certainly for the first few days.

The pattern was set for the summer term and Edith was thrilled with her place in it. She found her homework rather tiresome at first since it reduced the amount of playing time she had hitherto enjoyed before and after tea. But help from her competent brother was always available and she soon became adept at dispatching an evening's homework quickly enough to allow her some time for her other activities.

She was a rather solitary child and although she had complained at leaving her school friends in the village, she had, in fact, rarely played with them outside school hours. Her brother's company was sufficient and when he was not available she was well content with her own. She loved the woods and coppices of the farm and knew every one intimately by the wild flowers that grew there, and as a small child had often wandered far to gather them, much to the consternation of her parents. However, her favourite haunt was Bennett's Wood, three acres of ash, alder and silver birch, fairly close to the farm and to the road, for it was here that the bluebells grew in magnificent profusion. The wood was thick and fairly dark with plenty of top growth providing the ample shade which the bluebell prefers. There were clumps of brambles here and there, surrounding a stump or the trunk of a host tree, and some of these patches had been hollowed out into caves by the Felton children and, according to Edith's mother, by the Ratcliffe children before them.

Bennett's Wood or, as it was more frequently called these days, the Bluebell Wood, lay a few hundred yards down the road towards Repton, separated from it by one grass field, and as April turned into May the blue sheen in its annual glory showed as a delicate patch on the short horizon.

On this particular evening Edith had completed her homework, with a nonchalance which never failed to surprise her family, on the big kitchen table before the evening meal. This was timed for six o'clock when farm work finished for the day and the two lads who were living-in clumped into the scullery. In earlier years, as when Bob Felton had arrived at the farm as a sixteen-year-old before the War, it had been the practice for the farm lad to have his meals with the family. After the War, when Meg had assumed responsibility for the farmhouse, she decided to revert to the usual practice of the district and feed the male farm servants away from the family. She persuaded herself they liked it better this way, for at their little table in the scullery, free from the constant surveillance of the mistress, they could be less inhibited in their table manners. Gladys, the burly maid, saw to it that they lacked nothing, for they were served with food from the family table.

The effect of this segregation was that the children could do their homework at one end of the huge kitchen table without restricting the preparations for the evening meal. The kitchen was warm and companionable and the approach of the meal set a target for the completion of the paperwork.

The sun was bright and hot for early May and the bluebells had rushed into bloom as though anxious not to miss the year's first warm spell. Edith knew this and determined to gather a large armful of the woodland's colourful offering for her bedroom. She slipped out of the house immediately after tea, as the huge meal was modestly called. Arthur went out at the same time to look at the milking cows which had that evening been turned out to grass after the long winter in the sheds. Edith well knew of the satisfaction the menfolk seemed to get from watching the cows relishing their first taste of freedom and of rich spring grass.

Instead of following the drive to the road she took a short cut through the West Pasture which was set aside for the cows' use in the daytime. The grass was ankle deep and her feet left marks as if walking on snow. It was dewy wet too, and the leather of her sandals soaked up the moisture quickly, becoming dark, limp and uncomfortable. There was a handy rail-place in the hedge which separated the field from the wood – not exactly a stile but easily climbable. She sat on the top rail for a few seconds then dropped into the shivering mass of blue flowers which reached almost to her knees.

Young as she was she could appreciate the overwhelming sense of beauty in the profusion of blue-grey heads which stretched as far as the eye could see into the dim recesses between the trees and bushes. 'Nearly like being in church,' the girl said to herself and started humming 'All Things Bright and Beautiful'. She gathered a few handfuls of flowers as she walked further into the wood, pulling the stems upwards so that the whitened end of each left the damp ground easily. Still humming, she approached a large clump of brambles which surrounded a low thorn bush, one of their leafy 'caves' of the previous summer. Intending to peer into its dark interior she moved closer but to her surprise and fright there was a rustling within and a man burst noisily out of the entrance.

His clothes were ragged but had been patched many times, while the uppers of his heavy boots were parting from the soles in more than one place. His hair was long with a few leaves sticking to it, and a cap with a crumpled peak shaded a dirty face which had several days' growth of beard. His eyes were hostile and his whole manner unfriendly.

Edith knew him at once for what he was – a tramp. She knew about tramps. They were old, dirty and ragged people who spent their days walking from workhouse to workhouse and their nights in the casual wards of these institutions. When they left each morning they were given a spoonful or two of tea and to brew this they would call at any likely cottage on their route, for hot water or anything else they could beg. She had been told, as indeed were all children, to keep away from tramps, for in parents' eyes at least they were unsavoury characters. This one seemed more unsavoury than most, Edith thought, with a sad feeling akin to alarm, and when he spoke his voice did nothing to soothe her.

'Wotcher doin' 'ere, youngster?' he said angrily.

Edith trembled but kept her head.

'I'm picking bluebells. I can, you know. This wood belongs to our farm.' She looked over her shoulder towards the Oakleigh chimneys three fields away. The upper half showed above the rise in the ground. How strong and comforting they seemed and yet how distant and unhelpful in her present plight. She tried not to show her nervousness.

'This is our wood,' she said again, 'and you are trespassing.' She added hastily, 'Not that my daddy minds trespassers so long as they don't do any damage!'

'Huh! You're a cheeky little nipper, aren't you? You'd better come along wi' me.'

'Oh no, I can't do that! I must get back home. It's nearly bed-time and I've got to go to school tomorrow.'

'School won't see you tomorrow, gel. You're comin' wi' me,' and he seized her right wrist.

'Don't do that! Leave go of my arm, you horrid man.' Her eyes showed tears and she felt terror within her. 'If I'm not back in a few minutes all the farm men will be out looking for me and they know where I've gone.'

'Shut your trap and come on.' He dragged her towards the hole in the brambles. She struggled but made no impact.

'My brother's about,' she panted as a brain wave struck her. Then she suddenly screamed 'Arthur! Help! Help!'

'Quiet, you little rip,' said the tramp and put his hand over her mouth. It was dirty and smelly and nearly choked her. Utter fright took possession of her and she whispered a silent prayer, imploring Arthur's presence.

In fact, he was within earshot, walking pensively back across the thick grass of the day pasture when he heard his sister's yell. For a second he thought she must be spoofing him, but instantly realised that he could not gamble on that supposition and turned and raced towards the sound which had obviously come from within the bluebell wood. Sprinting with the speed of an athlete, as he had learned to do in the Boy Scouts, he reached the rail-place and, putting one hand on the top rail, he vaulted over. Edith and her captor, standing as if petrified, heard the twigs crackle as he landed. Then he came into their view through the bushes, leaping through the clinging bluebells with undiminished speed.

'Let go of my sister, you filthy bastard,' he yelled, and jumped straight at the tramp without pausing. No doubt he thought his appearance on the scene would frighten the man into surrender. He jostled the tramp casually but to his surprise, and Edith's dismay, the fellow lashed out with a huge fist, caught Arthur full in the chest and sent him sprawling among the branches of an elder bush.

'That'll teach you a lesson, young feller. Keep out o' my reach, else you'll get 'urt.'

Breathless and very red in the face Arthur scrambled to his feet, picking up as he did so a rotten oak branch which had fallen from the tree behind him.

'All right, tramp. Maybe you are stronger than me, but you can't frighten me away and as long as I'm here you can't do anything to my sister. You'd better give up, old sport. The milk float'll be coming by here from the station in about five minutes, too, so you can't get away.'

The tramp looked doubtful, and muttered something under his breath. He still gripped Edith's wrist tightly with his left hand but the girl, feeling that a crisis was near, started struggling violently. The man turned his head towards her and snarled 'Keep still, you little bitch!' At the same time Arthur sprang forward, raised the piece of oak in both hands and brought it down on the head of the tramp, who did not see it in time to avoid the blow. The branch was so rotten that a cloud of wood-dust and fragments of bark showered over the man's face and shoulders. The hard core of the wood hit him on the crown of the head and broke off behind him like a carrot. The effect was so comical that Edith giggled. The tramp swore in his surprise and removed his grip to scrape the dust and mouldiwarps from his face. Edith snatched herself away, turned and sprinted through the bluebells in the direction of home, to her own surprise still carrying her huge bundle of drooping flowers. Arthur threw down the wood, jumped in closer and landed two telling blows on the tramp's jaw and neck. But although shorter than Arthur, the man was as unyielding as a rock and returned the blows, his hardened fist crashing into the boy's face, sending him to the ground once more. Angrily he followed up, raising his foot to kick Arthur as the boy lay on the crushed flowers.

'I shouldn't!' Arthur warned him, wriggling out of range. 'It'll only be the worse for you and you'll get a longer spell in prison.'

The man spat in disgust. Arthur struggled to his feet, watching the other warily, for he had no intention of encountering any more such hammer blows.

'You'd better give up, I say. Maybe I'm no match for you but I won't let you out of my sight. In about two minutes my sister will be at home and they'll be on the phone to the police.'

'I didn't mean the little gel no 'arm . . .'

'You didn't mean her any good, either! Why couldn't you leave her alone. The kid's entitled to pick bluebells on our own property without being frightened by such as you.'

'I don't know what got 'old o' me, Gaffer.' He became suddenly obsequious for he realised that with the arrival of the village policeman on his bicycle, aided by the farm staff, some of whom would also have bikes, he stood no chance of getting away, especially if Arthur kept within shouting distance as he had indicated.

'I s'pose I'd better come back to th' 'ouse and apologise to the lass.'

'Hmm. You might not get away with it as easily as that,' Arthur warned him, but he was gratified nevertheless. 'Come on then!'

He indicated that the man should walk in front towards the road. They skirted an arable field being prepared for mangolds and just as they reached the road Charlie came down from the farm on his racing bicycle. When Edith had reached the kitchen and blurted out her story, her father, whose lame leg prevented rapid movement, had called Charlie from the tool shed and sent him to Arthur's assistance via the road, and despatched Tommy, who was in the stable getting Shandy ready for the milk-run, to the wood by the field route. Bob himself limped to the barn to get the motor out. With these two stalwart youngsters available, the police could wait awhile, he decided.

'Everything all right, Arthur?' Charlie said excitedly, but not without a trace of disappointment, as he braked to a dead stop beside the stranger.

'Yes, Charlie. Thanks for coming. He's given himself up.'

'Best thing he could do,' grunted the older youth. 'Here's Tommy now, just come out o' th' wood. This feller'd better not try owt on agen the three of us.'

The tramp said nothing but plodded on with a resolution which surprised Arthur. The Oakleigh car edged out of the farm drive but when Bob saw the group approaching he turned round and drove back into the farm. He was in the kitchen with his wife, his father-in-law and Edith when Arthur, Charlie and Tommy arrived with their prisoner.

Edith regarded him with equanimity. In her own home with her family round her she felt no fear of this strange man. Her mother uttered a cry of dismay when she saw Arthur's battered face and Bob stiffened visibly. Charlie and Tommy remained standing by the scullery door, having decided between themselves that this would prevent any attempt at escape.

'What the devil's the meaning of this?' demanded Mr Felton angrily. 'Trespassing on private property, molesting a little girl and fighting my son! You've got some explaining to do!'

'It were all a mistake, Gaffer,' the tramp said sullenly. 'I warn't goin' to 'urt the lass. I just wanted to talk to 'er. And it were the lad what pitched inter me. Clumped me over the 'ead, 'e did, with a bit of oak!'

'What did you expect him to do when you were frightening his sister? Pat you on the back and say "Well done!?"' With his daughter safe and sound indoors, Bob felt he could be free with his sarcasm.

'You will 'ave your little joke, Mr Bob,' the man said spontaneously.

'Mr Bob? Now, who the hell are you?' He peered at the tramp closely, as did Mr Ratcliffe.

'Why, it's Albert Kent,' declared the old man suddenly, delighted at being the first to recognise the man. 'Well, I don't know! You lived in this house nearly all through the war like one o' the family and now you come back and assault my grandchildren. If that isn't base ingratitude, I'd like to know what is!'

'It warn't like that, Mr Ratcliffe, honest . . .'

'And what are you doing tramping? Disgraceful! You were a good all-round farm chap when you left here for the Army. Don't tell me you couldn't get a job when you were demobbed!'

'Ah've 'ad a bad do, Mr Ratcliffe,' the man muttered, addressing himself entirely to the old man and lapsing into farm dialect. 'Ah were shell-shocked i' 1918, just after Ah got out theer, and took prisoner, too. When Ah got back to Derby after th' War, me 'ead was a bit funny and it still is, sometimes. Ah dunna allus know what Ah'm doin' but Ah've bin on th' tramp for nigh on twelve year. When Ah found meself at the Burton Spike last night, Ah thowt Ah'd come this way for owd times' sake and Ah were goin' to spend the night i' th' Bluebell Wood, altho Ah've no snap wi' me. Then Ah saw the little gel and recognised 'er straightaway as Miss Meg's – 'er's exactly like 'er mother – and Ah felt Ah wanted to get her alone and talk about the owd times 'ere. Then young Arthur come up and laid inter me an' Ah 'it back. Sometimes Ah don't know me own strength,' he concluded, lamely.

Everybody seemed to be waiting for someone else to speak first. Albert Kent looked around the kitchen and spoke again, visibly swallowing a lump in his throat.

'Ba gum, th'owd kitchen looks just the same as it allus did. Th' way Ah'd pictured it over all these years.'

'Well, this is a sad story,' commented Meg at last. 'You've had a rough time, Albert. What are we going to do, Bob?'

Her husband was not too sure himself. He had intended giving the man in charge, not only for his conduct towards Edith, but because of the possible danger to other girls. But his resolve was weakened when the man was revealed as an old employee who had lived in the house with them, had been there when Arthur was born and had probably helped the child with his toddling. His patriotic enlistment while still under age in the last few months of the War, had brought injury, imprisonment and mental instability. Bob felt the farm owed a duty to this unfortunate young man.

Kent must have sensed the farmer's thoughts for he said, speaking slowly, 'It were good to be 'ere i' th' owd days, workin' on th' farm wi' you, wi' Mr Sam and owd Ernie. Plenty o' good grub and a comfortable bed to sleep in. I mind the day Arthur 'ere were born. We were all that pleased! Ah s'pose Ah were thinkin' o' them days when Ah drifted back. Ah just don't know what made me frighten the little lass!'

Bob Felton thought hard. He knew his wife and father-in-law were waiting for his decision and would not offer an opinion until they knew his plans.

'Have you ever seen a doctor about your mental troubles or had any treatment?'

'Ah don't rightly know, Mr Bob. Ah conna remember. Ah think there must a' bin times but nowt ever come of it.'

The farmer thought deeply again.

'Tell you what, Albert. I'm going to give you another chance. Have a good wash in the scullery. Mrs Felton will give you a meal and you can sleep in the barn tonight and have some breakfast in the morning. We'll look out some better clothes for you and after breakfast I'll run you down to our doctor and he can examine you and tell us what's best to be done. If you have to go away for treatment, I'll give you a job here at Oakleigh when the treatment's over. I can't say fairer than that.'

Tearspots oozed out of Kent's eyes and trickled down his dirty cheeks.

'It's reight good o' you, Mr Bob, and you too, Missis. Ah don't deserve all this.' He laid his head in his arms on the kitchen table and sobbed into them.

Meg nodded the children out of the room and got food out of the larder, helped by a reluctant Gladys.

Arthur was piqued by such a summary dismissal and confided his feelings to his sister as they went upstairs together.

'It's a rum do, Edie. You get scared to death and I get a split cheek and a black eye and now they're killing the fatted calf for the chap that did it!'

Edith giggled.

'It's all over now Art, and we're back at home. Just another big adventure for you and me.'

'A bloomin' painful one, that's all I can say,' grumbled her brother.

The next day was an ordinary school day and the children had to be up by seven o'clock. But Arthur was out of bed much earlier than that and went down across the yard as the cows were brought in for milking. At that hour of the morning everybody was intent on getting the cows tied up for milking. No one other than Arthur had time or thought for the tramp in the barn. He went in there and saw the scanty bed of empty sacks where the tramp had slept, the disarray of old clothes and boots which had been left behind; but Albert Kent himself was not there.

Chapter 4

Kent's disappearance was the only topic of conversation at the Oakleigh breakfast table.

'You just can't help some people,' Mr Felton commented sorrowfully, and Mr Ratcliffe reluctantly nodded his assent.

'He certainly is a bastard,' remarked Edith casually, and her mother sat bolt upright in her chair.

'Edith! How dare you say such a word, you naughty girl! Where did you hear it?'

'It's only what Arthur called the tramp when he first saw him holding my wrist. "You bloody bastard!" he said. I left out the swear word.'

'Don't you dare use those nasty, wicked words again, Edith! I won't have it! Bob! Stop grinning! Arthur, you ought to be ashamed of yourself, using such bad language in front of your sister! Dad! What are you muttering about?'

'I was just saying that if it'd 'a been me, I'd have called him much worse than that,' her father said unrepentantly.

'Oh dear! How can I bring my daughter up in a ladylike way with you coarse-mouthed men around! I'm very surprised at you, Arthur, I must say.'

Her son was far from pleased at this second rebuke and rounded on his sister.

'You little fool, Edie,' he hissed across the table. 'You know perfectly well you shouldn't have said that in here, in front of the old folks. Just causing a sensation for the thrill of it, you cheeky madam!'

'That's enough, you two,' their mother said crossly. 'Let's have no more of this! Be off to school before I give you both a box on the ear.'

Arthur and Edith departed, still wrangling, while their parents tried to soothe their own mild indignation.

'Did you hear Arthur refer to us as "the old folks" Bob? The young rip! How old are we? Only thirty-six!'

'That lad's getting a bit above himself,' Bob agreed, but Mr Ratcliffe only chuckled.

'Now you know what it's like to have a young family catching up with you. It's the same with all parents and with all youngsters – at least it was so with us. If they could, they'd put us on the shelf

34

as soon as they leave school. I'm very disappointed about young Kent, though. I hoped we were going to do him some good. I'd like to know the reasoning behind it all.'

'That's simple, Dad,' Bob said. 'He played us for suckers last night to avoid possible punishment for his crime or intended crime. He took us all in, got a good meal and a suit of clothes and a pair of boots and avoided being questioned by the police. I shall be very wary about being kind to tramps after this.'

'I can't believe he was as wicked as all that, Bob,' Meg protested. She probably knew the man better than any of them, for she had been running the farm herself during part of his employment. 'I think we should give him the benefit of the doubt and put it down to his weak mind. We shall never really know what caused him to act as he did, for I'm sure we shan't ever see him again.'

Albert Kent's visit was soon forgotten as everyone at the farm revelled in the unfolding warmth of May. The calves were turned out in the sheltered orchard, the meadows had their winter drabness harrowed away and were then smartened by rolling before shutting them up for haymaking; the potatoes were planted and the mangolds, swedes, cabbage and kale were all sown by the middle of the month. The hoeing would not start until early June and in the meantime the main task was to remove the irrefutable evidence of winter – the manure. All hands – and all carts – were engaged in hauling the manure from the fold-yards and muck-hole and stacking it in a corner of the field where it was to be applied in early autumn. Farmer Felton took no part in this strenuous work for he had plenty of men, but spent an easy week or two walking or riding over his extensive acres, appraising his crops and livestock, spending more time at market, talking to his neighbours. He spent rather more time indoors too, rather to his wife's dismay, for he came in earlier to his meals and sat longer over them.

One dinnertime he and his father-in-law remained at the table drinking extra cups of tea. Meg was with them, also taking her ease while Gladys got on with the washing-up in the scullery. The air in the kitchen was warm and sleepy, for the windows were tightly closed to keep out the pungent tang of the newly-disturbed manure. The first cart of the afternoon rumbled by, stacked high with smoking muck. At the same time the village policeman rode up on his bicycle.

'Well, I'm blessed,' said Meg who was facing the window, 'here's Jack Ryder turned up. What ever can he want? It's not sheep-dipping time yet.'

In that law-abiding community in which Oakleigh Farm was the prime example the policeman rarely called more than once a year, that annual visit being for the purpose of seeing that each ewe was immersed in the prescribed arsenical dip for the statutory period of one minute. Meg went to the back door and asked the policeman in.

'Good afternoon, Mr Ratcliffe, Mr Felton,' said the constable politely as he entered the kitchen. 'By gum, there's a good healthy smell round your yard this afteroon!'

'Good afternoon, constable,' Felton replied formally. 'Sit down and have a cup of tea with us on this pleasant day and tell us why you're here. You didn't come up from Hartnall to talk about smells, healthy or otherwise.'

'I wouldn't be too sure about that,' the policeman said, gratefully sipping the mug of strong milky tea. Pushing a bike was hard and thirsty work in the unaccustomed heat. 'But that's an unpleasant approach to the business. The fact is, Mr Felton, a man's body has been pulled out of the river at Newark . . .'

'Has it now? Well, that's not surprising, constable. The Trent is the third longest river in the land which gives plenty of room for people to fall in! Beyond the fact that the Trent also flows through Hartnall, I can't see any connection.'

'Not yet, Mr Felton, I daresay. The corpse is said to be that of a young man – in his early thirties, they think – and had been in the water two to three weeks.' He consulted his notebook. 'His hair was long, ragged and dirty, but he had shaved recently. It is thought he may have fallen – or jumped – into the river round these parts. Have you any idea who it could be?'

'No, I'm afraid I haven't, Mr Ryder. Why should I have? This isn't the only farm with Trent-side meadows. I think you're holding something back!'

'Sorry, Mr Felton. We have to follow our enquiries in a set way. The fact is, this man was wearing an old hacking jacket made by Ellis and bearing your name on a Cash's label. Of course, there may be other Robert Feltons about, but you're the only one with a Trent-side farm who buys riding clothes from Ellis'. Now, have you had any clothes stolen, or have you given any away recently?'

Meg and her father groaned at the same time.

'Oh dear,' Meg said, 'poor little Albert Kent.'

The three of them, frequently speaking at the same time, described the incident to Constable Ryder who wrote it down very rapidly in his notebook.

'Was he a feeble man, Mr Felton? Could he have wandered along the bank and tottered in?'

'No, he was as strong as a horse. He had a fight with young Arthur and twice sent him flying. He must have rested on the parapet of Willington or Swarkestone bridge and slipped in!'

'I understand there was no sign of bruising, sir. No injury, and death was definitely by drowning.'

'As if he slipped gently into the water and died,' Meg said, feeling rather foolish as she swallowed a lump in her throat.

'That's about it, Mrs Felton. But if there was this fight as you say, why didn't you charge him with assault?'

'There was a history of mental illness following shell-shock and imprisonment, and for old times sake we wanted to help him. We were going to take him down to the doctor's after breakfast.'

'I see.' The constable stood up, returning his notebook to his upper tunic pocket. 'Perhaps if you'd called us in he might still have been alive. Anyway, I'm sure you acted for the best. We won't ask you to identify the body, Mr Felton – it's hardly recognisable anyway – but we may ask you to have a look at the clothes and the boots. You realise you will be wanted at the inquest? I'll let you know in due course.'

'Well, that's a sad end, I must say,' Mr Ratcliffe commented when the policeman had gone. 'Was it remorse, shame for what he'd done to Arthur and Edith, or misery in comparing his early life here with the present? Or was it just that he had a screw loose that dropped out of its socket at the crucial time?'

'Or was it an accident?' put in Meg. 'We shall never know, Dad, so it's useless speculating. I'm a bit cut up about it. He was a good lad and lived in our house for four years at a very awkward time. Should we keep it from the kids, do you think?'

'No point,' said her husband. 'It'll be all over the village in no time.'

The tramp's drowning was a nine days' wonder in Hartnall, for many of the older people remembered him. At Oakleigh Farm, Arthur and Edith were subdued for several days. This was the first death they had known and they seemed particularly involved. Edith visited Bennett's Wood no more. From being joyous with bluebells it had become dank and melancholy, haunted by the ghost of the black-haired tramp with the iron grip.

In farming, however, the seasonal work presses on regardless of human emotions and the next item on the programme and on the calendar was haymaking. Like all country youngsters of the period and district, Arthur and Edith regarded this as the most thrilling event of the farming year. They watched intently as the mowing machines were rolled out of the cart-shed, oiled, tested and the knives sharpened. The fore-carriages were manoeuvred out of the dim recesses of the rickyard shed and were linked up to the carts, converting them into hermaphrodites, or 'mophreys' as they were commonly called, for bringing in the towering loads. The very anticipation was an excitement in itself, not only to the children but to the whole farm staff. At Oakleigh, the mowing was still done by the horses, the tractor being used for the arable work only. Bill Marshall and Gerald Long set off soon after four o'clock in order to achieve their stint in the cool dampness of the morning, returning to lighter work in the heat of the afternoon. Arthur looked forward to some swath-turning or horse-raking when it did not interfere with his schooling, while Edith's chief delight was to ride back to the field in the empty mophrey.

The pleasant weather of May and early June was a mere flash in the pan this year. The main explosion of summer never materialised. The hay from two small fields was secured in good condition and by then the summer of 1931 was as good as over. Little or much rain fell on most days up to St Swithin's and for the inevitable forty days afterwards. Every remaining hayfield needed much turning, tedding and even shaking out by hand. Most days the sun managed to appear for a short spell, but every night it rained. The thick black clouds could be seen massing as the day's final, perhaps only, load was unloaded in the grim dusk. On every bright afternoon the farm staff, with horses, machines and vehicles, would hasten to the field and move the hay sufficiently to allow a couple of loads of the greyish-black material, clinging and dusty, to be taken in and added to the stack or barn. It looked so unpalatable that Mr Felton decided to revert to an old practice he had read about during the wet summer of 1912 – adding a sprinkling of salt to each layer of hay as it was built on the stack. As he said to his father-in-law: 'It's doubtful if the salt improves the quality of the hay, but at least it will encourage the cattle to eat it.'

In between his bouts of heavy breathing, which at times made even speech difficult, Mr Ratcliffe agreed with this. 'I wish we could do something about the dust,' he said, for one unexpected result of the rain on the hay, producing as it did black dust and dry mildew, was the aggravation of Mr Ratcliffe's asthma. He was so badly affected that he was unable to assist with the stacking, and this depressed the old man, for never before in his life had he been excluded from the haymaking.

The same rain which blackened the hay caused the weeds to grow thick and rank in the root crops. Since every dry period was spent in attempting to make hay, the hoeing could only be done in damp or dull conditions. The weeds refused to die but took root again instantly. The feet of the hoers pushed the newly-disturbed weeds firmly into the damp earth, making their regrowth a certainty. Progress was so slow, so uncomfortable and depressing that the men, without exception, thoroughly hated the job. Arthur certainly did when his school term ended at the end of July, for even at that time neither the hoeing nor the haymaking was more than half finished.

The absence of sun had delayed the ripening of the corn so it was clear that the harvest would not start until nearly the end of August but it still seemed likely that the haymaking would overlap into the corn-carrying. Arthur was much concerned and his attitude of identifying himself so completely with the management caused some amusement to his father and grandfather.

After tea one evening, there being no haymaking following a damp morning and dull afternoon, he disappeared on his bicycle and returned to a lamp-lit kitchen about nine o'clock. The family was seated round the cooking range for they had not yet dropped into their winter habit of spending the evenings before a log fire in the parlour. Arthur sat down in his chair and, although out of breath, plunged into his subject without preamble.

'With weather like this we ought to make some ensilage,' he declared with just a touch of defiance.

'Whatever's that?' asked his mother but no one took any notice of her, apart from Edith who said, 'He's just trying to look big, Mum!'

Mr Ratcliffe lowered his newspaper and took off his spectacles.

'Ensilage? You must be daft, Arthur. We haven't the equipment to do that. It would be quite a costly business to get it, and take months of preparation anyway, wouldn't it Bob? Those silo things have been advertised in the *Farmer & Stockbreeder* for years, but I've never seen one close to. According to the pictures they seem to be something like fat factory chimneys made of metal and you chop the grass up and blow it in through a pipe to the top. That's so, isn't it, Bob?'

'True enough, Dad, although I haven't been close to one, either. Seen 'em from the train from time to time, especially in the latter part of the War when feed was getting short. Nobody round here had one that I heard about. In fact it never took on very well – certainly not with tenant farmers. I daresay a few institutional

39

farms might have put them up and perhaps still use them. Only big farms would have a tractor powerful enough to chop the grass and blow it up there. I don't think our Fordson would do it.'

'When you two have finished reminiscing,' said Arthur rudely, 'perhaps you'll listen to what I've got to say. Of course I'm not suggesting erecting a tower silo like you see in the *Stockbreeder* adverts. I daresay it would cost £500 and we wouldn't need it in a dry summer. No! I mean cut the grass and carry it green and make it into a low stack or camp.'

'Carry green grass!' echoed his grandfather. 'That'd fire for a certainty.'

'It wouldn't, Grandad,' said the boy positively. 'You need air to cause fire, and the grass would be trodden down so tight that the air would be kept out. Nothing can burn without air!'

'You sure of that?'

'Yes, of course. We learnt that in physics.'

'Where have you been tonight, Arthur?' asked his father.

'I've been over to Egginton, Dad. There's a farmer there – Riley of Manor Farm – who's given up trying to make hay and is making the rest of his grass into ensilage, like I said. His waggoner mows a few rounds every evening – he was at it tonight – and in the daytime he has a gang of three or four youths picking it up and making it into a round stack. It steams a bit of course but it doesn't catch fire.'

'That's all very well, but how do we know what it'll turn out like?'

'It's been all right before, Dad. There was a lad at school – Jimmy Long – who came from Egginton and I remember him telling me last year that Riley had ensiled a crop of oats and beans, cut green. It was all eaten last winter. I had a word with the waggoner, Harry Fearn. He said it's hard work getting it together, but the beasts eat it readily enough.'

'It seems to me Arthur, that it would ha' been better manners to have gone to the house and seen Mr Riley, not sneak round his fields talking to his man. However, I'll have a word with him next time I see him at market.'

The boy flushed. He did not take kindly to rebukes.

'What are the snags?' said his grandfather. 'There must be some!'

'As far as I can make out, only two, apart from the hard work forking it. There's a fair bit o' waste round the outside where you can't tread it so solid and it stinks to high heaven!'

'I've heard enough,' said his mother. 'We won't have any of

40

that round these buildings!'

'Not round the buildings, perhaps,' said her husband. 'But Arthur's got something here, you know. We've still to mow the two seven-acre fields in Cowslip Lane. We'll get cracking on it with two mowers tomorrow and all hands on picking it up. Now, it's your idea, Arthur, and you'll bear the responsibility of failure, although we'll all help with the work. What do you think of that?'

Arthur looked pleased.

'Well, it won't take long for two machines to mow as much as we can carry in one day, so after an hour or two the waggoners can help with the picking-up. My own idea is that we should work the fields on alternate days – it'll give the ricks more time to settle. They don't need to be built too high too fast.'

Much to the astonishment of the farm staff the ensiling of the last two fields of mowing grass was started the following morning. Bill Marshall looked askance when Charlie and Len started forking up the grass on to the mophrey as soon as the mower had been round the field twice. Later, Arthur and Frank loaded a second mophrey and soon the two vehicles were shuttling to and from the circular stack which Mr Felton, helped by the cowman Ned and the silent but disapproving Ernie, began to build. The grass was long, wet, heavy and clinging and called for strenuous efforts in loading and unloading. Although the loads were small and the grass was not trodden in by a man on top, the grass was difficult to separate when it came to throwing it off. Unused to handling such material the men grumbled, mostly under their breath if any member of the management was present. Robert Felton himself soon found it particularly fatiguing and was glad to relinquish his job to Gerald Long when in mid-morning the mowers ceased their chattering. Mr Ratcliffe strolled over to the scene before dinner, gazed at the activity for a few minutes, then wandered away, shaking his head sadly.

By the evening the solid green mass had reached a height of eight feet, and as all the cut grass had been cleared work was stopped for the day. After tea, people from the village and men from other farms paid a surreptitious visit to the deserted ensilage stack, then withdrew to the local pub and sneered loudly at 'Felton's Folly'.

The next morning the stack was steaming strongly but Mr Felton adhered to the original plan of working the two fields alternately and started another stack. On the third morning they returned to the first stack and found that it had sunk to half of its original height. By dint of much labour over the next fortnight two

41

large round stacks of solid, steaming and stinking material were left as witness to their efforts.

The next task was to cover them with earth to consolidate the top and divert the rain. This was another herculean task, made a little less arduous by ploughing a narrow strip round the stack, digging the ploughed ground out with a spade and throwing it into a cart while another man stood in the cart and transferred it to a man on the top of the stack who spread it in a layer a few inches thick. 'Rather like icing a cake,' Arthur remarked enthusiastically.

'Bloody sight 'arder work, though,' one of the men said crossly and all the others agreed with him.

Perversely, the weather which had been dull, cloudy or wet for so long, relented for the ensilage and the work was carried on in bright warm weather. On several days the green material had to be left to clear up another dilatory instalment of the tardy hay crop.

'Niver done so much 'ard and dirty graft for such a long spell in me life,' grumbled Bill Marshall, voicing the thoughts of all the men. 'And as for the gaffer, it seems to 'a knocked him up entirely.'

Only Robert Felton himself knew just how true this was. He had started the ensilage with enthusiasm, pleased at his son's resourcefulness, but found himself unable to produce the strenuous effort needed to handle the heavy material and each day his energy diminished and he could do less and less of the heavy work.

Chapter 5

A start was made on the corn harvest during the last few days of the ensilage. Bill and Gerald each drove a binder, with Charlie and Tommy leading the fore-horse on each team. Three generations of the farmer's family – grandfather, father and son – were on the scene with their shotguns and the remainder of the farm staff were there for the stooking. Edith was present too, but she found herself neglected and solitary in the harvest field for when Arthur had his gun he was too grown up and important to bother with his young sister. If the afternoon were fine, Meg would find time to visit the scene for she still remembered her teenage years when she had helped regularly with the field work. Mr Ratcliffe's asthma did not prevent him from using his gun so long as he did not move too quickly. He rode to the field in the float and kept it there until it was needed to take the milk to the station.

The wet summer had caused weeds to grow in the corn and the frequent rain had weakened the straw so that it tangled in the gales. The binders often clogged and jammed, either the greenstuff or the crumpled straw proving too much for the mechanism. The ground was soft, even muddy sometimes, and such blockages would cause the main driving wheel to skid on the west surface, forcing the horses to a halt. The normal, pleasant harvest smell of dry earth, stubble and sun-warm grain, was replaced by the pungent tang of mud and milky thistles. The untidy sheaves did not make good stooks. They collapsed with a monotony which dismayed the farm labourers who did not relish having to restook them day after day.

The waggoners sought to offset this tendency to jamming by urging their horses on faster, hoping that the extra speed would force the tangled crop through the knotting mechanism, and to a certain extent it did so. This evidence of the value of extra speed caused Arthur to remark that it was about time the tractor took over from the horses for corn-cutting.

The weather was not good but allowed the work to proceed at a slow pace. When the time came to carry the sheaves it was necessary to throw them down a few hours before, then turn them over so they could take full advantage of the furtive sun. Much time was spent in getting the oats dry enough to stack, but the wheat was often carried in rainy weather which meant that the ricks could not be thrashed until the spring.

Arthur took a full part in the harvest this year for he had left school at the end of the summer term. He had passed his matriculation very easily and this would give him entrance to Cirencester Agricultural College when he was eighteen, and both he and his father considered this was sufficient. There was no point in carrying on at school, building up credits on academic subjects which were of no use to a farmer. So it was decided that he should put aside schooling for two years and concentrate on helping with the farm work.

Disconsolately Mr Ratcliffe brought up the subject of studying for the auctioneering profession. He had already resigned himself to the fact that this would remain a dream of his own. To his surprise, however, Arthur told him that he proposed to call in at the office of Arnold & Son the next time he visited Burton to get some information about the professional exams.

He was as good as his word. On a dull Wednesday afternoon when no harvesting was possible he announced that he was going in to Burton to see Charlie Chaplin in *City Lights* and he intended to get there in office hours so he could call on the auctioneers before going to the cinema. Edith begged to accompany him and surprisingly he agreed, to her huge delight. Bob, who was feeling very low again, merely said glumly, 'It'd be better manners if you asked if you could go, not take it for granted.'

'Don't be a spoil-sport,' whispered Meg. 'They don't often go out together.'

The youngsters returned at about 8.30, Edith unwillingly, as she had wanted to stay and see the programme round again, and Arthur had to adopt a stern, older-brother attitude to get her home. They enjoyed a belated supper in wrangling privacy at one end of the kitchen table, Arthur vowing he would never take his sister out again.

'I'll bet you didn't call at the auctioneer's,' their grandfather said during a lull in the exchanges.

'I jolly well did, Grandad. I saw Mr Upton and he was most helpful. There are one or two young chaps in the office studying for their exams. He said I could take the AAI or the RICS or both and gave me the addresses where I can get the question papers of previous years. He reckons that after two, or at the most three, winters of home study I should be able to take the exams with a fair chance of success, and he's going to get from his young people a list of the text books I shall need.'

'Ah! Arnold's were always a good friendly firm,' said his

grandfather, 'and Charlie Upton's the pleasantest man you'll meet in a day's march. Are you going to do all this, Arthur?'

'Yes, of course, Grandad! I said I would, didn't I?'

Mr Ratcliffe pulled himself slowly to his feet, the effort causing him to pant heavily. He shambled across the room, stood behind Arthur's chair and put his hand on the boy's shoulder.

'You're a right good lad, Arthur. You're doing this for me and I appreciate it. There aren't many youngsters would do it. And as for you, young Edith, you ought to be proud of this fine brother of yours, not keep on arguing and cheeking him!'

'I can be proud and still argue,' Edith said stubbornly tossing her brown hair.

'Edith, if you answer your grandfather back when he speaks to you, I'll clout you.'

'There's no need for that, Meg,' protested the old man. 'Edith wasn't answering back. She was just giving her point of view. I sometimes think you're a bit too strict with her. Much more so than we were with you.'

'Oh, I don't know! Mum gave me a hiding many a time!'

'Not often enough, I'm thinking. In any case, you had *two* brothers to spoil you. And you were far more wayward and headstrong than Edith.'

'For goodness' sake, Dad, don't say that in front of her! I'll never do anything with her!'

'I wish you'd all stop this idiotic, pointless chatter,' said Bob crossly. 'Say something sensible or keep quiet. Oh God, my head's splitting again. I'm going up to bed if I can get there.'

Meg Felton flushed. Her husband had spoken with real rancour and this was so unusual that she was hurt.

'I don't know what's come over Bob,' she said in a subdued voice to her father. 'He's like a bear with a sore head. Either he's tired or got a headache, and if he's got the energy to talk it's only to snap at you!'

'I can't understand it either, Meg. It worries me a bit. Bob's been here for more than twenty years and has always been as full of energy as a midsummer rabbit. Now he's like a watch with the mainspring gone. He must be sickening for something. Why not call in the doctor?'

'He just won't hear of it – yet. All the time I've known him he's never had a day in bed except with his war wound, and he thinks it impossible for him to be ill!'

'It's been a worrying summer, Mum,' Arthur reminded her.

'Your father can take those sort of worries in his stride,' Meg

45

said tartly. 'He always has done. But I don't know that we should be talking like this in front of you and Edith.'

'Oh, Mum, we're not kids any more – at least I'm not. Don't put your tongue out at me, Edie! If Dad's going to be ill, I'll have to take over the running of the farm.'

'That'll be the day,' muttered his grandfather. Then, remembering the boy's co-operative attitude over the auctioneering qualifications, he added, 'But no doubt you'd be very useful getting about and seeing how things are going on and reporting to us. If it comes to that, I'll have the pony and float outside all day and get around the place myself.'

'I jolly well hope it won't come to that,' Meg said, half to herself. 'I've never had a sick husband and don't think I'd quite know how to go on. Edith! Don't sit there any longer. It's long past your bedtime, and it's school tomorrow. These blessed pictures!'

When Mrs Felton went to bed she found her husband sleeping, but not very restfully. He looked feverish so she put her hands under the bedclothes and found him soaking with perspiration. She went downstairs and fetched a jug of lemon squash for she knew he would wake with a raging thirst. Then she got in beside him, but the moisture and the heat from his steaming body was so uncomfortable that she was unable to sleep for more than a few minutes at a time, or so it seemed. From time to time she threw the clothes back to let out the heat. Bob was restless, but seemed to be sleeping every time Meg looked at him. She dozed off towards morning and when she finally awoke about six o'clock the lemonade jug was empty. Bob was sleeping more peacefully and was free of perspiration. Normally he would have been out of bed by quarter to six, for the workmen all started at six o'clock and he liked to be out to see them arrive. After such a weary night she decided to risk his annoyance by letting him sleep on. She had not heard Tommy and Charlie go downstairs. Normally Bob called them and they had never been known to get up until he had done so. They shared an attic bedroom at the top of the house on the same floor as Arthur and Edith. Meg had no intention of entering the lads' bedroom in her dressing-gown but Arthur could do so. She ran up to his room and shook him awake.

'Get up now, Arthur. Your father's not well and the lads aren't up yet. Go along and rouse them out of it!'

Arthur needed no second bidding. He liked playing the gaffer. Hastily dragging on his trousers he hurried along to the end room, pushed the door open unceremoniously and said, 'Come on, you two, it's gone six o'clock!'

They sat up at once and rolled out of bed without comment while Arthur ran downstairs and put on his boots. His mother was in the kitchen making the tea.

'Have a cup before you go out, Arthur,' she suggested.

'No fear, Mum, thanks. I want to be out and see what's doing.'

Mr Ratcliffe entered the kitchen at that moment having also been unceremoniously aroused by his busy daughter. He gladly accepted her offer of tea.

'This certainly wants chalking up,' he grumbled. 'First time for twenty years Bob hasn't been out for milking.'

'Well, you'd better go out in the yard Dad, and see that Arthur doesn't chuck his weight about too much. If Bob's going to be ill we don't want complications with disgruntled workmen!'

She refilled the teapot with boiling water, put it on a tray with two cups and saucers, sugar, milk and a plate of bread and butter, and took it up to her own room feeling very important, for, as she kept telling herself, this was the first time she had so waited on her husband in their seventeen years of married life.

Bob was still sleeping but woke at her touch. He looked at his bedside clock and sat bolt upright, nearly knocking the cup and saucer out of his wife's hand.

'Good God, Meg, it's twenty past six! Why the blazes didn't you wake me? And why this tea up here? I must get out!'

'Relax Bob, and drink this tea. Arthur and Dad have gone out to see to things. The farm won't come to a dead stop because you're not there. You've had a bad night and you'd better take it easy for an hour or two.'

'I must get up!'

'Drink this tea first and have some bread and butter. You'll feel a lot better. I'll have a cup with you.'

She watched him drink two cups of tea voraciously, swallowing great gulps as if he had to quench a fire in his stomach.

'I'm sure you must be thirsty, Bob. You were very hot last night and sweating like a milk horse.'

'I'm cool enough now, anyway, and my headache's gone, thank goodness. I'll get up now.'

He swung his legs out of bed, stood up for a few seconds then sat down on the bed, suddenly.

'Meg, what's the matter with me? I haven't got the strength to stand up!'

'I'm going to call the doctor, Bob. You can't go on like this. Get back into bed!'

'I'm not going to stay in bed long,' he protested as he obeyed her. 'I'll get up as soon as I can stand.'

Doctor Whittaker's visits to Oakleigh were so rare that he invariably treated them as emergencies. The family were all private patients, of course, but farmers, even if well-to-do, did not call in the doctor on frivolous grounds.

Robert Felton was sitting beside the kitchen fire in a melancholy frame of mind. He had tried to walk down to the cowshed and round to the stable but, finding himself so weak as to be on the point of collapse, he returned to the house to await the doctor's coming with resignation. Meg was more impatient. She had great faith in their new young practitioner, for his father had been the family doctor in her childhood.

Doctor Whittaker listened carefully to the symptoms described by both Bob and Meg, with Mr Ratcliffe, who was very concerned, chipping in with a comment now and again.

'I can't really see why you should be so debilitated,' the doctor said when he had examined his patient thoroughly. 'Your lungs are all right, blood pressure normal, heart one hundred per cent as far as I can tell. I'll take a sample with me to see if there's anything wrong with your kidneys. These headaches keep recurring, you say. Do they come on suddenly? Can you think of anything which precedes the headaches? Sudden noise, for instance, or worry, or long periods of extra concentration? This summer has been very trying for farmers, I realise that.'

'It's certainly not worry, Doctor,' Bob said shortly. 'My farm is organised to cover any eventuality or any weather. I've got a good staff as well as an expert father-in-law and a competent son!'

Meg hastened to change the subject.

'There was all that sweating last night, Doctor. He must have been in a red-hot fever. It was almost impossible to lie beside him.'

'That's gone now, Meg,' her husband said testily. 'There's no need to bother the doctor with things which have cleared up!'

'There's no sign of fever now, certainly,' Doctor Whittaker said. 'It's most unusual for a feverish condition to disappear so rapidly. Take things easily, Mr Felton. Get as much sleep as you can, drink as much fruit-juice as you can. If you send someone down to the surgery this evening, I'll have some medicine ready. I'll call and see you again in a couple of days.'

'I don't think he knows much about it,' grumbled the farmer when the doctor had gone.

'Don't say that, Bob,' said Mr Ratcliffe. 'If you don't have absolute faith in your doctor you're never going to get well.'

'I'm well enough. This is just a temporary weakness. Nothing to worry about.'

'That remains to be seen,' said his father-in-law discouragingly.

Try as he might to make light of his condition, Bob Felton was forced to admit later that day that he was far from well. At the afternoon milking he got up from his chair to visit the cowsheds, found himself barely able to stand and his head began to throb furiously again. He almost shed tears of despair as he climbed slowly up to bed. When Meg went up later she found him in a high fever, sweating from every pore in his body. When she got in beside him at bedtime the sheets were hot and sticky, which offended her sense of cleanliness. She would have liked to change the sheets but did not wish to waken him for he was sleeping, though not soundly, so she resigned herself to another night of damp heat. To add to her trials, her perspiring husband appeared to give off strong odours which made her feel quite sick and contributed to another broken night.

She got out of bed at six o'clock feeling faintly light-headed. Bob had stopped sweating and was awake but quite lacking in energy. Meg came to the point at once.

'You'd better have a bath as soon as the water's hot, Bob. When you were sweating so much in the night you smelt like a cowshed!'

'Oh? What's wrong with the smell of a cowshed?'

'Nothing – if you're in a cowshed! But I don't like it from my husband and in my bedroom! Perhaps it's something to do with whatever complaint you've got.'

'Rubbish!' Bob was angry and hurt by the imputation.

'Anyway, have a bath this morning and again tonight when you go to bed, and you'll have a bath every night in future until you're well again. And if this smell persists you'll have to move into Betty's room until you're better.'

Her husband swallowed a lump in his throat.

'I never thought the time would come when I'd be turned out of my own bedroom and by you of all people, after what we've been to one another these last twenty years!' He turned away from her.

'Oh Bob! I'm sorry I sounded so cross, dear. Of course I don't *want* to turn you out of our room, but you're sweating so much every night and it's so unpleasant for me, so hot and sticky and now the smell as well. I'm not getting any sleep and at this rate I'll soon be knocked up too. If that happens, who's going to run the house and look after Edith and Arthur and all of us? We can't expect a maid to do it all, good as she is. You must see that, Bob. We'll try one more night here. Perhaps you're over the worst!'

'I don't think so, Meg. I don't mind saying to you that I'm a bit worried. I'm getting weaker and weaker. Of course I mustn't interfere too much with your rest. All this means extra work for you. So if I must, I'll go into Betty's room as soon as you can get it ready. It's a good idea for another reason too – this might be contagious.'

'Tomorrow, Bob, not until tomorrow!'

Apart from being weak and tired the farmer felt better than he had been over the last two days. Still he did not feel energetic enough to venture outside, although the harvesting was by no means finished. At mealtimes he questioned Arthur closely on progress and, much to the old man's annoyance, his father-in-law as well.

'Don't think the farm's going to fall in ruins or float away, just because you're ill, Bob,' he said crossly. 'You can leave it perfectly well to me and Arthur. I can make the decisions and he can do the running about, while you can be ill with a contented mind.'

'Dammit man! I don't want to be ill with a contented mind. I want to be out and about attending to my business!'

'No doubt. So do we all. I didn't want to get landed with this asthma which stops me doing practically anything worthwhile – can't even walk across the yard without blowing!'

'But you're seventy, Dad,' Meg reminded him, 'and Bob's only thirty-six.'

'Illness takes no account of birthdays and calendars as everybody in this house should know. We've got to take what comes and make the best of it. You going to bed already, Bob?'

'Yes, I am. I've got a hell of a headache again and your conversation doesn't improve it.'

'Don't forget to have another bath, Bob,' his wife called as he mounted the stairs.

When she went up to bed he was sleeping normally and he lay in an aura of strong carbolic soap. Meg got into bed in a more comfortable state of mind and quickly fell asleep herself. At midnight she was awake again, stifled by the heat from Bob's perspiring body. The strong animal smell had completely overpowered the carbolic and this added to her discomfort.

In the morning she referrred to this again, to her husband's pained disbelief.

'I think it's your imagination,' he said sorrowfully, 'but if it'll please you I'll sleep in Betty's old room tonight.'

Later in the morning Doctor Whittaker made his expected visit and Meg made a point of explaining everything to him.

'It's the same every night, Doctor. He gets these dreadful fits of sweating which go off by morning. But while he's sweating his body smells so awful. I can't understand it.'

'No need to tell the doctor all that rubbish, Meg!' Bob said, feeling incensed and humiliated. 'That's nothing to do with the fever.'

'What sort of a smell, Mrs Felton?'

'Well, you know – sort of cowy.' Meg coloured in embarrassment for herself and her husband.

The doctor made notes.

'I'm sure that's relevant, Mrs Felton. What you've told me is possibly very significant. I will look into this further and call again tomorrow. In the meantime, continue with the medicine and the fruit drinks.'

'He doesn't eat much, Doctor – quite lost all his appetite.'

'Then make sure that what he has is nourishing and easily assimilated – soups, Bovril, eggs and so on.'

'And milk, Doctor? He generally likes milk dishes and takes a lot in other ways.'

'Yes, for the time being – certainly.'

That evening Robert Felton sadly left the marital bedroom and tossed and sweated in the guest room which his young sister Betty had occupied in her long spell at Oakleigh.

When Doctor Whittaker arrived he had the air of a man who had positive news to impart. Bob was too listless to get up – the exertion of his now regular morning bath seemed to use up his reserves of energy – and he rolled back into his newly-made bed. Meg took the doctor up to him.

'Tell me, Mr Felton, how long is it since you had a case of abortion among your cows?'

Bob stared at him.

'That's a thing farmers don't talk about, Doctor. They keep it quiet and shut the cow up for a few weeks. Until she's finished discharging, that is. The other cows might pick up the germ.'

'But you must have had cases,' persisted the doctor.

'Generally it's confined to farmers who buy and sell cows in the market,' parried Bob. 'Our herd is self-contained and has been for many years. That means we breed our own replacements.'

'You mean you never had an isolated case?'

'What's all this leading up to?' the farmer was becoming impatient. 'These are matters to talk over with the vet, not the family doctor!'

'No doubt! I am merely trying to establish the cause of your own illness. Now tell me – if one of your cows aborted, what would

51

you do with the milk?'

'Why, it would go in with the rest, of course. There's nothing wrong with the milk, Doctor! It's the discharge from the cow's breeding passages that carries the infection!'

'It used to be so accepted, I agree. But modern thought inclines to the view that the milk is also infected. A good deal of research is going on which tends to support this. Have you in fact had an abortion here?'

'Well yes,' the farmer said, very reluctantly. 'A second-calver cast her calf at about six months a few weeks ago.'

'And the milk went in with the rest?'

'Yes, of course, every farmer does that. What else could we do with the beast? We're prevented by law – an Act passed in 1922, I think – from offering her for sale on the open market. She'd be no good to the butcher in that condition and we certainly couldn't afford to send her to the knacker. That would be unthinkable!'

'You could rear calves on the cow.'

'Now look here, Doctor, if as you say the milk is infected then the heifer would get the disease and there'd be no end to it.'

'But don't you sometimes rear male calves for fattening?'

'Oh, yes, of course. We could do that.' Bob was visibly annoyed that he had not thought of this himself. 'But what are you trying to tell me, Doctor?'

'Simply this, Mr Felton. You are suffering from a fever transmitted to you from the milk of this aborted cow. The pattern fits exactly – regular night fevers which subside in the morning, headaches, general debility, and these animal odours from the body. I don't quite see how abortion comes to be in your herd, but it must be there!'

'We certainly haven't bought it in,' the farmer said thoughtfully. 'But of course we oblige one or two neighbours by letting them use our bull. That practice will have to stop, althought I don't know what they'll do – they're only small men. But what about me? Why have I got it and no one else? Everybody in this house drinks the same milk. It seems to me this knocks your theory into a cocked hat.'

'It's no longer a theory, Mr Felton. But disease tends to be selective and we don't always know the reason, I'm afraid. Now, the first thing to do is to remove that cow from the milking herd. You can identify her, I suppose? Drink less milk for a while. There might be other cows in who carry the disease latent in their system. Then I'll put you on a diet and a course of treatment which must be rigidly adhered to. I'm afraid it's going to be a long job, Mr Felton. At least, every other known case has been.'

'What do they call this illness, Doctor?' asked Meg who had been listening to the dialogue with growing dismay.

'It's been named undulant fever from the characteristic undulating pattern of the symptoms. But the technical name is the same as the veterinary profession uses for the disease among cattle – brucellosis. Now Mr Felton, you've a splendid constitution and there's no reason why you shouldn't be back at work, in full health, by the spring!'

'By the spring?' Bob shouted. 'Good God, man, this is only September!'

'It may sound a long time,' said Doctor Whittaker, 'but it's relative, you know. If you could survive four years in the trenches on the Western Front, then I'm sure you can tolerate a few weeks in a sick-bed in your own home, surrounded by your family and with every comfort.'

'If you put it like that . . .' Bob said and groaned.

Chapter Six

Robert Felton was not a good patient. The thought of lying in bed weak and helpless while his beloved farm disintegrated (as he imagined) was almost too much to bear at first. He had felt quite differently when he was in hospital at St Albans in 1916–17. His army life severed him from the farm in any case and prior to the War he had been a workman only – a favourite workman perhaps – but not involved in the management. Since the War, Oakleigh had been his whole life and he begrudged every hour away from it. Now he was forced to lie inactive, hearing the familiar farm sounds only through his window, which in the sunny October weather was frequently wide open.

At first he was consulted often, even down to small details, Arthur running up to him every mealtime to report progress and to receive comments, but as time went on this attention to his feelings and reliance on his flair for organisation dwindled. Because of his asthma, Mr Ratcliffe mounted the stairs once a day only, which was when he went to bed. Each night when he had recovered his breath he visited his son-in-law to talk shop. Since Bob had come home in 1919, newly demobilised, Mr Ratcliffe, still grieving for his older son Sam, had allowed the whole of the management to slip into the returned soldier's hands. But he had never forgotten that he was a competent farmer in his own right. He had occupied Oakleigh for over forty years, knew every square yard, every brick and post, every animal, and had not lost any of his old skills. This illness of his son-in-law was a blessing in disguise for the old man, giving him a rejuvenated interest in life. Within a few days he had taken over full control as if he had never relinquished it and although he made full use of Arthur as an errand boy he took major decisions without consulting the boy's father. He told himself that by so doing he was taking worry from Bob's mind, but in fact it had the opposite effect. The younger man fretted because he could not take every minute decision and he had to keep reminding himself that Meg's father was, after all, still a partner in the farming business.

Much to his own and everybody else's alarm Robert Felton got progressively weaker and by the time harvest was over he was unable to leave his room for the kitchen. The potatoes had been lifted and camped without his involvement, the last load of mangolds had rumbled out of the carts without his knowledge; he felt weak and unimportant for the first time in his life and he did not seem to care that he could no longer go downstairs. A log fire was kindled in his room every day, not because the temperature was low, but because as his wife said 'the place looks more homely with a fire going'. She bought him another wireless set and had it fitted within reach of the bed, but he rarely used it and evinced no interest.

Dr Whittaker was deeply concerned at his patient's total withdrawal, as he preferred to call it, and did not hesitate to communicate his fear to the farmer's wife.

'We must keep his mind active, Mrs Felton. He needs plenty of visitors, preferably someone with him most of the time.'

'Do you think we should move his bed downstairs, Doctor, into the sitting-room?'

'That might not be a very good idea,' the doctor said thoughtfully. 'He would hear the household conversation in the kitchen and would feel frustrated at not being able to join in. Besides, there are the practical considerations, your bathroom is upstairs.'

'I could do my homework in Daddy's room,' suggested Edith who, quite unwarrantably, was hovering within earshot before setting off for Sunday school. The doctor's concern had compelled him to make a Sunday morning call, which was quite a rare event.

'Edith!' said her mother sharply. 'How dare you be so rude as to listen to our conversation and to interrupt! When you come back from Sunday school you'd better go straight to bed and stay there for the rest of the day!'

'Don't be too hasty, Mrs Felton. Your daughter has something there! Edith, that's quite a brilliant suggestion. Take as much homework as you can get up to Daddy's bedside – tell him what you are doing and ask his advice. I am sure he will begin to look forward to his evenings and we have a long dark winter ahead of us.'

'We'll certainly arrange that if you say so, Doctor.' Meg was secretly pleased to know that she had such an intelligent daughter, but she would not show it. 'You can go up there this evening Edith and if you've already done your homework, which you should have, you can read him one of your books. Now run off, or you'll be late.'

'The fact is, Doctor,' Mrs Felton continued when Edith had left for church, 'I've kept the girl away from her father as much as I could in case she worried him.'

'I don't think that's very likely, Mrs Felton. Edith's obviously very fond of her father and she is such a lovely child I am sure he is very fond of her and would welcome her company. She is so very much like you were when I first started Sunday school at Hartnall. You were the prettiest girl in the village and all we little ones loved and admired you!'

'Hang it all, Doctor, I wasn't all that much older!'

'No, but when one is very young even two or three years seems a lot. Anyway, you were very beautiful and still are, if I may say so, and Edith is taking after you.'

'Careful, Doctor!' Meg smiled deprecatingly, but was gratified by the warmth of the remarks.

The pattern was set accordingly. A suitable table was moved into the sickroom and every afternoon Edith rushed upstairs with her satchel of books as soon as she arrived home and remained there until bedtime, except for her hurried supper at six o'clock.

At first Bob was surprised and perplexed but he soon came to enjoy it. He went through her work, asking her this, and telling her that. Sometimes their discussion went on well after Edith's normal bedtime and her mother, thinking that the girl had gone straight to bed, would go up and find her sleeping soundly on top of the quilt beside her father, also asleep. This was a satisfaction in itself for normally he had difficulty in sleeping at all.

When there was no homework, or if it finished early, Edith would read to her father. Her English class was taking Scott and she would read lines from *Marmion*, for the vivid descriptions and grandiloquent setting of the narrative fascinated them both. When Edith, soldiering through the introductions came to the lines,

> To mute and to material things,
> New life revolving summer brings,
> The genial call dead nature hears,
> And in her glory reappears.

'Read that again Ede,' said her father and when she had repeated it: 'And again!' Then he said, half to himself, 'I hope it'll be like that for me, but sometimes I doubt it!'

Tears welled up in the girl's eyes as she flung her arms round his neck and kissed him.

'Oh Daddy! Daddy! Don't be so sad! We're all praying for you to get better, and you *are* better than you were, you know you are!'

'Sorry Ede. I shouldn't have given way to melancholy, especially when I've got such a loving and lovely daughter looking after me!'

Arthur continued to visit the sickroom during the dinner hour, and inform his father of the scope and progress of the day's work, but in the evenings the boy, intent on keeping his promise to his grandfather, studied hard for the professional qualifications which the old man thought so desirable. Mr Ratcliffe went to bed much earlier now that he had such a busy life but never failed to spend half-an-hour with his son-in-law before retiring, discussing policy and finance in an endeavour to keep his partner's interest alive. The fluctuating nature of Robert Felton's illness seemed to reflect his keenness, or lack of it, on farm topics.

The rector, Mr Bagnall, called in twice a week. He was now a very old man having held the living for more than forty years. He easily remembered Bob's advent as milk lad, for it seemed to him quite a recent occurrence and it affected his attitude. The farmer found it amusing or annoying according to the level of his spirits.

Several farmer neighbours called once or twice in the early days but their visits did not persist for, as Mr Ratcliffe said, farmers are not usually good sick visitors.

'They sit there with a faraway look in their eyes as if they're half thinking about tomorrow's weather or when to order the thresher, or the price of store cattle.'

'Then why don't they say these things aloud instead of just thinking? That's just what a sick farmer needs to make him feel he's still part of it all!'

'I'm sure you're right, Meg, but it just wouldn't occur to 'em.'

There was one other regular caller – Jim Wheeler, whom Bob and Mr Ratcliffe had helped to buy his farm ten years previously. An honest man with a simple scale of values.

'You 'elped us once, Master Bob,' he said, maintaining the old master/servant relationship, 'and sin' then me and Pam 've niver looked back. We owe everything to you and Ah'd be a poor thing if Ah couldn't come and 'ave a word with thee when thee's ill and lonesome.'

'Always glad to see you, Jim,' Bob said and meant it; after such a visit he felt that he was not entirely losing touch with his farming connections.

Arthur brought him a great surprise on one of his usual dinnertime visits.

'What do you think, Dad? Major Mortimer Ratcliffe stopped and spoke to me today. We had quite a conversation, in fact.'

His father reared up on one elbow.

'Mortimer? That *is* strange! As you know, there's no love lost

57

between those Ratcliffes and us.'

'I know that it is so, but I've never known why. Anyway, I was talking to Dick who's ploughing over at Clayfields and the Major came along on his new black horse. I've never spoken to him direct before, but of course I've seen him at the meets and been close to him at the Scouts and on the cricket field. Well, the Major stopped and I could see he wanted to say something, so I gave Dick the nod to go on.'

'And what did Mortimer say?'

'At first he chatted on general lines – about the difficult harvesting weather and how fortunate we were to have got ours all in. Then he got on to cricket and said he hoped I'd join the club and play regularly next year as he thought I had the makings of a good opening bat. He used to go in first, he said, before his arm was crippled. I suppose he got that during the War, and yet I fancy somehow I can remember seeing him play when I was six or seven!'

'Never mind about the cricket talk, Arthur. Come to the point.'

'Well, then he said he'd heard you were very ill and how sorry he was and that he would like to come and see you!'

'The devil he would!'

'"It would be a neighbourly thing to do," he said. I asked him what on earth there was to prevent him. Other neighbours came in freely!'

'"Our families haven't always seen eye to eye, although we bear the same surname," he said to me. "But your grandfather was my father's tenant over forty years ago and there's a long and intimate connection." What was the trouble years ago, Dad?'

'Part of it was that your grandfather bought his farm and that didn't please them!'

'But that doesn't make sense,' objected Arthur. 'He couldn't have bought it unless they were willing to sell, could he?'

'There was a lot more to it than that,' his father said hurriedly, anxious not to get involved in lengthy explanations. 'Have you told your mother?'

'Well, no. It was you he wanted to see.'

'Better tell her, then, but not when your grandfather's there.'

'Why ever not?'

'He had a serious argument with Mortimer personally, much later!'

'Well, I'm blowed! I'll ask him about it.'

'You'll do no such thing Arthur! He's very touchy over it and it's no good raking up the past. Thanks for telling me. Now you'd better get back to work – whatever it is you're doing, for I'm blessed if I know.'

'But what am I to tell Major Ratcliffe if I see him? I got the impression that he's going to look me up for an answer.'

'Your mother and I will talk it over and tell you later.'

After dinner Arthur waited until his grandfather had left the house with Charlie, whose job it was to harness the nag and hitch him in the float for the old man's use, before telling his mother of Mortimer Ratcliffe's request. Her reaction astonished him, for she whispered fiercely, 'Don't say a word of this to anybody else!' and rushed upstairs leaving Gladys to cope with the washing-up single-handed.

Subconsciously Meg noticed that her husband was more alert than she had seen him for some days, but the significance of it was momentarily submerged in the importance of her visit.

'Bob, what are we going to do about Mortimer?' she exclaimed as she entered the room.

'That's what we've got to decide,' Bob said, sitting up with animation. 'Will it be opening up old sores, or should we take the opportunity of burying the hatchet?'

'From his point of view it must be a wish to bury the hatchet. If we don't accept his gesture we shall get all the blame from the village for wanting to stay enemies for ever with our nearest neighbours.'

'The man's got a nerve, Meg, but that class of people always have. Generations of superiority you know, right up from feudal times.'

'I wonder he ever had the cheek to come back to Hartnall at all!'

'He stayed abroad for two years and I reckon he knew by then that Betty would keep quiet about it for good. He would have heard from the Home Farm bailiff – Gillespie, it was then, wasn't it – that she and Edwin had gone right away from here.'

'Yes, but what about Betty's reaction to all this? Won't she think it disloyal of us. After all, it ruined Betty's life at the time and ours as well. How pleasant it would have been if they'd been living next door all these years!'

'I'm sure Betty's got over it by now – it's more than eight years. At least, she never mentions it. I have an idea that Mortimer wrote and apologised, although Betty's never actually said so. Not to me, anyway, nor to you, has she?'

'Apologise? Apologise for tearing a girl's clothes off and having his way with her in her own hay-shed? It would need some apology to wipe that out!'

'I dare say. Genuine respectable women place more importance on that sort of thing than men of Mortimer's type. Probably it wasn't the first time he'd done it!'

'Don't *you* belittle it, Bob! I bet it was the first time he'd met an angry farmer just outside! It's a wonder Dad didn't kill him! He would have if the blow had landed in the right place.'

'Well, your Dad's no weakling and he had a hefty walking-stick. Mortimer's left arm's never been the same since that day.'

'What are we going to do about Dad? He might burst a blood vessel if he meets Mortimer in our house.'

'I don't think so, Meg. Your father's sensible in most matters. He wouldn't want things to blow up so that Arthur and Edith got to know. You'll have to tell him quietly, though, and warn him that Arthur's beginning to get curious already.'

'Should I phone Mortimer do you think, and invite him to come along?'

'No – let him make the running. He approached Arthur in the first place. Let him meet the lad again if he really wants to come. Arthur can tell him casually that he can visit us if he likes. We certainly don't want Mortimer to think he's doing us an honour by calling!'

Major Ratcliffe drove his Sunbeam into the Oakleigh yard a few afternoons later. The break-up of the estate ten years previously had not entirely extinguished his penchant for expensive cars and high living. He dwelt at the Home Farm where the farmhouse had been suitably improved for his use, and the farm was well and profitably run by the Scottish bailiff Laing. Hunters were kept for the owner and a pony for their first child, Belinda. He accepted as his right the same respect and subservience from the villagers as had been automatically accorded his father in the spacious days when the Squire ruled the village from the Hall. Since the War, the fine old mansion had become a girls' school. The coach-houses, stables and other outbuildings were little used other than for storage, and the whole place carried an air of postponed decay. Major Ratcliffe accepted the changed profile and his reduced status without any noticeable resentment.

Knowing the general farming customs as well as the habits of his neighbours, Major Ratcliffe chose a time when his namesake, Arnold Ratcliffe, was supervising the potato-lifting at the far end of the farm where he would remain until five o'clock, when the pickers – some village women and unemployed factory lads, would return to their homes. The visitor correctly ignored the

60

front door, walked round the house, through the cooling-shed and rapped on the back door which was ajar. Gladys answered his knock.

'Come in, sir,' she said bashfully, 'Mrs Felton's in the sitting-room. I'll tell her you're here.'

The Major's tall figure seemed to reach the ceiling as he entered and took off his checked tweed cap. Gladys returned and ushered him into the front room, where Meg stood nervously awaiting him.

'Good afternoon, Major Ratcliffe,' she said awkwardly.

'Good afternoon, Mrs Felton, or may I still say Margaret? We have known each other for so many years it seems a pity to be entirely formal.'

'All our lives, Major, not just so many years!'

'Even so I don't think I've ever been in this house before.'

'I daresay not, but your father called in here several times during the twenty-odd years my family were his tenants.'

'They were the spacious days, Margaret. A pity they had to pass away. But I called to see your husband, having heard that he was ill. Is he not about?'

'Bob's in his bedroom, Major. He doesn't come down these days.'

'Oh dear! I'm sorry to hear that. He must be more seriously ill than I realised. May I go up and see him?'

'Yes, of course.'

Mrs Felton led the way up the stairs to the pink bedroom at the front of the house. The colour scheme had never been changed from Betty's choice so many years before.

'Major Ratcliffe to see you Bob,' Meg said nervously, then added: 'If you'll excuse me, I'll leave you together. I've things to do downstairs.'

'Sit down, Major Ratcliffe,' Bob said stiffly, indicating Edith's homework chair, 'and tell me the reason for this surprising visit.'

'Do neighbours need a reason for visiting each other, Felton? Especially when one of them is ill – seriously ill, it appears, which I am sorry to see.'

'Thank you for your concern, but I don't feel particularly ill. Just weak in the legs after an intermittent fever.'

'At any rate, I'm glad to find you're able to make light of it.'

'Talking of neighbourliness,' Bob persisted, 'we haven't really been the sort of neighbours who make sympathetic calls on each other in time of sickness, and you know the reason, well enough!'

'Ah, you mean the affair with your sister. I'm sorry about that,

Felton, and I've never ceased to regret it. She was such a lovely girl, quite ravishing in fact. I could not help being attracted to her!'

'She was a married woman!'

'Quite so, I shouldn't have gone as far as I did. But I paid for it, you know. Arnold Ratcliffe nearly cut me in half with his walking-stick. Ruined this arm for good, unfortunately. I never played cricket or golf properly afterwards. I probably came off worse – very much the worst, I should think. Betty would soon have got over the incident, which was only high spirits, really.'

'In fact she had a nervous breakdown and it ruined her life in that she couldn't stay at Manor Farm. They moved away on medical advice! But we've been all through this before – in Gammon's time.'

'I did write to Betty and apologise. She didn't reply!'

'Did you expect her to?'

'Well, yes, after such an interval. Most women would have done so. Perhaps I had underestimated her sensitivity.'

'I suppose there's no point in going over this same ground,' Bob said grudgingly. He was feeling tired and he hoped his unwelcome visitor would soon go.

'We shall be farming side by side for many years possibly,' Major Ratcliffe answered. 'I have no intention of leaving Hartnall and I am sure you haven't either. I thought it would be worthwhile trying to clear the air of past misunderstandings . . .'

'Past misdeeds, more like,' interrupted Felton.

'Well, if you say so . . . and live together amicably. We are the two largest farmers in the parish, employing the most people, so any co-operation between us must be for the good of the village. I should like to see Hartnall remain a close-knit community.'

'I quite follow you,' the farmer said, stifling a yawn. He was becoming tired and did not attempt to disguise it.

'Of course if you wish to reduce your activities after this obviously exhausting illness, I am quite prepared to take over any land you may wish to relinquish.'

'I am not likely to do that,' Bob said crossly as the reason for the Major's visit became apparent. 'I have an able family.'

'Quite so! I am much taken with your son, who as well as being a budding farmer, shows great promise as a cricketer. But I fear I am tiring you with my conversation. No doubt your illness has affected your powers of endurance and concentration. Nothing like it was on Coronation Day, what? I will leave you now, Felton. I am sorry to see you so ill and I hope there will be considerable improvement when I call again. Goodbye! I am sure I can find my own way out!'

'Well, I'm damned!' Bob said to himself when he was alone. 'I'll bloody well show him!'

'What are you swearing to yourself about?' his wife asked as she came up the stairs.

'Mortimer, of course. The nerve of the fellow! I should have known. He didn't call here out of sympathy, you know!'

'What then?'

'To see how close I was to the grave so he could put in a stake for any land that might be available when I'm dead!'

'Oh, surely not, Bob!' Meg was amused at her husband's vehemence, but delighted that he had so miraculously regained his old interest. 'Didn't he talk about Betty at all?'

'Oh yes! He brought that up as preliminary. Wants to scrub that from the slate and be good neighbours with us. Said he was sorry to see me so ill, but he made it sound as though he was really glad. Then, in case I'm not well enough to continue farming such a large place, he'd be prepared to take over some of our land! My God, Mortimer, just wait until I've done with this sick bed!'

'Don't get excitable, Bob.'

'Excitable be damned! I suppose I can be angry in our own house? When's that doctor coming again? I'll have a long talk with him.'

Chapter Seven

Major Ratcliffe's unexpected visit marked the turning-point in Robert Felton's illness. If the Major had been hoping to accelerate the farmer's withdrawal from active farming he was disappointed for the implications of the conversation struck deep into Felton's mind and reinforced his will to survive. The doctor was delighted at the change in his patient, for after weeks of lethargy Bob became enquiring, argumentative and impatient.

'I'm glad to see you taking such an interest in life again, Mr Felton. The change in your attitude is quite remarkable. But I must warn you that full recovery is still a long way off. The undulating nature of the fever may continue for several months yet – hopefully on a lower level. If you can retain the zest you are showing now you should be back at the helm by the spring.'

'I'm aiming to be fit by Christmas,' Felton said boldly.

'Let's hope your marksmanship is as good as your intention,' Doctor Whittaker said as he rose to go. 'I shall not need to come in so frequently now – not more than once a week unless you send for me. I'm sure your womenfolk will continue to attend to your wants as admirably and devotedly as they have done in the past.'

'I've no complaints on that score Doctor, I can assure you! It's bad enough to be ill, certainly, but with my family taking such care of me and the farm, it's not so bad as it might have been.'

'That's a bit of soft soap, Bob Felton,' his wife said, entering the room at that moment. 'A pity you don't tell us, as well as the Doctor. Of course we've looked after you as well as we could! We want you out of the house, out of our way. We can't get on with the housework with you under our feet!'

'You just see how my wife speaks to me, Doctor.' Bob said plaintively.

'I think I'll get on with my calls and leave you to sort out your own problems of cause and effect,' Doctor Whittaker replied, smiling with real amusement. 'Everybody in this district knows that you're a model couple – a fair example of the perfect marriage – and you don't have to pretend otherwise to me!'

Every member of the Oakleigh household was affected by the change in the master's condition. It was if a giant thundercloud with its depressive humidity had been static over the farm for weeks and had now moved away, leaving blue-patched skies.

Meg's feelings were of relief and gratitude bracketed with the hope that her husband was reverting to his normal character and would soon resume the life of a vigorous and still young married man. Mr Ratcliffe was glad to think that his son-in-law might soon take over the bulk of the farm management again, for the novelty had worn off long since and the old man felt his age. Arthur had privately worried that his father might not recover, and to have this load removed from his mind was a delight. Now he began to wonder what effect his father's return to duty would have on his own recently-acquired status.

Edith's joy was obvious to everyone and she asserted with tiresome frequency that it was her own efforts in providing her father with company and interest which had brought about the change. Gladys, the willing and friendly maid, was pleased to think that her own work-load would be reduced but she was, and always had been sympathetic towards her mistress' distress and problems, for in her eyes the Feltons were ideal employers. The farm lads who lived in felt similarly for they too enjoyed their employment and to be members of a household where the master was ill seemed vaguely embarrassing.

The married workers were understandably pleased when news of the Gaffer's progress filtered out to them. At first, receiving their directions from the Old Gaffer or young Arthur had seemed a pleasant novelty, but after a few weeks they all longed secretly for the return of Mr Bob's masterful presence which left no one in any doubt as to his own share in the day's or the season's programme.

To give added point to his own determination to recover quickly, Robert Felton insisted on coming downstairs in between his bouts of fever and sitting beside the kitchen fire. As the doctor had forecast, these recurrences of fever were inevitable and each time Bob was exhausted and dispirited for a day or two and fretted because he was too weak to leave his bed. But as he regained his strength, his resolve to get well quickly took possession again and he resumed his daily visits to the kitchen. Meg and Gladys thought this a mixed blessing, but tried not to show that they were being inconvenienced. However, Meg did mention as casually as she could that if Bob intended to come down regularly she would have the sitting-room fire kindled in the morning instead of the late afternoon. To her relief Bob said he thought this a good idea and added that he had not liked to suggest it himself although the windsor armchairs beside the kitchen range were not *too* comfortable to sit in for hours on end. Of course it was satisfactory to be able to overlook the main farmyard from the kitchen window all the time, but the extra comfort of the deeply-upholstered three-piece suite in the parlour more than compensated for the view of the muck-hole, and anyway he now had a good head-on view of the farm drive.

However, he did not spend all his time gazing down the well-known approach road for he had latterly taken to reading – mostly library books chosen by Edith, who insisted that she knew better than anyone else what Daddy would want to read. One drab December afternoon he sat in his usual regal comfort enjoying the new farming novel *Farmer's Glory* written by A. G. Street, a fellow farmer of similar age. He was so engrossed that he failed to notice Major Ratcliffe's long car bouncing down the rutted drive.

'Major Ratcliffe to see you, Bob,' Meg Felton said unnecessarily as she ushered in the visitor and quickly excused herself.

The farmer put down his book with noticeable reluctance and rose to his feet.

'Glad to see you, Major,' he said as he shook hands, but his tone quite failed to match the cordiality of the words.

'I am certainly surprised and delighted to find that you are about again, Felton,' the Major said, equally unconvincingly. 'A remarkable improvement since my last visit. You will soon be taking up the reins again, no doubt!'

'I hope so, Major, although I must say Meg's father and young Arthur seem to be coping adequately. I'm sure the farm hasn't suffered through my absence. There'll be no need to consider selling off part of the land, after all,' he added maliciously. 'In fact we might be trying to buy some more from you!'

'You're joking, of course,' said the visitor coldly. 'Although it is ten years since the estate was broken up, I have still not become used to farming a relatively small acreage and shall recover as much of the land as I can, if and when it becomes available.'

'Well, none of Oakleigh land will become available in my lifetime, that's certain,' Felton said positively. 'However, it's good of you to call and see me. Perhaps I can return the compliment when you are unwell. Do sit down. How are your wife and little daughter keeping? No doubt they will be looking forward to their Christmas skiing holiday in the Alps!'

Major Ratcliffe clearly did not appreciate this hearty and semi-intimate approach.

'I am sure you are aware that such holidays are not provided by the income derived from farming only, Felton. There is little enough profit in it these days, as you must know – certainly not enough to allow for Continental holidays. In our case, other funds are available. But I did not call to discuss these private family matters, as I am sure you are aware. I am impressed by your splendid, clean and apparently heavy crops of potatoes which I have seen your staff dressing out for market on several occasions. My crop was badly affected by blight, which is not unusual in a wet summer, but yours seem to be little affected.'

'That's probably because I grow only whites and choose varieties less susceptible to disease. They may be worth less per ton on the market, but the heavier unblemished crop more than compensates. That's the art of farming, Major.' After the snub about the holidays, Felton could not resist this final dig.

'We ought to get together more, Felton. I'm sure if we combined our knowledge and ideas it would be advantageous to both of us. However this is not really the time to pursue the proposal. Later on when you have fully recovered, perhaps. Although you have clearly made great strides since I saw you last, you are still far from well and unlikely to resume your normal life for some time. I think I will leave you now and look forward to seeing further improvement when I call again in a month or two, perhaps.'

He smiled as he left the room. The farmer smiled too, although he was fuming inwardly at Major Ratcliffe's overtly discouraging attitude.

'That villain always manages to have the last word,' he said angrily to Meg when she returned after showing the visitor out. 'But I'll have the last laugh, I'll warrant!'

'Don't bother about him, Bob! If it pleases him to act superior, why should we worry? We've got everything we want and he can't take it from us. We can be civil to him without getting into his pocket or eating out of his hand. He can't force us into selling him any of our land – nor scare us into it, if I know you. Just concentrate on getting well, dear, so we can show him that the Feltons are a force to be reckoned with!'

Felton put his arm round her and hugged her tightly.

'Thanks for your loyalty and faith, Meg,' he said huskily. 'That's what'll keep me going over the next month or two. I haven't got rid of these damned fevers yet, worse luck! I can feel it coming on again, blast it!'

'It's just that Mortimer's visit has caused your temperature to go up,' Meg said, not very convincingly. 'He makes every male member of this family see red every time he turns up. But I should go to bed now, dear. Don't stay down here and tire yourself out making plans. Time enough for that when you're back to normal.'

The winter dragged on sombrely – for Robert Felton at least – in a succession of black, grey and lighter patches. To everyone's unfeigned delight Christmas coincided with one of the brighter periods and Oakleigh enjoyed the festival in much the same way as usual. Arthur and Edith were still young enough to revel in the traditional glories of Christmas, the decorations, the seasonal music on the wireless, the exchange of presents secretly planned weeks in advance and, above all, the unending supply of rich food, which Edith helped to prepare proudly. Mr Felton was still not well enough to leave the house and as his wife had never learned to drive the car, Arthur had to drive his mother to the village in the milk-float on her Christmas Eve visits to the homes of their employees. She carried a farm-fed chicken and a bottle of port for each family, plus cigarettes for each man, artificial silk stockings for each wife and a toy, lovingly chosen, again with Edith's help, for each child. Of course, Edith had to accompany her mother for Edith had heard her say many times that it was the part of Christmas she enjoyed the most.

'Next year I'll be old enough to drive you round in the car, Mum,' Arthur said as the pony trotted out of the farm drive. His mother replied, 'Next year your father will be able to drive me again, as he has done every year since we first had a car,' and there was silence for a few minutes.

On Christmas Day the farm lads were invited into the kitchen to have their meals with the family and, by tradition, the farmer made a speech at teatime, reviewing the past year with its trials and welcoming the coming year with its hoped-for successes. He mentioned that it was the twenty-first Christmas since he had first come to Oakleigh and added forcefully, 'By gum, it's not the worst either, in spite of everything. When I think of the miseries of Christmases in the trenches, when you couldn't help thinking that every day might be your last . . . but all that's well behind us, thank God. I think we all ought to spare a thought on how lucky we are to be on a farm and have plenty of good, fresh, homeproduced food. In some parts of the country, in the big manufacturing towns where there are thousands on the dole, they'll be having a thin time, poor devils.' And having made them all feel slightly guilty, he sat down to a subdued silence.

As the January days lengthened, Bob the invalid moved slowly and almost imperceptibly back into the character of Bob the farmer. He asked casually for the account books, secretly intending to criticise his family for neglecting them, but was agreeably surprised to find that they were quite up to date. In fact, Arthur's neat round figures and legible schoolboy handwriting showed a great improvement on the farmer's own bold lettering. Wisely, he made no comment, deciding to allow his son to continue with the book-keeping unless he asked to be relieved of it.

On a gently warm day in February he made his first visit to the farmyard. The waggoners, just bringing their horses in for dinner, were so loquaciously pleased to see him that he forebore to criticise minor items of untidiness, which he felt would have been churlish. He certainly did not wish to make his presence felt in that way – yet. The cowman also shouted a hearty greeting from inside the mixing-place.

Bob stood in the cowshed doorway – open because of the unexpected warmth of the day – surveying the long lines of shorthorn cows as they stood in front of him, two by two by two, side by side, down into the dim distance of the shed. They were eagerly consuming their midday feed of the ensilage which had been made at Arthur's instigation. Their chains jingled musically as they tossed their heads in delight, devouring the evil-smelling stuff with a relish which the farmer found difficult to understand. Sensing his presence, some of the nearer cows swung their heads round to regard him with their huge friendly eyes. He fancied that they, too, seemed glad to see him, which raised his spirits and he greeted his father-in-law cheerfully as the old man appeared at the door of the mixing-place.

'B'guy, Bob, I'm glad to see you about again, lad,' Mr Ratcliffe said heartily as he walked up the cowshed to join his son-in-law. 'It's what I've been waiting for these three or four months. I thought I could do it, but I find I get tired very easily and I'll be thankful when you take over again. The cows look well, don't they?'

'Aye! A bit too well, perhaps. I hope they're not being overfed!'

'They're not getting too much, I can assure you, and the milk is keeping up. Must be the ensilage.'

'That stinking stuff? I'm surprised they eat it!'

'So was I at first. When we started using it, I said to Alf, "You're carrying muck into th' shed instead of out o' it." But they really go for it. Sometimes it comes out quite warm, especially from near the top o' the stack where it's not settled down tight enough – at least, that's what Arthur says – and it steams just like a muck heap. Alf said it was the first time he'd given his cows a hot dinner!'

69

'Don't they grumble about handling it?'

'The chaps don't, but I fancy their wives don't like the smell o' their clothes when they get indoors and sit down by the fire.'

'I've noticed it a bit with young Tom. They ought to wear overalls for the ensilage and take 'em off when they go home. Perhaps we should supply 'em.'

'It's an idea, Bob. We certainly didn't think of it. That's surprising really, 'cos young Arthur's coming out with new ideas every day. What it is to be young! I keep putting him off by saying we'll leave it until you're about again. And now you are, thank the Lord!'

'What's he doing today, and the others?'

'Riddling 'taters for the Co-op. Just started the last camp. It's become a slow job. This lot haven't kept as well as the others. Too wet last summer, I reckon. This was the only field that took the blight, though.'

'Are the waggoners and hosses there too? All of 'em?'

'Aye, well, there's seven tons to put on rail. That's six cart-loads you know, and Arthur likes to load the bags straight off the riddle and send each cart off as soon as it's loaded.'

'It's a slow job going to Willington six times a day, certainly. I'm beginning to wonder why they can't pick 'em up themselves. They've got plenty of lorries!'

'That's what Arthur's been saying all season!'

At the dinner-table Arthur said it again, quite forcefully and seemed prepared to pour out a flood of other suggestions and criticisms of the farm policy and practices. His mother quickly put a stop to it.

'That's enough of that tack, Arthur,' she said crossly. 'This is your father's first day out for months and you want to spoil it with arguments about changing things.'

'I don't want to spoil anything, Mum. Just a few suggestions for improving the work on the farm.'

'I'd rather see your father improve first, if you don't mind! Your improvements can come later, and a bit slower, too. Rome wasn't built in a day!'

'I wasn't the boss' son on that job.'

'Very sharp aren't you? Mind you don't fall down and cut yourself. Anyway, that's enough! Get on with your dinner young man. The farm can quite well go on as it has been doing for many years, before you even came on the scene.'

Meg should have known that her son was irrepressible. He returned to the subject at the evening meal when discussion was

70

more readily tolerated since there was no urgency to return to work. His seniors were listening to him good-humouredly when Tommy was heard driving the nag and float up to the door of the cooling-shed. Charlie got up noisily from his place at the scullery table and walked across the brick floor in his nailed boots to help load the churns.

'That's another thing,' Arthur said argumentatively. 'Running the milk to the station every night with a horse. Takes an hour or more. If we had a trailer for the car we could do the journey in a few minutes.'

They all sat bolt upright at this revolutionary suggestion, and Edith looked at her brother in open-mouthed horror. She had begged a ride in the milk float hundreds of times and loved it. The tang of the sweating horse, the milky smell of the metal churns, and the company of the farm lad, also smelling of stale milk and manure – these thrilling occasions had been the highlights of her middle childhood. An unchanging ritual which was part of life itself on a Derbyshire farm. She tried hard to think of something to say which would wither her brother, but it was her father who spoke first.

'Now wait a minute,' he said, his voice vibrating with surprise and shock. 'This is fundamental. We've always done the evening milk run without any trouble – never caused any disorganisation that I know of. I used to love it when I was a lad. It was my first regular task at Oakleigh and I looked forward to it. The unfailing urgency, the company of the hoss, the chat with the porter and the other milk lads sometimes. Then the trip back home, sometimes on frosty nights in bright moonlight, sometimes so pitch black you had to leave the direction to the hoss!'

'It's all very well for you to reminisce in that touching way, Dad,' Arthur retorted. 'What about those wet nights when the milk lad comes home like a drowned rat, water running down his neck, off his nose and eyebrows. And what about those haymaking and harvesting nights? I've heard you grumble often enough, having to take a lad away from the gang to take the milk. When you were doing it, all those years ago, I reckon you just liked showing off with a smart hoss which was faster than anybody else's. That was the style of those days o' course, but we're moving on now.'

His father grunted but did not argue on this point for he felt he might be forced to acknowledge there was some truth in Arthur's summary. He decided to revert to practicalities.

'The milk hoss is useful for many other jobs, and it costs no

71

more to keep him. He doesn't need extra food for each mile, but a motor needs petrol, which has to paid for in cash!'

'Yes, but a motor doesn't need petrol when it's standing in the shed, but a hoss still needs grub! So it's as broad as it's long. The milk hoss' other jobs can be done in other ways. The bit of outside foddering can be done by one of the heavy hosses, nearly as quickly. We just wouldn't need the float hoss for anything. Sell him and save so much feed and grazing!'

Edith could restrain herself no longer. She alone had noticed her grandfather's drooping countenance.

'Oh shut up, Arthur!' she shouted. 'You're talking rubbish! If we don't have a horse and float, how about Grandad?'

'Don't bother about me, none of you,' the old man said, sadly sarcastic. 'I don't matter at all! I suppose I can stay in the yard for the rest of my life!'

Arthur was instantly penitent.

'Oh, Grandad, I'm sorry. I didn't think about you using it. Of course we must keep the milk hoss and float for you until – I mean, as long as you want it. Forget about the trailer, Dad!'

'Until I'm dead, you were going to say, Arthur. Well, you're probably right about the milk job, and I daresay I shan't last much longer, so you don't have to keep a nag hoss specially for me. A trailer behind the motor might well be quicker, and certainly more comfortable on wet nights. By gum though, these changes make me think. I took this place in March 1888, and now it's February 1932. That's nearly forty-four years we've driven the milk hoss to Willington station, every night without a break! We allus thought it'd go on for ever. But nothing does that, it seems.'

'Don't be unhappy, Grandad,' Edith said, leaving her place, going up to him and putting her arms round his neck. 'We don't want you to die! We want you to stay with us for ever and I shall insist that Daddy keeps the horse and float for you!'

'Sit down, Edith,' her father said. 'No need to get maudlin. Dash it all, this is a four-hundred-acre farm and surely we can afford to keep a light horse for the use of the old gaffer, even if things are bad generally. We'll think about a trailer, Arthur. It'd probably need a more powerful car than ours to pull it. But *I'm* not going to be milk lad! You'd have to take it on yourself. Anyway, you're not seventeen until June and then you've got to learn to drive.'

'I can drive now,' Arthur interrupted swiftly, hoping to strike while the iron was hot.

'Oh, can you? I think not! I'd like to know when you had the time and opportunity to learn.'

Arthur started to speak, then changed his mind, thinking it might not be wise to acquaint his father of the occasions when, during the master's absence he had taken the family car out of the barn. As an additional precaution, he flashed a warning glance to his sister.

'You learn to drive,' his father continued, 'and then I'll buy a big second-hand car and have a trailer made, and you can run the milk yourself every night. And to get used to it, you can take the milk in the float every night from now until then!'

Chapter Eight

As the spring advanced Robert Felton regained his full health in time to supervise the sowing of barley and oats in a dry and dusty March. Mr Ratcliffe heaved a deep sigh of relief which seemed to last for days. He contented himself with pottering around the yard in the morning and usually made a part-tour of the farm each afternoon in the float, carrying the odd bag of seed or fertiliser to meet an emergency, or simply just to look on.

The farm men were also vastly relieved at Mr Bob's return, for they had often been rendered breathless by young Arthur's impatience and hustling methods. Oakleigh Farm reverted to its old unhurried pace, every detail of every operation planned carefully in advance so that no time was wasted and the business as a whole again ran as smoothly as a sewing-machine.

Arthur was unwilling to give up his newly-acquired mature status and made many suggestions for improvements in management, most of which were firmly but fairly disposed of by his father. The boy was resentful but tried to console himself with the thought of his approaching seventeenth birthday which was to bring with it a car and trailer mainly for his use. In the meantime he made a show of learning to drive the family's new Ford, taking it out to the Rickyard Pasture on dry evenings. He had an aptitude for mechanics as he had shown with his tractor-driving, and he manoeuvred the car on the bumpy turf with suspicious ease. Watching him, his father smiled ruefully, but did not voice his conclusions. He merely reiterated his instructions to Arthur to procure a licence on his seventeenth birthday.

'And as you're going to drive for the farm, the five bob fee can come out of the farm accounts,' he said magnanimously.

'Do I have to wait until then, Dad?' Arthur asked testily. 'There's really no need. The Post Office people don't know how old I am – at least, not to the day!'

Unfortunately he made this remark at the meal-table when his mother was present and in fact standing behind him.

'There'll be no hanky-panky of that sort Arthur,' she said wrathfully. 'The very idea! Falsifying your age for the sake of a few weeks. That's downright dishonest and would make you into a liar! I've a good mind to box your ears for thinking of it!'

Arthur pulled a long face and hunched his neck down into his shoulders as if to lessen the effect of the threatened blow.

'All right, Mum! Keep your hair on. I was only joking.' This was an afterthought and convinced no one. Nevertheless, he wisely decided to wait patiently until June 5th.

Mr Felton kept to his original instruction that Arthur should do the evening milk run with Polly until the arrival of the new trailer, but this had an unforeseen result. Tommy, whom he superseded, enjoyed the job and the sixpence-a-night overtime which it earned him. He refused to accept the withdrawal of this precious perquisite and surprised everybody by immediately handing in a month's notice. His employers were shocked at his decision but, as a matter of principle, Robert Felton refused to change his plan in order to humour a disgruntled employee. Hoping that the lad would change his mind, he refrained from advertising for a replacement, but Tommy was too proud or too stubborn to withdraw and at the end of the month said his farewells with a lump in his throat. He was nineteen and had been living-in at the farm since leaving school five years earlier. The Feltons and Mr Ratcliffe, too, were subdued for they took an interest in their workpeople and regretted changes.

As was customary, Tommy left his employment after milking and the evening meal on Saturday. It was the middle of April, a cold wet evening and all the family were round the fire discussing farming topics, the chief being the gap caused by Tommy's leaving.

'You'd better get something off to the *Derbyshire Advertiser*, Bob, and the *Burton Chronicle* too, I should think. We can't manage for long with a man short, or can we?' This was Mr Ratcliffe's contribution.

'I think we could manage without another lad,' Arthur said swiftly before his father could reply. 'Sell the older of Charlie's team of hosses, then let him help Ned with the cows and work the odd horse part time.'

'An instant solution from the youngest farmer present,' his grandfather said with a sigh of amused resignation. 'Why do we bother to puzzle things out Bob, when Arthur here can give us an immediate answer?'

Bob smiled a his son's discomfiture.

'Arthur may have something there Dad, but it needs a fair bit more consideration. I wouldn't mind if we *could* get by with one hand less. We paid Tommy a pound a week plus three-and-six for taking the milk – that's about sixty pounds a year plus his keep.'

'I hope you're not going to cut the housekeeping just because

75

there's one lad less,' Mrs Felton said shortly. 'One mouth doesn't make any difference in this household!'

'All right, Meg, we're not as poor as that – yet,' her husband replied. 'But that sixty pounds a year is worth saving. We're not making much profit you know, if any. We farm well and live well, but we're only just keeping our heads above water.'

'I hope all this talk about being poor doesn't mean that I'll have to leave the High School,' Edith said glumly. 'Now that I've got used to it, I like it there.'

Everybody grinned at her obvious concern, but the girl looked tearful and sidled up to her grandfather who put his arm round her waist.

'Don't worry yourself, lass. I won't let 'em take you away from school. I've got a bit put by that'll cover your school fees and a bit more besides, I daresay. It might even run to buying you a sports outfit when the time comes. I think your Dad's in a pessimistic mood tonight. I shouldn't worry too much, Bob. We've had bad years before!'

'Yes, I know – some of 'em quite recently. But practically everything's bad just now. Wheat only just pays its way, even with this new subsidy. Barley and oats are worth four or five pounds a ton, which is nowt; taters only pay if you get an extra heavy crop, and as for beef cattle – well, the trade's so bad they'll soon have to bring in a subsidy on that!'

'But most of our corn goes for seed, doesn't it?' Meg interposed. 'Surely that must make some difference!'

'You're right, Meg,' her father replied. 'It does make a great difference. The Lord only knows how farmers go on who sell their crops to the merchants at ordinary prices.'

'Some of 'em are going bankrupt, Dad,' Bob said gloomily. 'It's a threat which hangs over all of us.'

'I don't see why. You can stand a small loss on your farm accounts for year after year without it affecting your farming or your living.'

'Well, I daresay some of 'em have been showing a loss every year since about 1921 and that's a long time. I s'pose we've been luckier than most.'

'Well, you are a grim lot tonight, I must say,' Meg observed. 'All this frightening talk of poverty and bankruptcies seems to have sprung from Tommy leaving. That's not like this family. We generally take those little things in our stride!'

'The sugar beet and the milk show a profit, don't they, Dad?' asked Arthur, privately agreeing with his mother and anxious to divert the conversation into pleasanter channels.

'The beet does, yes – it gives a good return but the few acres we grow doesn't have much impact on the general scene. It takes a hell of a lot of labour, so we can't grow any more without reducing the potato acreage. As for the milk – that's our mainstay of course, as it is of everybody else round here. But if we costed it out properly and separately, I reckon it'd be like giving a penny for two ha'pennies.'

'It seems to me then that we ought to try and do with even less labour,' Arthur said briskly, eager to show off his practical and analytical mind. 'There's old Ernie for instance – sentiment's all very well, but can we afford to go on paying him half wages for a bit of pottering about? He must be about seventy-five, and after all, they have their house for nowt!'

There was a choking sound from his mother as she struggled to get her words out.

'Arthur, I'll clout you good and hard if you dare to suggest such things about Ernie! He's been here since I was three years old, and that's as far back as I can remember. The old chap's been a good servant to Oakleigh, and so has Mrs Wagstaff. She helped us in the house here every day for more than twenty years. I won't have them touched. They only get the old age pension – that's a pound a week between them, but with that and a few shillings from the farm, they can just about manage. I will not have them end their lives in dire poverty, so there! And they'll stay in that cottage as long as either of 'em need it!'

'You've had your answer on that subject, Arthur,' his father told him, grinning widely. 'Your mother said it far better than I could.'

'Then I'd better not go to Cirencester,' pursued the irrepressible youth. 'Three years of doing nothing is a big drain on the exchequer.'

'Don't be ridiculous, Arthur,' Edith said imperiously. 'You don't go to college until a year next September anyway and things will be better by then.'

'Out of the mouths of babes and sucklings,' muttered her grandfather.

Arthur was not to be subdued.

'All right, then. What about fitting a milking machine and getting rid of another man?'

'Oh dear! He's at it again,' sighed Mr Ratcliffe. 'Don't you ever give up, Arthur?'

'That may well come in time,' Mr Felton observed, not wishing

77

to dampen his son's ardour entirely, 'but not just now, I think – not on this farm anyway. They need to be developed and improved a great deal more yet.'

'But milking machines are not new,' his son protested. 'They've been about for years. All my life, I should think.'

'So they have, and they'll have been about a good few more years before we use 'em at Oakleigh. We're free of mastitis here now, but we wouldn't be if we installed a machine!'

'That's because the operation of them is faulty!'

'Maybe, but as we haven't got a skilled operator, the result would be as I said. We'll just carry on with hand milking for the time being. Tell you what though, Arthur. If you're still so keen on machine-milking when you're through college, we'll put one in and you can be the non-faulty operator!'

'It's no good, Arthur,' his sister consoled him, 'they just don't like your ideas. The only change you're allowed is your motor and trailer and you'll have to be content with that. And I'll come along to the station with you to see you do it right.'

Mr Felton kept his word to his son, but he had no intention of allowing Arthur to use the family Ford, new last year, for trailer work. In the first week of June he purchased a four-year-old Austin sixteen, and had a drawbar fitted by the blacksmith. The local wheelwright constructed a trailer and Arthur was presented with his new turn-out. In the afternoon he practised diligently round the muck-hole, in forward gears and reverse. After tea he drove out of the yard with style and pride, the churns bouncing slightly on the more flexible springs of the trailer. Edith kept to her declared intention to accompany him, to which he agreed good-naturedly. To everyone's surprise Charlie went along too, telling Arthur that he would need some help to unload the churns. Privately Charlie thought there was no reason why he should not enjoy a free motor-ride now and again, for such luxuries seldom came the way of farm lads.

Mr Felton, his wife and the old man stood at the farm gate watching the little vehicle bounce and sway as it was drawn along irresistibly by the powerful car.

'I don't know whether I've done the right thing now,' Bob grumbled to his companions, 'There's seventy pounds for the motor, twenty for the trailer, licence for the car, insurance – that's about £125 without petrol and repairs! That would 'a kept old Polly going for a long time.'

'Too late to think o' that now, Bob,' his father-in-law said unsympathetically. 'Anyway, Arthur's a good lad. It won't do any harm to humour him a bit.'

'That's all very well *now*,' said Meg whose notions of progress were even more conservative than her menfolk, 'but what's going to happen when he's been through college? He'll want to turn the place upside down!'

'That's how it always is with youngsters,' her father reminded her. 'Bob brought in some new ideas when he came here as a lad, and you were more in favour of 'em than anybody else, as I remember it. The wheel's turned right round now and you're underneath instead of being on top.'

'That's altogether different,' Meg said shortly, but did not explain how or why.

The summer of 1932 was nearly as wet as the previous year and the dismal haymaking which, again, at Arthur's instigation expanded into silage-making, kept everyone's nerves on edge. The weeds grew strongly in the roots and in the corn crops, which meant that harvesting would be a long and arduous task unless there were long sunny spells, which seemed unlikely. While his family and the farm staff were foreseeing heavy difficulties, Arthur had another brainwave and suggested that at least one of the binders should be converted for tractor-power.

'With all this rubbish in the corn, the hosses are soon going to get tired,' he asserted, 'whereas the tractor can go on idefinitely. Not only that, it'll travel a little faster than hosses and the extra speed will help the mechanism to clear itself. At horse speed the machine will block every time the ejector comes over.'

Try as he might, his father could think of no argument to counter this suggestion, nor could his grandfather, so the change was made. Arthur and Dick went out proudly with the lurching tractor coupled to the better of the two binders to cut the first field of wheat. In a long day they finished the seventeen acres and drew the silent binder to the gate, well satisfied with their day's work. Mr Ratcliffe sat there in his float, watching the three teams of stookers coping with the hundreds of sheaves which still lay in neat rows in the centre half of the field.

'How's that for bindering, Grandad?' Arthur called across gaily as he and Dick prepared to pack up the machine. 'It's a lot more than your old hosses could 'a done in a day!'

'Aye, true enough. You've been running at full speed all day, I reckon. How many times did you stop to oil the machine?'

Arthur looked blank and Dick looked guilty and they looked at each other, but said nothing.

'I thought so! Didn't stop at all, did you? With the hosses, we

79

used to stop to oil up whenever they needed a blow, and the machine lasted longer! It's no good running on to finish a field in twilight it if means dry bearings! You remember that next time, and don't be so cocky!'

This incident was typical of his handling of the staff and spending his days. Robert Felton's illness had forced Mr Ratcliffe to take a renewed interest in the management of the farm. Although when his son-in-law recovered the old man had professed to be glad to give up active participation, he actually remained totally involved and spent most of his days, certainly in fine weather, driving round the farm in the float behind Polly who he now regarded entirely as his own.

During the school holidays he was accompanied by his granddaughter more often than not, for Edith too had a healthy interest in everything that went on at the farm. She loved her grandfather's company and she enjoyed the ride in the swinging float behind the gentle but underworked Polly. It was certainly preferable to walking or biking round the fields – she had enough of that exercise in term-time. She was not obliged to spend the whole of the summer holiday at home. For years it had been customary for her and Arthur to spend two or three weeks with their Aunty Betty at Stokenchurch, but since Arthur had been old enough to help regularly on the farm he had been unwilling to leave it. Edith quite failed to enjoy her holiday there without him, much as she loved her aunt and her twin cousins. Harvesting was noticeably earlier in Buckinghamshire, so this year she had spent one week there at the start of the school holidays, and had returned home at full speed when she heard that harvesting was in progress at Oakleigh.

One sunny morning she was hovering about the yard as usual when she heard her father ask the old man to drive up to Clayfields farm. There had been a heavy dew and the grass round the farm was very wet and Bob wanted to know if the stooked oats on the higher ground would be dry enough for carrying that afternoon. Edith was in the float picking up the reins while her grandfather was still clambering aboard.

'Are you going to drive, lass?' he said genially. 'All right, carry on then. I'll just sit back and relax.'

Edith was thrilled. She had once or twice begged a few minutes' driving from the milk lad but had never been allowed to hold the reins officially. To drive her grandfather, the expert of experts, was a prize indeed. Not that Polly needed much driving. She trotted smoothly along the farm drive, out on to the village road and then turned off into Clayfields Lane. Their own land was on both sides all the way and Mr Ratcliffe gave his attention to the fields, leaving the care of the horse to the proud Edith. As she let Polly relax and walk up the slight incline, Mortimer Ratcliffe appeared over the hill on his big hunter. Seeing the float and its occupants he stopped and pulled his horse halfway across the lane.

'What the devil does he want to talk to us about?' the old man muttered crossly. 'Better pull in and stop, Edith.'

Mortimer smiled in charming fashion and raised his cap to the girl.

'What a delightful scene, Mr Ratcliffe! I do envy you your lovely and competent driver! My word, how pretty she is – and so very like her charming mother at the same age!'

'What do we owe the pleasure of this meeting to, Major Ratcliffe?' the old man said shortly, determined not to be fooled by this flattery. It was the first time he had spoken to the Major since that tragic day nine years before when he had met him outside Betty's stable and had tried to exact vengeance on the young villain with his walking-stick.

'Chance, Mr Ratcliffe, simply chance,' said the other. 'You would not wish us to meet and pass without a word! We are still neighbours!'

'I could wish a lot worse things on you than that,' the farmer said to himself. Aloud, he replied, 'Neighbours aye. But it's easier to be pleasant to some neighbours than to others.'

Edith looked across strangely at her grandfather. There was an edge in his voice which was unfamiliar to her. Irritable she knew him to be – bad-tempered, never. He was beginning to breathe heavily too.

'I cannot recall that you have ever been an unpleasant neighbour to anybody, Mr Ratcliffe – certainly not to the other tenants on the old Hartnall estate. My father used to say that you were the most friendly of all his tenants.'

'Your father was in a different category,' the old man said shortly. He was nettled by the pointed reference to the fact that for many years he had been in a subordinate position. 'Your father never abused his position, that's certain. I'm afraid in this instance I can't say "Like father, like son", much as I wish to.'

Major Ratcliffe frowned.

'Each generation has its own moral standards, Mr Ratcliffe. It isn't altogether just to compare them.'

'It's not a comparison of moral standards.' The old farmer's chest was heaving now and the words burst out between deep gasps. 'It's a comparison between a gentleman and a blackguard!'

The horseman coloured with anger, turned his mount round in the road, then faced them again.

'You're not still harking back to those little incidents of 1911 and 1923, surely. You've got a malevolent memory, old man, and you give those two escapades an importance they don't deserve. Each time I came off worse, but I don't brood about it!'

'You were lucky to be left alive to do any brooding after our last encounter,' the farmer reminded him grimly. He was fighting for breath and his weather-beaten face was turning slate-grey. 'I did my damnedest then as I'd do it again. And it's not very gentlemanly of you to bring this matter up in front of my granddaughter. You've a daughter of your own, young man, and you ought to know better!'

Edith sat motionless on the wooden seat of the float, gripping Polly's reins tightly and staring straight before her. She was frightened at the rising tone of the men's voices, speaking as they were, right across her as if she were not there. The Major was livid at the last remark and edged his horse closer to the vehicle.

'Damn your impertinence, man,' he snapped, his voice rising in a sharp crescendo as if he were on the barrack square. 'How dare you question my manners or my motives? You ignorant curmudgeon! You uncouth peasant! You would not now be a landowner were it not for my father's generosity and over-scrupulous sense of fairness! You should have been pitched out of Oakleigh according to our original intention. Allowing you to buy your farm was the most stupid thing my father did in his whole life. Damn you, Ratcliffe! I was prepared to hold out the olive branch and in return I get nothing but insults and condemnation. My God, you seem well on your way to hell already and the sooner you get there the better it will be for everybody in Hartnall!'

His face was suffused with passion as he reined back his horse to deliver the last part of his tirade from a more telling distance.

The effect on the old man was dramatic. He rose to his feet, his eyes bulging, his features strangely contorted. He sucked in great gulps of air, but could get no word out. His face turned quite blue and it seemed to the horrified Edith that her grandfather was about to burst. His hand went up to his throat but it could give no relief for his shirt collar was already open. He swayed, then slithered to the floor of the vehicle, his stomach moving in and out like leaking and wheezy bellows.

Major Ratcliffe recovered his composure and spoke sharply.

'Turn your horse round, child, and get your grandfather home as quickly as you can. He needs relief very urgently!'

He backed away, and Edith, not conscious for the moment that this was the first time she had been in charge of a horse and vehicle, backed Polly with voice and rein until the back of the float struck the hedge. Pulling the mare's head round, she steered her for home, flapping the reins agitatedly and urging the horse on with every threat and encouragement that she could think of, hoping against hope that her grandfather would not die before she reached home.

Chapter Nine

'Whoa!' shrieked Edith as the indignant Polly swung into the yard and slithered to a stop outside the kitchen window. Ned looked out of the upper cowshed door and called, 'You shouldn't be driving like that, lass,' but his admonition was drowned by the girl's own cry as she bent down over her grandfather.

'Mummy, Mummy! Help! Oh, do be quick! Grandad's not well.'

This was an understatement, for the old man was still crumpled on the bottom of the float. His eyes were open but he was still breathing in great gulps of air, slowly and painfully, apparently unable to release any air from his congested lungs. Edith's mother and Gladys ran out of the house and Ned strode up from the shed.

'What on earth's the matter, child?' Then Meg saw her father's condition. 'Oh, Dad, what's happened? Oh my God! Gladys, we must get him indoors and into his chair!' They tried to move him, Ned climbing into the float and grasping his shoulders. But in its inert condition the enormous frame could not be moved without putting unacceptable strains on his limbs.

'Fetch his armchair out here, Gladys. We'll set him in it and carry it in. It'll be easier on him that way. Ned, get a fencing stake.'

'Leave me a bit and I'll be all right,' the old man managed to gasp, but Meg preferred to organise his removal to a more manageable position in the kitchen. The backboard of the float was let down and the seat removed. Then with tremendous effort he was edged out of the vehicle into the Windsor armchair, a thick stake was put through the legs of the chair, Gladys and Ned each seized an end and as they lifted and shuffled forward, Meg held the back of the chair upright and with much advice to each other and with many stops, they gradually manoeuvred him into the house and set the chair down with a creak in its usual place.

'Run up to Grandad's room Edith, and get the tin of Potter's on his dressing-table,' Meg said as they all struggled to regain their breath. 'Thanks ever so much, Ned, we'll manage now.'

'Ah 'ope the owd Gaffer's goin' to be aw reight,' Ned said, disregarding the fact that although Mr Ratcliffe could not speak easily, his hearing was unimpaired, 'Ah've niver sin 'im look so bad!'

Gladys nudged him vigorously out of the kitchen while Meg took the tin of inhalant from Edith and set some of it burning in a saucer on a small table beside her father's chair. The old man moved his head over the pungent fumes and breathed in deeply, gaining an immediate measure of relief.

'Now Edith, we'll go in the front room out of this smoke and you can tell me exactly how this happened.'

'I don't quite know how to describe it, Mum,' the girl said sadly, 'it was all so horrid! We met Mr Mortimer on his horse and everything was all right to begin with. He said how pretty I was and how like you when you were my age. Then Grandad was rude and hateful and the Major got very angry and shouted unkind things and called Grandad names. Mummy, it seemed as if those two had a fight years ago, or more than one. I just can't believe it! I've never known Grandad act so awful before. Then he fell down in the float and I thought he was dying!'

'There, don't upset yourself, love. It's a pity you were there to see it. If you hadn't been, Mortimer would probably have ridden by with just a nod. He just can't resist paying a compliment to a pretty face, even of a schoolgirl. I always thought this sort of thing might happen if they met in the right place and in the wrong temper. Your grandfather can't control himself over some things. Not much hope of a reconciliation with Mortimer now, that's certain. But you must forget about it, dear. Put it right out of your mind.'

'But what was it all about, Mum? Do tell me!'

'No Edith! It happened a long time ago. I'll tell you when you get older. And you mustn't talk about it, either. This is a private matter between the two Ratcliffe families.'

'Does that mean we can't talk to Major Ratcliffe? I always thought he was so nice. When he visited us at the village school we all thought he was so grand!'

'In my day we thought the same thing about his father, the old Squire. Mortimer's nice enough when he wants to be. Probably he won't want to talk to us after this. But if he does speak to you, of course you must answer him. As a family, we are not beholden to him or his any more, but you must always be respectful and ladylike. Now we'd better go and see how your grandad's getting on.'

The sickly smell of the fumes still drifted about the kitchen, but Mr Ratcliffe had regained his breath and most of his composure. He looked pale and exhausted.

'Sorry about all this, Meg – and you, Edith. Sorry I frightened you, lass. You did splendidly in bringing me home. I don't know what came over me!'

'Well, we soon will know, Dad. I'm going to 'phone Doctor Whittaker. Probably a heart attack. What possessed you to get so worked up with Mortimer?'

'I couldn't help it Meg, when I thought about what happened the last time we met face to face.'

'That's ridiculous after nearly ten years. Mort was trying to heal the breach and although we don't care much for him we were prepared to remain civil. Edith, don't stand there listening. Help Gladys put the dinner on! And don't you say any more Dad, either.' She lowered her voice. 'We've been trying to keep this thing from the kids and you have to blurt out the whole story apparently. Edith will never rest now until she knows. You're not fit to have the girl along with you!'

'Don't say that, Meg! I love taking her with me!' The old man now added misery and contrition to his appearance of exhaustion.

'Control your temper better, then. Now I'll 'phone the doctor.'

When the menfolk came in to dinner Arthur was frankly curious, his father perturbed.

'Just the sort of confrontation we've been trying to avoid for the sake of peace in the village. I've talked pretty frankly to Mortimer myself but have stopped short of downright abuse which you seem to have indulged in, Dad!'

'Everybody's blaming me,' the old man said bitterly and did not speak for the remainder of the meal.

Doctor Whittaker was equally condemnatory when he examined the patient privately in the sitting-room.

'You've had your first heart attack, Mr Ratcliffe! We don't want another one. Your heart's got enough to do coping with your weight and your breathing restrictions. It won't take any more overloading. You know, Mr Ratcliffe, you've got two lungs, two kidneys and two testicles and you can manage quite well without one of either. But you've only got *one* heart and when it goes you're finished. Now – no more excitement, nor getting steamed up over things that are past or you can't help. That is, if you want to stay alive. Your next attack might finish you!'

'All right, Doctor, as you say,' the old man sighed in resignation. 'You must keep me alive a bit longer. I want to see young Arthur pass his exams before I go!'

Mortimer Ratcliffe did not continue his visits to Oakleigh. He would not risk another meeting with the fierce old man who appeared to grow more bitter with age. Arnold Ratcliffe, for his part, was equally determined not to meet his namesake closely again if it could possibly be avoided. He was wary of his route as he drove round with Polly and if he saw the young squire in the distance he took care to drive another way. He did not know fear, certainly not in connection with a human being or animal, but he recognised, and was prepared to observe, the limitations imposed on him by his weak heart. He wanted to see his grandchildren grow up, and shaped his life accordingly.

Arthur settled down to the normal life of a yeoman farmer's son, working on the farm harder than any employee most of the time, but taking a half-day off for his own pursuits whenever he chose. He found that life was easier if he asked permission, which was never refused by his father. He played cricket on Saturday afternoons and in return helped with the milking on Sundays. In the winter he hunted at the Saturday meets, along with Edith and her pony. Their mother also went occasionally, mostly to display her horse, for she refused to sell him. She had never re-kindled the enthusiasm which possessed her when Betty had lived at Oakleigh and later at Manor Farm. Robert also hunted now and again, mainly to keep up contacts with neighbouring landowners and as a social necessity. When the four of them were out together he would say it was like deserting the farm entirely, adding that it was a good job Meg's father was still with them.

They often encountered Major Ratcliffe or members of his family at the meets and both parties maintained an air of strained civility. The old man no longer attended the hunt so there was no fear of another confrontation which in such august company would have disgraced everybody involved. Arthur was friendlier to the Major than his parents for he met him frequently at the cricket club of which Mortimer was an enthusiastic patron. Edith, in spite of being alarmed by the Major's vehemence when he had abused her grandfather, seemed to have developed an admiration for the young Squire, as he was still thought of. She often manoeuvred her pony close to his massive hunter, hoping to receive his friendly smile. She generally succeeded but recognised the disdain in his expression. Her parents did not check Edith in her attempts at friendliness with their old enemy. When Arthur was in charge he tended to encourage it, for he admired the Major more than he was prepared to admit at home.

The summer of 1933 had everything the three previous summers had lacked. Heatwave succeeded heatwave in one of the hottest summers of the century. Just like 1911 and 1921, Mr Ratcliffe said, and Bob agreed with him. There was just sufficient rain at intervals to keep things growing and the highly fertile fields of Oakleigh showed heavy crops of grass, grain and potatoes.

The unending sunshine made of haymaking a dusty, thirsty and continuous job. The mowing was still done by horses in spite of Arthur's efforts to persuade his father to mechanise it. The hay was pitched with long handforks and towering loads were brought in on the mophreys to the barn at Oakleigh and Clayfields. Arthur never stopped trying to get more machinery in the hayfields.

'All this pitchfork stuff is out of date,' he complained. 'You really ought to be more modern, Dad.'

'And how do you think we should get the hay in?'

'Fit a haysweep on the front of one of the cars and sweep the hay to an elevator at a stack in the field. Probably clear a field every day.'

'Perhaps, but that system's no good to us. We want to feed the hay at the buildings, not out in the fields. I maintain it's better to get the hay up on wheels and haul it straight to the place where it's going to be fed. It's got to be hauled there sometime, so why handle it twice?'

'Most of the big farmers down south use the sweep,' objected Arthur.

'You've been reading too many journals, lad. On the chalk downland that you're thinking of, they do outdoor milking – the cows live out on the fields all winter and are milked in a portable shed. They call it bail milking, I don't know why. The hay is fed in the field where it's been made and when one stack is finished, the cows and the tackle are moved to another field. Of course, the soil on those downs is light and dry. Used to be arable until a few years ago. Here, we still milk in cowsheds and keep the cows in during the winter, so the hay must be handy to 'em.'

'Why not get a hay-loader, then and save all this pitching?'

'Getting hay with a loader is damned hard work and unloading it is harder still. And if you don't have wires round your waggon, you'll lose half of it. No, we'll stick to the pitchfork and the mophreys for some time yet, eh Dad?'

'I agree, Bob. We've got all the field machinery and an elevator for the stackyard, which is more than most farmers have round here, so I don't know what you're grumbling about, Arthur. You want to go too fast, lad!'

'Old fogeys!' muttered Arthur under his breath and added aloud, 'I shall be glad when I get to Cirencester. I'll bet they do things in a modern way there.'

'Getting impatient about that now, are you? Well, it's only

three months away. Don't forget you promised to qualify for a Land Agent, though.'

'I haven't forgotten, Grandad, but I might not have time to carry on with it while I'm at College. But when I'm through and have got my Diploma, I'll carry on again. I'll keep my promise, Grandad!'

'I think you will, Arthur. You're a good lad in spite of your impatience with your father's methods. We don't want changes for their own sake, lad. They've got to be seen to be worth while!'

The hot dry weather continued on and on. The harvest was secured quickly and cleanly, the manure carted out and spread on the stubbles. The farming programme was well up to date when, at the end of September amid great excitement, Arthur's bags were packed and he set off for the Royal Agricultural College. Edith was wistful at the sight of her brother's departure for they had scarcely been separated before. Tears were not far away but she indignantly denied this when Arthur told her not to be a cry-baby. Meg's face was flushed as she controlled her own sadness and she fussed over her son like, as Arthur said, a hen with one chick. Bob pretended to be nonchalant but privately wondered how the devil he was going to run the farm without the energy and the stimulating proddings of his son. Arnold Ratcliffe was quiet and thoughtful but hid his deeper feelings in a burst of generosity by presenting his grandson with a secondhand Morris Minor for his use at the college. Arthur was delighted, for this was unexpected. He had secretly hoped that he might be allowed to take the old Austin milk car but had not dared to ask for it. The little Morris was newer, handier and his very own and he set off in it on his hundred-mile journey with a light heart. He would show them all how to farm when he came back!

He had another reason to be pleased, for his father had told him he would be paid the same pocket money, thirty shillings a week, he had received for working at home. The fine summer had rekindled Robert Felton's faith in farming and he felt in an expansive mood. After all, agriculture was improving, albeit slowly. A Milk Marketing Board had been formed to handle all milk produced in Britain and to arrange the payment, so that was another annual headache disposed of. Each October he had worried in case the London dairy no longer required Oakleigh Farm's milk. Now he had an assured market and it was a pleasant feeling. There was talk of the introduction of a beef subsidy to help that branch of the industry – important at Oakleigh and capable of expansion. For these reasons, and perhaps pride too, he was content to pay Arthur enough for him to play the part of a yeoman farmer's son.

Arthur's absence from the home circle was keenly felt by all. The two men found that the relief from Arthur's constant goading to mechanise was not quite so acceptable as they had anticipated. The arguments between Arthur and his sister, which at the time had irritated everybody, now seemed, in retrospect, to have been entertaining. Robert was drawn closer to Edith who had already established a very intimate link by her efforts to interest and amuse him during his illness. Grandfather Ratcliffe also made a greater fuss of his granddaughter, and so did Meg. She loved both her children with a fierce possessive passion and the absence of one inevitably caused her to concentrate her affection on the other.

Girl-like, Edith soon sensed she was receiving extra attention, and she revelled in it, especially indoors where she held her head extra high and carried herself with a pronounced air of superiority which did not always meet with approval. On the farm however she adopted the opposite behaviour, mixing with the men rather more freely than before when Arthur had always been there to keep her in check. On Wednesday and Saturday afternoons she jumped up on the carts and mophreys, rode the sweating plough-horses astride when they came in from the fields, and sat on the wide mudguard of the tractor when she located Dick ploughing or cultivating. Dick did not mind at all, for he had watched the girl grow up from babyhood and was as fond of her as he might have been of a very young sister. His father, however, did mind and had something pointed to say on the subject. He made his views known one morning in the stable when Gerald and Charlie were present as well as Dick.

'That young lass is sprawling about the farm just a bit too much lately,' Bill Marshall said. 'Missin' Arthur's company mebbe. But don't you chaps encourage 'er so much! Gie 'er the cowd showder a bit. And dunna let 'er spend so much time wi' you on that tractor, Dick. That's no place and no way for a young wench to sit!'

'Damn it, Dad, 'er's only about twelve – just a kid!'

'Mebbe 'er is, but 'er's growin' up fast and afore we know wheer we are 'er'll be kickin' ovver the traces, and we dunna want that. Lasses 'a got to be kept in check and showed their place, especially when it's the Gaffer's daughter!'

The three young men pulled long faces behind the waggoner's back, but they knew better than to ignore his bidding entirely. He had sown the seed which would bear fruit in time.

Meg had also noticed this tendency in her daughter and thought it high time that she exercised her authority. One evening Edith arrived home from school, rushed upstairs to change into an old skirt which was very short, having been outgrown, and was leaving the kitchen when her mother stopped her.

'Where are you off to in such a hurry?'

'Down to the lower fields. Bill's been drilling there and I like to ride up on the horses.'

'You've been doing too much of that lately, Edith, and it's about time it stopped!'

'But why, Mum? There's no harm in it!'

'Sitting astride on a steaming horse with that short skirt on! Enough to give you a chill as well as getting your underclothes in a state. You show far too much of your legs when you're with the men.'

'The men don't mind!'

'I'm quite sure they don't! The point is, I mind because it's not lady-like. You're thirteen next month and you shouldn't be rambling round the farm like a tomboy at your age. You must wear longer gymslips too. You're showing far too much of your legs above the knee. It's about time you started acting like a young lady, Edith!'

'Plenty of time for that, surely,' old Mr Ratcliffe observed as he came in for a cup of tea which he hoped was ready. 'Don't make our little girl grow up too quick, Meg. I like her fine as she is!'

'She's growing pretty fast, Dad, whether we like it or not. Outgrown all her clothes, too. Some of her skirts are hardly decent any more.'

'There's no fun if I can't get around the farm like I always have,' grumbled Edith. 'I'm a farmer's daughter and I want to stay a farmer's daughter, not a lady.'

'I hope you'll be both my girl, when the time comes,' her grandfather said affectionately. 'What's all the fuss about, anyway?'

'I like riding in from the fields on the horses. There's no harm in it. You've seen me plenty of times, Grandad.'

'Yes, well – er – of course, you're not exactly a toddler now, to be lifted up and down by the waggoner. It's not a good idea . . .'

'If you want to ride a horse round the farm, you must take the pony,' her mother interrupted. 'That's what he's for! And put proper riding clothes on as well, so you look respectable.'

'But if I have to get Turpin in after I get home from school, saddle him up and change myself, there wouldn't be any time to go out,' Edith objected, pouting.

'That problem's easily solved,' Mr Ratcliffe said brightly. 'Just tell us in the morning before you go to school and one of the men – Ned or Charlie – will get the pony in for you – aye, and saddle him up as well, ready for when you get home.'

'You grown-ups have an answer to everything,' the girl said disconsolately. 'Anyway, there's no point in going out tonight now. Here's Bill Marshall just coming in to the stable with his team.'

'Yes, and your father's just coming in here for a cup of tea. Move the kettle over the fire, Edith, and don't look so glum. You've got to grow up sometime, you know.'

Robert Felton walked into the kitchen and stopped, looking at his family in surprise. He sensed the atmosphere at once.

'Hello, what's this? Nothing like a Mad Hatter's tea party so it must be a Cabinet meeting. And what was that remark about growing up?'

'I was just telling Edith to be a bit more ladylike on the farm. She'll soon be in her teens, and it's time she gave up her tomboy tricks. Putting ideas into the lads' heads!'

'Oh Mum! You don't have to tell everybody!' Tears formed in Edith's eyes at the embarrassment. She hated being made to look small in front of her father.

'Well, don't cry lass,' Bob Felton said, putting his arm round his daughter's waist, 'and your father is not "everybody".' As he sat down he pulled her on to his knee. 'Of course you're growing up. But you'll always be my little girl – my angel of the sick-room and my sunshine of the kitchen. But I've noticed myself that you've been a bit careless about your modesty lately. It isn't worth crying about, love. I must say you did show a big chunk of your drawers the last time I saw you swing up on old Jewel. Bill Marshall looked most disapproving. I thought he was going to lecture me about it, so I cleared off!'

Edith giggled and laid her head against her father's chest.

'In future love, when you go out on the farm, wear your jodhpurs. You can scramble about as much as you like then, as far as I'm concerned.'

'Well, that's a compromise,' Meg said grudgingly. 'I was hoping she'd start to be a bit more genteel . . .'

'That'll come in time,' Edith's grandfather interrupted proudly. 'Don't push her too much. In a few years, our Edith will be the finest young lady in South Derbyshire!'

Chapter Ten

By the time Edith was sixteen she had fulfilled in good measure her grandfather's prophecy. A little taller than her mother, she had the same rich hair just a shade darker in colour. She had the same deep blue eyes, too, and the same bold rounded features and so resembled Meg at the same age that Robert Felton often drew in his breath with hurt admiration as he compared his daughter with his wife as he had first seen her more than twenty years before. Edith had not achieved Meg's stalwart figure because she had not worked on the land to the same degree as her mother. The daughter had enjoyed more of a lady's life, her experience of farm work being confined to driving a pair of horses for a few minutes when keeping Bill Marshall company and to frequent lessons in tractor-steering from Dick Marshall.

However, she was quite expert at driving a pony in the trap or float, for she still accompanied her grandfather on his tours of the fields, and he was pleased to delegate the driving to her as a mark of confidence. Her pony had been replaced by a grey hunter known as Silver, of which she was very proud. She loved to display her skill as a horsewoman at the Saturday meets during school holidays.

Mortimer Ratcliffe and the older members of the Hunt told each other that she was Meg Ratcliffe all over again. Some added that she carried a look of her Aunty Betty Felton as well, at which remark Major Ratcliffe would change the subject and saunter his horse over to have a word with Edith and with Meg as well if she were present.

At the High School it was customary for girls to leave at the end of the term in which the pupil became sixteen. As Edith's birthday was in November, she was not expected to leave until Christmas. This annoyed her a little for Arthur's three-year course at Cirencester ended at the summer term of the same year and at first she felt belittled by having to attend school while Arthur resumed his normal work at home. This feeling soon wore off, but secretly she was envious of her brother's diploma and a few weeks later she astounded her family by announcing her intention of enrolling with a business college for three terms – long enough to get a certificate. Her mother was surprised and almost affronted.

'The very idea!' she exclaimed. 'I was looking forward to

having you at home to be company for me. You wouldn't have much to do, and in the afternoons we could go out with the pony, or perhaps the car if you learned to drive it.'

'Um, I don't know about driving the car,' Robert Felton said. 'We don't want it wrecked by women drivers. Take the pony by all means, so long as Dad doesn't want it.'

'Driving around in the afternoons calling on people is right out of date, Mum. Nobody in our set does that now. It went out before I was born, I should think. And anyway, Dad, I can drive the tractor and I'm sure I could soon drive the car. If I can't have the Ford I'll save up and buy one of my own. Dick will teach me to drive if you and Arthur are too mean!'

'I didn't say anything,' protested Arthur. 'I s'pose I can teach you, but most girls make an awful fist of it. The only woman I know who can drive a car properly is Aunt Betty.'

'We're getting off the subject since you came into the discussion. We were talking about my intention to take a business course.'

'I like your last remark, I must say! Anyway, I think you're daft, going in for more schooling when you could stay at home and take it easy like most farmers' daughters do!'

'Do stop arguing, you two,' their mother said crossly. 'It's nothing to do with you, Arthur. You've just been away for a three-year course, and probably Edith thinks she ought to do something similar. I just think it's unnecessary and I'd like to know why you think it is necessary, Edith.'

'Oh, I don't know, Mum. It's just that I want to have something of a trade at my fingertips, so that I can do other things besides being a farmer's wife to the first young buck who eyes me up and down like a prize heifer . . .'

'Don't be vulgar, Edith!'

'Well, that's what it used to be like, didn't it? I want to be able to type, keep accounts and so on, so I can get a secretary's job if I want to, or if I have to!'

'If you have to! What are you saying? We may not be exactly rich, but we're well enough off to keep you without you working for someone else!'

'Don't be a snob, Mum! There's nothing wrong with working for a living, especially if you're doing it from choice and you know your job. If they allowed women to do it, I wouldn't mind taking an auctioneers' exam, like Arthur's doing for Grandad. Perhaps he'd be more pleased with me, then.'

'Don't bring me into it, Edith,' Mr Ratcliffe said from behind

94

the *Farmer & Stockbreeder*. 'I must say, though, I can't see any harm in gaining a few more accomplishments although they can't be much use on a farm.'

'Can't they, Grandad? From what I hear from the men in this house, farming has got to be a highly-organised business in the future with proper accounts, records, copies of letters and all that. Well, if I'm to marry a farmer, and you're all determined I shall, then I'll be in a position to do all his office work for him!'

'By gum, you've got a point there, Edie,' her father said, rousing himself up to take a further part in the conversation. 'Indeed you have. You could do all our office work, couldn't you? Accounts, records, letters. It's getting more and more involved and if I do it, or Arthur, it means we're taking time off from outside work.'

'You mean, I can do it so that you and Arthur can be free of desk work in the evenings, Dad! I know you!'

'Well I think it would be a good idea for you to take this business course and I'm prepared to pay for it, so you won't have to find the money yourself.'

'I never had any intention of finding the money myself,' Edith replied with spirit. 'If we're so well off, you and Mum can easily afford it!'

'Well, I don't know!' Meg said in disgust. 'I was hoping to forbid this stunt and now we end up with paying the bill and being criticised for ever thinking otherwise!'

'That's how it is, Mum. She's got her own way again, and will do, if you keep giving way to her,' Arthur said reprovingly, and ducked swiftly to avoid Edith's open hand on his ear.

'I suppose we musn't grumble, Bob,' Meg said later when they were alone. 'Edith's been pretty good. She's given us less trouble than most girls give their parents.'

'Do they do that?' Bob enquired in surprise. 'I didn't know. Edith hasn't given us any trouble at all as far as I can see.'

'I mean, she hasn't brought home any young men of the wrong type,' Meg persisted.

'Of course not! She's got too much common sense for that. But as I remember it, she hasn't brought home a young man of any type, and a good thing too! Dash it, she's only sixteen!'

'I know, but some girls are courting at that age nowadays, and a good deal younger! I thought at one time she was getting interested in some of Arthur's college friends, but I'm glad nothing came of it.'

'I should think not, at fourteen or fifteen as she was then! By gum Meg, how your feminine minds work! Why, you and I lived in the same house from sixteen until we were nineteen and didn't even hold hands!'

'Ah, but things are a bit different now, Bob. Besides, all boys are not as slow as you were!'

'Huh! You weren't so forthcoming,' Bob grunted and immersed himself in the *Farmers Weekly*.

In fact, Edith had been quite interested in Arthur's friends and had anticipated their coming with secret thrills. She had examined each one from afar, met him, enjoyed his unfamiliar company and, since each only remained a week, had quickly mourned their departure.

Most of the students at Cirencester were, like Arthur, sons of farming families, but there were a few others also seeking a career in agriculture who had no farming background. These young men were naturally anxious to visit the farm homes of their fellow students and Arthur usually had a series of them every vacation. There were so many candidates that Meg decided to limit the stay of each student to a week and declined to accommodate more than one at a time. A morning departure was followed by an afternoon arrival. They all left sorrowfully; the excellent food, the experience of living and observing on a large well-run farm was something they would have liked to prolong indefinitely. Naturally they ate with the family and had ample opportunity of admiring at close quarters the pretty and lively daughter of the house.

Edith accepted this as a shy princess might have done and sometimes her mother was glad that the current visit was so short. The girl quickly memorised each visitor's name and mentally catalogued his qualities, his background and his possibilities, secretly of course for she knew her mother would be shocked and angry at such precocity.

In such a short time it was not always possible to gather details of his family, but his presence at Oakleigh indicated that he was from a non-farming family, otherwise he would assuredly have returned home to give assistance there. The first of the batch was usually Edgar Collins, tall, fair and assured, who needed a diploma for a job abroad. He was shy and tongue-tied at first, but he came to Oakleigh every vacation for three years and towards the end was noticed casting appreciative glances at the developing damsel. Edith would have liked to string him along but dare not try it under the eyes of her parents.

David Ensor, who usually followed Collins, was dark and sleek, talked very fast and carried an air of superiority. He paid much attention to Edith at first, thinking her to be much older, but when he discovered her real age, dropped her like a stone, much to the girl's indignation.

Bill Haines was a burly, red-faced Yorkshireman whose father was a butcher in a substantial way and proposed taking a farm for his son when qualified. Edith liked him for his bluff ways for he treated her exactly like a sister. However he overdid the brotherly act when he playfully turned her up to smack her bottom, a procedure which drew disapproving looks and coughs of remonstrance from the parents, and from Edith utter fury at the humiliation. Prior to this incident, Bob and Meg Felton had been hinting to each other that Bill might prove a suitable friend for Edith in a year or two.

Maurice Lee intended to try for an advisory post with the Ministry of Agriculture. Polite, studious and ineffective, he was grateful for the opportunities his stay at Oakleigh provided and his attitude to the whole family was diffident and respectful. He reminded Edith of a shop assistant and she treated him as one.

Reg Oliver had intrigued her more than the others. He was red-haired, jovial and pretended to be simple, but the quickness of his wit belied that impression. His main reason for studying agriculture was the hope of securing a post as agent on a large estate, disregarding the fact that in 1936 such jobs were scarce. He took a liking to Edith which increased with every visit, and did not hesitate to tell her nor to show sorrow when he had to leave. For her part she felt drawn towards him but only as she might have been attracted by a bouncing sheepdog puppy.

Norman Roach she had not liked at all. Pale-faced with stern and narrow features, excessively tall, he practically ignored her, but whether from shyness or ill manners she could not decide. He never spoke to her nor to the servant Gladys, reserving all his remarks for the seniors of the household other than Mr Ratcliffe whom he treated in a very condescending way. After his first visit the old man had said abruptly to his grandson, 'I hope you don't bring that chap very often.'

In the last two vacations Arthur had introduced another colleague, George Stringer. He was something of a dandy and gave himself the airs of a Don Juan. His mother was a woman of means living in a town house and his presence at the Agricultural College was due to his disliking it less than anything else he had considered. By this time Edith was in her sixteenth year, a strapping but beautiful girl and Stringer wasted no time in paying court to her. She was flattered at first and welcomed his attentions, but when he manoeuvred her into secluded corners, became over-familiar and tried to take outrageous liberties she became frightened. It was not easy to avoid him altogether though she tried hard to do so. Of course, she was big enough and strong enough to repel advances from any man other than a professional wrestler, but the thought of having to fight to protect her chastity was quite distasteful.

When Arthur returned home from his last term at college Edith summarised the position and felt that her brother's friends had been no use to her at all and that she must find her experience elsewhere. She had always been strongly attached to the tractor-driver Dick Marshall who looked after her pony and the other horses. For a time she developed a girlish crush on him but as he was nearly twenty years older the absurdity of this soon became apparent, even to the girl. Moreover, he was happily married to Mavis who had been Edith's nursemaid when work in the farmhouse allowed. They had three splendid children, known and liked by everyone on the farm. Edith pulled a wry face whenever she thought of the sensation she would cause at Oakleigh if she made her fondness for Dick too obvious.

The tractor-driver was fond of this child who had grown up under his eye and as she got older he delighted in telling her stories of her Auntie Betty who had lived on the farm at the time of Edith's birth. In particular Dick never tired of repeating the dramatic story of how Betty had saved him from drowning when he had been trapped under his mowing-machine in a deep part of the river. Dick had been very fond of Betty and the story lost nothing in the telling as he tried to over-glamorise the girl's part in the incident.

Because of Dick's friendliness and his fondness for reminiscing, Edith, who had never lost her curiosity about the cause of the strained relations between her grandfather and the young squire, decided to probe Dick for his version. She knew well enough that farm men were always fully aware of every aspect of their employer's business and family matters, however private. She would have to wait her opportunity, though. It was of no use asking while they were on the tractor together for the noise made ordinary conversation impossible. Nor was it sensible to ask him while the tractor was idling, for if he wished to evade the question he would simply drive off and leave her standing. Neither could she ask him whilst around the yard for someone else might be within earshot.

One Wednesday afternoon in mid-May she was having lunch

at home after arriving from school. Glancing through the kitchen window she observed Dick leading Polly in float harness in the direction of the rickyard. She finished her meal hastily, hurried upstairs and changed into her old jodhpurs then sauntered casually round to the rickyard. Dick was loading up some piles and rails from the stack in the corner. She went up and noticed he had the mallet, saw, hammer and a tin of nails already in the float.

'Going fencing, Dick?'

'Ar – the 'osses have bust down a rail-place atween th' Rickyard Close and Long Seeds and let 'emsens and the dry cows through wi' th' young beast. Dunno wheer the 'ell everybody else is, but Ah th'owt Ah'd better get 'em back and fence the gap.'

'I'll come with you if you like.'

'Will you, gel? Good! You'll be able to 'elp me sort 'em out and hold th' rails while Ah nail 'em. Jump in an' drive th' mare. Ah'll oppen th' gate!'

The weather was warm and bright and the urgency of late spring was manifest everywhere. The grass, dark green and growing fast, the hedges in full leaf, the stock full and contented, or would have been if they had not broken out. They left the mare beside the gap in the hedge and advanced into the next field on foot to find the truants, expecting some difficulty and the need of quick footwork in sorting them out. But the riding horses apparently possessed a strong sense of guilt, for as soon as they saw the man and the girl heading in their direction they put up their heads and cantered back to their own enclosure with penitent dignity. The half-dozen dry cows who shared the field with them also returned obediently when singled out and driven in the right direction. The younger cattle quickly bunched themselves and drew off to a distant part of the field as if to announce they had no part in this escapade.

Edith felt triumphant for she felt she held Dick captive. Having sorted out the stock he could not now leave the scene until the fence had been repaired. Automatically she sized up the job – an hour-and-a-half at least, she calculated. Dick went to the float and took out the saw and mallet. He had his back to the girl when she opened the subject.

'Dick, what's the story behind the old row Mort Ratcliffe had with my grandfather?'

Dick stopped dead for a moment then continued his movements towards the hedge, saw in hand.

''Owd this branch out o' th' way, Ede, while Ah saw the other one off. It's i' th' way o' swingin' th' mallet.'

She did as she was bid, waiting for a reply. He sawed vigorously for a moment or two until the branch crashed down.

'Now Ah'll want th' crowbar to mek a couple o' holes for th' piles.'

She went to the float and got it, and as she handed it to him she moved round to look at his averted face.

'Dick, I asked you a question!'

'Yes, Ah heard you, and you know darn well you shouldn't ask me that. It's allus been understood on this place that we niver mention it. If you'd bin a few year younger Ah'd a' turned you up and smacked your be'ind for asking!'

'Well, don't try it now!' Edith, thinking of the erring Bill Haines, was indignant.

'Ah'm not likely to. Ah know what's proper and what ain't, Edith Felton. Fetch me one o' them piles!'

'Oh come on, Dick! We've always been such pals!'

'Er – well, maybe, but this is different. And don't come up close and ogle me like that! Somebody might be watching!'

'You must tell me, Dick. I insist!' Edith said imperiously. She could sense Dick was weakening.

'Ah don't know all the story – nobody does. Onyway, you were i' th' 'ouse yourself. Why don't you know it?'

'But I was only about two years old! Tell me what you do know, Dick. I'll keep it a secret and I'll promise you won't get the sack!'

'Thank you for nowt! Ah know Ah shan't get th' sack but Ah couldn't look Mr Bob i' th' face, nor your mother neither if they knew Ah'd been talking about their private secrets. There's such a thing as loyalty, you know!'

Edith felt rebuked.

'Dick, I know and we all know at home that there's never been a more loyal chap than you, nor a better one. But I feel such a fool with this dark mystery hanging over me. Do tell me Dick! Please!'

'Just 'owd this rail up for me while Ah stand back and size it up for being level. Just a bit 'igher – an inch. Now 'owd it theer! Ah'll just put a nail in.'

He hammered home a four-inch nail with precise and vigorous blows. Then he stood a moment, tapping the head of the hammer gently into the palm of his other hand.

'Your Aunt Betty were just about the grandest lass Ah've ever seed or will see. After 'er'd pulled me out o' th' Trent, there's nowt Ah wouldn't 'a done for 'er, and me dad were the same. By gum, Ah believe 'e'd try to clump me now if 'e tho't Ah were talkin' about 'er be'ind 'er back!

'Ah were reight fond o' 'er, Ah can tell you and tho't at one time
. . . but 'er were a cut above me, and it just couldn't 'happen. But
Ah'd do owt for 'er even after 'er'd married young Salt. Ah still did
onything Ah could for 'er – cleaned 'er 'oss up or owt like that ivery
time she come to Oakleigh from th' Manor. We'd better get
another rail lined up! Wunna do to stand about talkin'.'

Edith held up one end of the ash rail while he nailed the other
end and when he came along to her he continued, 'It wor a reight
muck-up that day – grand weather it wor, too. Well, Mr Bob and
Edwin Salt went off to Leek or somewhere to buy some store beast.
It were a fair way off and they reckoned to be away all day. Your
mother 'ad a sprained ankle and couldn't go with 'em so Betty
wouldn't go either. It were the maid's afternoon off too, so p'raps
your aunt felt a bit lonely. Onyway, 'er goes off ridin' on 'er black
'oss – owd Beauty. Me dad were rolling spring corn wi' th'
cambridge roller on one o' th' top fields and Betty come across
theer and chatted to 'im quite pleasant, then went on. About ten
minutes later 'er come back, galloping full out, reight past me dad
wi'out speakin'. A bit later on young Mortimer rides up and asked
Feyther which way the lass went. 'Course, me dad wouldn't tell
'im and 'e went off swearing.'

Dick fetched another rail from the float and slid it into place.
Betty stood watching him, her heart thumping quickly in
anticipation of the revelation she expected, but she would not
interrupt the story.

'Then the owd Gaffer comes walkin' through. 'E'd sin both of
'em i'th' distance – 'ad a word wi' Dad, then set off for th' Manor
on foot. Carried a big stick wi' 'im, as 'e does now.

'Th' next bit Ah got from Mavis. Betty, lookin' a bit rough,
drives into th' yard at Oakleigh i' their milk float, full o' loose
straw and your grandfeyther sittin' among it. Mavis and 'Ilda put
'im to bed, cos 'e 'ad an 'ell o' a bump on th' back o' 'is 'ed.
Mortimer wasn't sin for months. We 'eard 'e'd gone abroad and
when 'e did come back 'is left arm were all crumpled up like it is
now. Nobody knows what 'appened at th' Manor that afternoon,
on'y Betty 'erself and Mort, and mebbe your grandfeyther. By
gum, Edie if Ah'd 'a knowed for sure that somebody 'ad done 'arm
to Betty Ah'd 'a found 'im 'an finished 'im and so would ony o' th'
lads who worked at the Manor – Charlie, George, an' Jack Long.'

'And that's all you know, Dick?'

'Not quite all.' Dick looked around him furtively. 'Ah've towd
you so much, you might as well 'ear th' rest. Mr Bob came back
from th' sale soon after, and Betty took th' float back to th' Manor

wheer Mr Salt would 've bin by then. About an hour later 'er drives th' little car into Oakleigh, goes in to see Meg and then runs off down to th' river. Mr Bob goes after 'er and your mother sends me dad down theer as well. Betty, poor lass was in a right state and was goin' to chuck 'erself in Ah reckon, but they got theer just i' time. 'Er went to bed in 'er owd room at Oakleigh an' stayed theer until 'er left these parts for good. Never went back to Manor Farm at all. So what went on theer atween 'er and Mort Ratcliffe and then atween 'er and 'er 'usband is onybody's guess, but poor little Betty was th' one to suffer!'

Chapter Eleven

Edith was far from triumphant at her success in wringing the story from Dick's unwilling lips. In fact, she felt quite nervous to be in possession of her newfound knowledge. Although only fifteen, she was shrewd enough to realise that something momentous must have occurred to influence her grandfather to exchange blows with the young squire; to force Mort Ratcliffe to leave England suddenly and to stay away for months, and to cause dear Auntie Betty to suffer a mental breakdown so severe that she never returned to her bridal home at Manor Farm. Edith tried hard to imagine what it could be and in her own mind succeeded. One day she would try to get the full facts from Betty Salt but did not see how it could be attempted just yet. In the meantime, she regarded her grandfather with more respect and Major Ratcliffe, secretly, with more interest.

For the first time in her life she did not confide in her brother for she was convinced that he would not understand the need for secrecy. He might carelessly reveal his knowledge and put Dick in the wrong for having divulged the story. However, Arthur was too busy trying to convince his father and grandfather of the pressing need to allow him to put into practice the methods he had learned at Cirencester to listen to what he would have described as girlish intrigue.

Before the end of the year a second tractor was purchased and Arthur insisted that it should be fitted with the recently-introduced pneumatic tyres. To his great surprise, his seniors agreed without demur, for as Bob said, if the rubber tyres were too limited in their scope it would be a simple matter to take them off and fit iron wheels. Arthur was proud to be the first to drive the smart blue machine and hoped he would be able to regard it as his own. To his chagrin, Mr Felton not infrequently assigned the new tractor to Dick who, as senior tractor-driver, was too valuable a man to be slighted or belittled. Bob was determined to keep his staff happy and to achieve this he tried not to show favouritism to his son when allocating the farm work. In the house it was another matter and Arthur was brought into every discussion as of right. The evening meal was often the occasion of fierce arguments among the males, and Mrs Felton, Edith and, to a lesser degree, Gladys were often heard to give sighs of relief when Arthur retired to his own room to continue his studies for the professional qualifications so earnestly desired for him by his grandfather. On these occasions Mr Ratcliffe would say, half proudly and half wearily, 'By gum, the lad's got tenacity, if nowt else. But I think he's got a lot more besides, and it'd be worth your while to humour him a bit, Bob!'

Arthur was an avid reader of the *Farmers Weekly*, a new publication which updated agricultural journalism and which provided the inspiration and the fuel for many of his ideas. His father and grandfather seldom did more than glance at it, preferring the established *Farmer & Stockbreeder* for their solid reading. After Christmas Arthur brought up another of his permanent fancies – the installation of a milking machine. To the rest of the household the discussions seemed endless for they continued throughout the whole of the summer of 1937. Word of the proposal seeped out to the farm men, presumably through Gladys who was by now reputed to be 'going out' with Charlie. None of the farm workers appreciated the idea of mechanical milking. For the cowman it was harder work, requiring more sustained effort than the restful, almost sleepy ritual of sitting on a comfortable stool and snuggling into a cow's flank with angled head and shoulders. True, it was hot and smelly in summer when one also had to contend with swishing green tails, but still it was a welcome break from hoeing, haymaking and harvesting. In winter the warmth of the friendly hide made hand-milking a pleasure on icy mornings. From the point of view of the labourers the introduction of the machine would mean no early morning work, much less overtime at week-ends and consequently lower wages which was a more important issue than extra leisure.

The faithful Ned, stalwart and reliable, was outraged at the thought of his cows being milked by a soulless pulsator and rashly let it be known that he would leave rather than use the machine. He was so forceful in his opinions that the other men, for perverse reasons known only to themselves, took every opportunity of egging him on. They liked to hear his positive views and in a sense he was fighting their battle. As a result of all this, Ned found himself in an entrenched position from which he could not escape without losing face. Robert Felton, having weighed up the advantages and disadvantages of the project over many wordy months, was hardly likely to be deflected from his course by a fierce-tempered workman even though Meg showed sympathy for the cowman's views. Once the decision had been made, opposition merely strengthened the farmer's resolution and before the cows were brought in for the winter the milking machine, with its level rows of pipes and endless tubes, was fitted to the Oakleigh cowshed. Angrily, Ned gave in his notice and he was not asked to stay on as he had so rashly assumed. The new man Alf was a modern machine-milking cowman and after many teething troubles, udder disorders and lowered yields, milking by machine became an accepted part of the Oakleigh programme.

As 1937 came to an end Edith completed her secretarial course, accepted the first class diploma and proudly presented it at home. Her family were all proud, too, and were indiscreet enough to be surprised. Edith's self-admiration turned to mild indignation but she was mollified when her father promised her a new typewriter – 'for the farm, of course'.

'All right, Dad, but I ought to have an office as well!'

'An office? Can't you use it in the front room?'

'I daresay I can but if I keep all the papers in there the room will be spoiled for bringing guests home and I'm sure I'll soon start that, even if Arthur doesn't seem to be making any headway.'

Her brother snorted.

'I'll start bringing girls home when I please! Farming and studying for my exams are more important to me than women! I see enough of them eyeing me up and down every time I go to the meet!'

'Ah, you're just like your Uncle Sam,' his mother sighed. 'He never bothered about girls either. But I don't see why you can't use the sitting-room, Edith. The old roll-top desk has always been adequate for our correspondence and bills.'

'But Mum, I shall want a flat-topped desk for the typewriter and at least one filing-cabinet. We can't get any more things in that Victorian jungle!'

'Victorian jungle be blowed!' Mr Ratcliffe said explosively. 'That room was newly furnished when your grandmother and I were married. Beautiful stuff – expensive too – and I wouldn't want to see a lot of modern rubbish squeezed in there!'

'Then I must have an office,' Edith said simply.

Her father looked glum.

'There's no end to the things you youngsters want! I thought a new typewriter would keep you quiet for a bit. But to provide and furnish a bloomin' office is a bit thick, Edie.'

'Oh come on, Dad!' The farm's prospering – I've heard you say so several times recently.'

'Well, that's true enough. The war clouds are gathering and farming allus picks up at such times.'

'Don't talk about war, Bob,' Meg said in alarm. Arthur was of military age and Edith approaching it.

'We're getting away from the subject,' Arthur said. 'I've got a brainwave. Why not buy a sectional wooden hut and set it up in a corner of the rickyard?'

Edith nearly burst with indignation.

'Not likely! Do you imagine I'm going to sit in a poultry house? I'm not a broody hen, am I Grandad?'

'Certainly not, love! The very idea. Tell you what, Edith, I'll build you an office if no else will. It's still my house,' he added defensively.

'Oh, and what site did you have in mind, Dad?' Meg could not keep a note of scepticism out of her voice.

'I'll tell you exactly where,' the old man said aggressively. 'We'll build a lean-to on the blank end-wall of the scullery. That old privy can be knocked down now. It's given this house good service for a hundred years but nobody ever uses it since we built the WC round the corner.'

'That's not surprising,' Edith said, half to herself.

'But that would be on the front of the house,' Meg objected.

'The shrubbery which hid the closet would also hide the office, if we want it to,' Bob interposed. 'That's not a bad idea, Dad, and I don't mind paying something towards it.'

'Very generous, I must say,' his father-in-law commented sarcastically. 'Now, this is what I suggest. We'll have a door in from the scullery so we can go in the office with farm boots on without going in to the house proper. We'll have one window looking out over the Croft as the parlour windows do, and another in the inner wall to look over the garden.'

'Yes, and another door in the angle so travellers could apply there without needing to call at our front door,' Arthur said brightly.

'All very prettily worked out,' his mother replied. 'Now I'll have *my* say. I'm not going to have the front of the house disfigured by a hideous shack of breeze-blocks and asbestos, put up by a half-baked handyman. The materials must match the house exactly, the work must be done by a builder and sufficient shrubs must be planted to screen everything except the two windows and the door!'

Her father and her husband looked at each other and grinned ruefully.

'Now we know exactly what we've got to do,' Bob observed without rancour. 'Arthur, you're a surveyor, or should be by now.

Get a plan drawn out. Room fifteen by twelve, say – and I'll drop it in to Brown's tomorrow and asked them for an estimate.'

'Oh good! I'll charge a fat fee. It'll be my first commission,' Arthur replied and yelped when his mother twisted his ear.

When something was needed for Edith, to think was to act in the Oakleigh household, and local tradesmen had learned to respond accordingly. The builder came along at once and produced an estimate which was accepted. The dry winter allowed the work to proceed rapidly and by the middle of March Edith was proudly and comfortably ensconced in her own domain with a new modern desk, filing cabinet and chairs, together with her own extension telephone.

Of course, even Edith realised that for such a small business her office was really an expensive luxury. Except for Fridays when she made up the wages, she rarely spent more than half-an-hour each morning on correspondence. But, as her father said, it was lovely having all the papers together in a place where you could find them and handier to go in to the office to phone rather than to remove wellingtons and walk through the kitchen into the hall.

In the same month the German armies marched into Austria among welcoming crowds and Europe trembled.

After a studious winter Arthur found a renewed enthusiasm for changing things as the spring of 1938 developed. The weather was dry but cold and growth was restricted, especially on the pastures, and the dairy cows reflected this shortage in their reduced milk yield.

'In a season like this we could do with a field of lucerne,' Arthur announced one evening when his father was bewailing the falling milk supply at a time when it should have been rising.

'Lucerne? What the devil's that?' Bob and Mr Ratcliffe said together, but as he said it Bob vaguely remembered reading of it from time to time in the *Farmer & Stockbreeder*.

'It's a deep-rooted leguminous crop which withstands drought like no other plant. It can be cut again and again; the more you cut it the more it grows.'

'Sounds like manna from heaven,' grunted Mr Ratcliffe. 'Fetch your books out Arthur, and let's look into it!'

'Nobody's ever grown it round here in my time,' the old man said later. 'Sounds as though it might be just the thing for Hilltop. What do you think, Bob?'

'Try anything once, Dad. We'd better stick to the rules though. It says here that the seed must be treated with live bacteria of some sort, especially in places where it hasn't been grown before.'

'No problem there, Dad. We did it every year at Cirencester.'

'All right, then. You take charge of the operation – order what seed and culture you want for that ten-acre field and if you can provide unlimited green feed in a dry time I'll take my hat off to you!'

Elated with the success of his proposition for the dry upland field, Arthur now turned his attention to the riverside meadows which he said were in need of drainage. This was a harder battle, for none of his elders would agree with him.

'Drain the river fields?' echoed his grandfather. 'Whatever for?'

'So we can get the water off 'em o' course, Grandad! We could outwinter cattle beside the river then!'

'That's contrary to commonsense Arthur,' his father explained so condescendingly that the boy was furious. 'The land there is free-draining anyway and we don't want to get the water off any faster. Just the opposite, we want the land to absorb water from the river in a dry time and keep the grass growing, and to some extent that's what happens. Anyway, I've certainly no intention of winter-grazing cattle beside the Trent. It might ruin our most productive grassland. You can forget about that!'

Arthur sulked at this positive rebuff but refused to forget the subject. He brooded over his scheme for several days and finally brought it up again when he, his father and the whole farm staff, even his grandfather, were singling mangolds in the Top Longfurrow.

This was the field where his uncle and namesake had met his death in a haymaking accident twenty-five years before. The recollection of it always put Arnold Ratcliffe and Robert Felton in a sombre mood and even after such a long time their conversation was always muted in this field, as though the ghost of little Arthur still hovered over the windswept acres. Otherwise it was a pleasant field to work in. There was plenty of air, for it was free of shading trees and from its high position one could enjoy a panoramic view of nearly half the farm. Two fields separated it from the highway and on the other side of the road was the series of the River fields, then the Trent itself, dividing the land like a strip of bent silver. Over the river other fields were in view, but they were farmed by other men and had no relevance to the Oakleigh staff. The men often muttered to each other that the gaffer and his family were right fond of Top Longfurrow, because from there they could see what everybody else was doing.

There was a thick plant of mangolds and they were growing so fast that the singling had become an urgent task needing completion before the plants and the weeds grew too strong to be dealt with. All the men worked together, side by side on a broad front across the striped field, Mr Felton, Bill and Dick Marshall, Alf, Charlie, Gerald, Frank, Len and Arthur, followed by old Ernie and Mr Ratcliffe. The talk was scanty and aimless for the men were always diffident in the presence of the gaffer. They would have considered it ill-mannered to hold private or grouped conversation in his presence and therefore kept their remarks general, raising only those subjects to which the gaffer could contribute if he chose. The farmer's presence was in itself an indication that the job was urgent and long conversations which might distract attention from the work were not encouraged.

Arthur, in his half-way position between the staff and the management, generally took a main part in any chatter, but this afternoon he was thoughtful and occasionally stood gazing over the lower ground. He frequently fell behind the main body of the hoers and in so doing impeded his grandfather and Ernie who excused their own slowness by claiming the privilege of age.

'You're holding us up again, Arthur,' Mr Ratcliffe said mildly. 'What are you doing back here? You ought to be up along with the younger men.'

'Still thinking about my drainage project, Grandad. I haven't changed my mind – I'm sure it'd be a good idea!'

'I thought we'd explained why it's not feasible or necessary,' the old man replied wearily.

'You haven't convinced me!'

Arthur increased his pace and soon caught up with the main body. Now that the site of the proposed drainage was in full view, it might be a good time to re-open the subject with his father.

'Dad,' he called out across the other hoers, 'I can see from here the advantages of draining River Fields one and two!'

'The devil you can,' muttered one of the men.

Robert Felton frowned slightly. He always tried not to discourage his son, but Arthur should have known better than to discuss farm policy in front of the men, and over their heads into the bargain, for the gaffer was at the head of the main squad and Arthur at the rear.

'There's no sense in what you say, lad,' he remarked quietly. 'The riverside land doesn't need draining. It's like pushing an open door.'

The men were uncomfortably silent.

'I don't agree at all,' Arthur continued stubbornly, reckless of good manners. 'Some o' the land beside the Trent may be free-draining as you say. But look, you can see from here – in the near left-hand corner of the first field there's a low-lying patch of a couple of acres or more. There's even a few rushes growing there, so don't tell me it doesn't need draining!'

'There's a pocket of clay there, I agree, but it's a long way from the river bank and it wouldn't be a paying proposition to run a pipe diagonally across two fields to get the water away!'

'Then don't run diagonally – take it through the willow clump and save a couple o' hundred yards!'

'Run a drainpipe through close-packed willows? You're talking plain stupid, Arthur!' Mr Felton was beginning to lose patience.

'Dammit Dad, we can grub out the clump altogether. It's no good, and we'd gain an extra half-acre of ground!'

'Grub out the willows? Hold your tongue, you bloody young fool and don't argue with your betters! Concentrate on the work you're supposed to be doing instead of hatching out fanciful ideas which are too bloody silly for words!'

Nobody present had ever seen such a wrathful outburst from the gaffer. The farm workers reddened and continued their hoeing with set faces as if trying not to take sides. Arthur flushed, then paled with resentment and humiliation. He had never been so addressed by his father in his life and to be so castigated in front of the whole farm staff made him feel sick and miserable. He would have liked to leave the field but he knew such a reaction would not be tolerated and it was not his custom to run away from problems. He knew he would have to stick it out for the remainder of the afternoon.

Robert Felton was furious with his son, but vexed with himself for losing his temper in such circumstances. At the end of the row he exercised the gaffer's privilege by placing his hoe in the hedge and leaving the field. His departure slackened the tension, but Arthur knew that only the presence of his grandfather a few yards away saved him from a broadside of leg-pulling. For the first time he felt dissatisfied and unhappy with his life at the farm. Although he now realised he had been wrong in pressing his argument in front of the farm staff, he thought his father's attitude was savage and unnecessary. Arthur felt the need to confide in someone, but his grandfather was only mildly sympathetic, 'You oughter've known better, Arthur, but there was no need for your dad to be quite so vicious.'

It was not a problem he could discuss with Edith for she was always unsympathetic towards his ideas and automatically favoured her father's point of view. That only left his mother and he had not taken his troubles to her for years for he was twenty-three and above feminine counsel, or thought he was until now. There was no opportunity during or just after the evening meal for there was always someone else in the kitchen. But Meg knew her family and had sensed that her husband and son were not on cordial terms. Consequently, when she went out to her flower garden after tea she was not surprised when Arthur joined her. No one else in the family was interested in gardening and they both knew they would not be interrupted.

'Well son, what's your trouble? I don't like to see my boy going about with a face as long as a retriever's.'

'I'm just absolutely fed up, Mum – fed up with life at home, the farm and everything. I think I'll join the army. It looks as if there'll be a war!'

'Oh no! Don't say that, Arthur.' Meg recalled the emptiness and misery of her husband's four-and-a-half year's absence in the last war. Bob had been in the trenches when this handsome son had been born.

'Well, why not? Everything points to it. Germany's kicking up a fuss about these Sudeten people just inside Czechoslovakia. On the face of it, I think Germany's got a good case, but from the tone of the papers most people feel differently. If war breaks out I'll go, of course, even if I don't agree with the reason. Dad fought in the last war without feeling too keenly about it, and it's up to me to fight in this one if it comes.'

'Don't be so depressed lad, and talk so wild! What's upset you so much? Something your father said?'

'Well, yes! I've never known him be so mad. He's never spoken to me like that – nor has anybody else, for I wouldn't stand it, I can assure you. He was livid with temper and made me look small in front of the men.'

'Of course, you shouldn't have been arguing with him in front of them. You know better than that, boy.'

'I realise that, Mum, and I've never done it before. But it was such a small thing and I thought it wouldn't matter referring to it in general terms. But Dad's reaction – oh dear!'

'But what was it all about? What did you say to rile him so?'

'I only suggested running a drainpipe from the roadside corner of First River Field down through the willow clump and doing away with the clump to gain a bit more grazing ground and he nearly exploded!'

'You suggested grubbing out those willows?'

'Well, yes. They aren't much good . . .'

'Oh Arthur!' His mother coloured prettily and looked at her son with a tender thoughtful smile. 'Dear, dear old Bob! You know lad, your dad's an incurable romantic!'

'Dad – romantic? What's all this nonsense? Have you gone off your rocker, Mum? You look a long way off, as if you're sleep-walking and dreaming of heaven!'

Meg laughed merrily.

'You touched your dad on a tender spot, son. That clump of trees which you want to tear out so casually was the place where he first made love to me on the night before he joined the army. I wouldn't want those trees taken away either. It was such a lovely hot August evening. We hadn't said anything to each other before that night, although your father had lived in the house for three-and-a-half-years. We found out that we were fond of each other and had to say good-bye all at the same time.'

His mother coloured more deeply, lowered her head and grasped her son's forearm affectionately then said, with an effort, 'Arthur – that – that was where – your life began!'

A strange look of surprise and shock passed over the young man's face.

'Mum – you don't mean . . .'

'I do, Arthur. That's what happened. Then Bob went away and I thought I might not see him again.'

Arthur Felton looked at his mother with a set face, lowered his eyes when they met hers, then turned and walked away without another word.

Chapter Twelve

Arthur did not mention land drainage again, nor did his father or grandfather. The subject was left alone by tacit agreement but the atmosphere in the kitchen remained quiet for several days. Meg was slightly more attentive to her husband and son than usual. If Edith noticed all this she made no comment for she was enthusiastic about a new plan of her own. From now on, she said, she intended to attempt some farm work every afternoon; it was ridiculous that a farmer's daughter should be unable to tackle farm jobs, and anyway her mother had so worked as a girl.

Meg pointed out that in her young days the family was not so well off. There was no financial need for Edith to work, so long as she helped in the house every morning after doing her office work. Her father smiled tolerantly at the new idea, Arthur was contemptuous, her grandfather disapproving and Gladys envious.

Having heard that the hoeing of mangolds and sugar beet was falling behind schedule, Edith selected a hoe from the toolshed and presented herself at the root-field. The men looked down their noses. They were all fond of the girl and admired her but assumed that her presence among them would inhibit their conversation and they were right. No one dared to swear or tell a blue joke in the presence of the gaffer's daughter. Edith even decided to learn to operate the milking machine and her presence in the cowshed pleased Alf even less than her hoeing. He had been inclined to swear at his cows in friendly fashion but now had to indulge himself under his breath.

When haymaking time arrived and the farm carts were converted to mophreys, Edith insisted on trying to load the hay which was quite a task since two pitchers were always used. Her father demurred at this, saying that her unskilled efforts would impede the flow of hay to the barn. He decreed that if she intended to learn to load she must be accompanied on the mophrey by Charlie or Arthur. Charlie was delighted, Arthur less so.

Sometimes Meg would wander out to the hayfield in the afternoon. The haymakers assumed that it was to ensure that the proprieties were being observed, but in fact the mistress still retained a child's fascination for the most fragrant farm task of the year. She would have liked to ride out to the field in the empty mophrey, but refrained on the grounds that clambering into a vehicle fitted with hay-raves was not the most elegant or modest thing for a weighty, mature woman to do.

At seventy-seven Arnold Ratcliffe was no longer able to assist. He could not keep up the pace of the younger men on the stack and it was not considered safe for him to work on a swaying load. Leaning heavily on his stick he ambled from rickyard to field and back again, sitting here and there for a few minutes to while away the long hot afternoons, smiling with deep content as the loads of hay or the empty conveyances passed him.

Arthur accepted the hard work of haytime with nonchalance. He took charge with natural ease if his father were absent and the men accepted this as a matter of course. This season, although outwardly composed, inwardly Arthur was bubbling with anticipation and had been so for weeks. In March he had taken the finals for the RICS and AAI and was now awaiting the result. He did not propose to allow these qualifications to affect his life, but the desire for achievement was there; also he was keen to please his grandfather.

Much hay was needed at Oakleigh to supply the large number of stock and the haymaking continued well into July. The River Fields which had been shut up for mowing late in the spring were consquently the last to be cut. Arthur was crossing the road with an empty mophrey when the postman, passing on his bicycle, handed him a large stiff envelope. He continued driving his horses into the field, holding the envelope high to show the old man, who was standing by the loaded wagon. Edith and Charlie had just slid down the rope when Arthur arrived. With sisterly impulse Edith flung her arms round her brother's neck and kissed him. He was more ruffled than gratified by this exuberance.

'Don't be a fool, Edith, you're smothering me,' he waved the envelope past her brown hair. 'I've got it, Grandad – the RICS which is the important one. I'm pretty sure to get the other as well!'

'Well, open it lad, and see exactly what you have got!'

Arthur shrugged his shoulders slightly but thrust his forefinger in the envelope and tore it open.

'Here it is Grandad! Pass with Distinction!'

The old man's face suffused with pleasure and he started to speak, but his breath was suddenly cut off. He staggered back to lean against the load, but the horse had moved on a few feet, Mr Ratcliffe's body met no resistance and he crashed to the ground, his face turning blue as he fought for breath. Arthur took in the situation at a glance.

'Watch him, Edith! You know what to do! Gerald, take this load home. I'll get the car!'

He turned and sprinted out of the field, across the road and up the farm drive.

Edith dropped on one knee and propped up her grandfather's shoulders, waving Charlie and Len away to start loading. Mr Ratcliffe looked at the girl with grateful eyes. His breath came and went in short gasps as his bronchial tubes adjusted themselves to the demands made on them, but by the time Arthur drove into the meadow and pulled up after a theatrical U-turn, he was breathing normally.

'I'm sorry about this, you two,' he said apologetically as they hauled him with some difficulty to his feet. 'I'll be all right but you'll have to take me home, Arthur. I've not enough breath to walk. I don't know what came over me. Must be the excitement I reckon. B'guy, I'm right pleased, Arthur. You've no idea how much. I've been thinkin' o' this day for nigh on thirty year, I reckon. Now I can die in peace!'

'Don't talk like that, Grandad,' Edith admonished him 'I won't let you die! You're good for years yet!'

'Years of sitting by the fire perhaps. I don't think I want that, you know. If I can't get about the farm, I might as well die. But don't worry, you two. I've had a good life and a grand family.'

'Get in the car, Grandad. I'll take you home before you start writing your epitaph and selecting a tombstone. You get in the car first, Edith.'

The hayfield saw no more of Arnold Ratcliffe that summer. He confined his pottering to the rickyard and his remarks to enquiries about what was happening elsewhere on the farm, nodding with satisfaction when the bumper yields of grain were reported to him day after day, indeed week after week, for the acreage of corn at Oakleigh was considerable. The harvest lasted well into September and a lot of the grain was threshed direct from the stook, much to Arthur's satisfaction.

While the Feltons and their employees toiled with the sheaves, the machinery and the sacks of corn, the politicians of Europe also toiled in their own inimitable way to sort out the problems dividing Germany and Czechoslovakia. Hitler could not be moved from his determination to protect the people of German origin in Sudetenland. Crisis succeeded crisis and war loomed very near. In the farmhouse only Meg voiced her fears. 'Please God, don't let there be a war,' she said again and again. She was afraid for Arthur and Edith, but everyone knew that the next war would bring air attacks on a large scale, possibly gas and even germ warfare. Nobody would be safe, no matter how far they were from the front.

Arthur, who considered himself well-read on such matters, stated flatly that there was no need for war. Hitler had fought in the trenches in the last war, knew how tenaciously the British could fight and for that reason would not declare war on us. For once, Bob agreed with his son, but Mr Ratcliffe, emerging from one of his quiet spells, pointed out that even if Germany would not willingly make war on us, that was no guarantee that we should not declare war on her, as had happened last time. This gave the family much food for thought and reassured them not at all.

Gas masks were issued and in the towns sandbag reinforcements were built round important buildings. Preparations for war went on at a pace which was frightening in its intensity, for it had been discovered that we were pledged to defend the territorial integrity of the troublesome land-locked Czechoslovakia. Mr Ratcliffe roused himself and said the whole problem was caused by the stupid break-up of the old Austro-Hungarian empire, and Bob certainly agreed with that.

The British Prime Minister made hurried flights to see Hitler at his country retreat at Berchtesgaden. The French Premier and Mussolini were co-opted to the discussions. Finally, in an explosion of publicity all four leaders met again at Munich and worked out a solution which was accepted willingly by all except Czechoslovakia. Mr Chamberlain returned by air from Munich, triumphantly waving a tightly-clutched document and quoting Shakespeare, 'Out of this nettle, danger, we pluck this flower, safety.' Later, he said earnestly, 'Herr Hitler has assured me that he has no more territorial demands to make in Europe.'

Everyone swallowed this German piecrust thankfully, especially Meg and Edith Felton who were firm in their belief that any war was undesirable. The country as a whole heaved a deep sigh of relief and the obvious signs of war preparations were discontinued. About a week after Chamberlain's dramatic return, various persons of the political Left spoke on the wireless to express their dissatisfaction of the Munich agreement, referring to it as 'appeasement'. Apparently they themselves could have achieved much better results but they did not specify the cost. Robert Felton was furious at this attitude and he was dutifully supported by his whole family.

'The utter fools,' the farmer said. 'Can't they see we've gained a respite which will be invaluable, war or no war? There's always some nitwit ready to chuck a spanner in the works.'

In Hartnall church prayers of gratitude were offered up and no one prayed more fervently than Meg, who so desperately wanted to retain her home and family intact. She did not know that war preparations were going ahead just the same, but they were less obtrusive and 'out of sight, out of mind' seemed the maxim to suit the hour. The Home Office intensified its training in the new Air Raid Precautions movement and enrolled more volunteers, while the factories of Britain, particularly those working in steel, increased production and engaged more staff, reducing unemployment to its lowest level for ten years.

After a succession of mild winters 1938-39 was very severe with deep snow and hard frost. The Oakleigh staff grumbled in their surprise at these arctic conditions, but in fact there was no crisis. There was plenty of hay, plenty of straw, grain and mangolds; the sugar beet had all been despatched before the cold weather struck, and the potatoes were well covered and could be dressed for market under a portable shelter which Arthur had constructed.

In the farmhouse the family passed a comfortable winter with the males listening intently to the Test Match broadcasts from South Africa, while the females groaned every time the cricket was switched on. Even Mr Ratcliffe, sitting silently in his chair, absorbed the details intelligently but remarked while the fifth Test was in progress, 'Seems to take them longer to play a match these days! It can't be the fault of the wireless, can it?'

This was in March and the spring work was in rapid progress, for the hard weather had not been prolonged and Len and Arthur were fully extended with a spate of lambings.

The papers reported that German troops had marched into Czechoslovakia and had annexed the rest of the state. This news was received with general indignation; clearly Hitler had broken his promise and was no longer to be trusted! Britain immediately started discussions with Poland to arrange a pact of mutual assistance. Meanwhile Italy, somewhat casually and for no apparent reason, launched an attack on Albania.

Meg read the papers closely – they had the *Telegraph* as well as the *Mail* now. She was worried and said so. Her father read them with equal absorption but said little. Arthur read them and remained thoughtful for a long time afterwards, while Edith refused to read the political news, dismissing it as too depressing. To most, war seemed inevitable sooner or later, but Bob tried to soothe his household by saying: 'If everybody keeps their heads, there needn't be any war. It's the bloomin' papers that are fostering the idea.'

Meg replied sorrowfully, 'You don't really think that at all, do you? You know better than anybody what's going on! The government's not calling up these Militiamen for nothing. Thank God, Arthur's too old for that!'

The headlines diminished and went back to reporting ordinary news, while Germany presumably consolidated her recent gains. On the farm, the spring work went ahead, as it must, in spite of political ineptitudes. Lambing, cultivating, fertilising, drilling; ridging, planting, sowing, corn, potatoes, sugar beet, mangolds, cabbage, to provide work without end for the farm staff. Work so pressing and so absorbing, the war scares of the early spring were quickly forgotten. Farming problems were paramount.

For the last few years Oakleigh Farm had been increasing its acreage of cash crops. Potatoes, sugar beet, swedes and winter and spring cabbage had spread the workload and increased the farm income. The city of Derby on one side and the busy town of Burton on the other provided excellent markets for the greenstuff which Bob usually sold on the field so that the buyer provided the labour for cutting, packing and transport. It was thus possible to avoid the long hard work involved in harvesting these crops, but not so during the growing season when there was perpetual work for the hoers. The inter-row cultivations with the horses were also a permanent chore and Bill and Gerald, with occasional help from Charlie, drove their horses up and down the green-edged alleys every dry day when there was no haymaking. Robert Felton was a stickler for keeping his crops as free of weeds as his wife kept her table-linen free of stains.

The tide of agricultural mechanisation was creeping slowly forward, but at present it was only a gentle flow. Most progress was being made on the large arable farms of the eastern counties, for on the smaller, mainly grass farms of the Trent Valley, horses were still the main source of power. In Hartnall parish only Oakleigh and Major Ratcliffe's Home Farm possessed tractors which were used only, apart from ploughing, for drawing converted horse implements at a slightly higher speed. The wheel-widths of the ordinary tractor were fixed and this made them unsuitable for inter-row work. Progressive manufacturers had now introduced a row-crop model with extendable front axles and rear axles on which the position of the wheel could be varied, thus giving a range of wheel-widths to suit any row-spacing.

Characteristically, Arthur kept abreast of all farming

developments, reading every word of the *Farmer & Stockbreeder* as well as the new *Farmers Weekly* with an infallible eye. Changes in tractor design were of particular interest and the reports and photographs in the journals fired his imagination. If revolutionary machinery could be made use of on other farms, then it could be used at Oakleigh, for nothing was too good for his own well-loved acres.

'We ought get one of these rowcrop tractors, Dad,' he said one evening as he sat at the table drinking his last cup of tea and perusing the new *Farmer & Stockbreeder*.

His grandfather jerked awake immediately.

'Rowcrop tractor? What's that, boy?'

'It's a tractor with its wheels moveable sideways so it can fit the rows of beet and cabbage, Grandad,' the young man said patiently.

'What, move those heavy wheels? Dangerous business I should think. They might fall and hurt somebody!' and the old man fell silent and appeared to have dozed off again.

'What's the idea behind that suggestion, Arthur?' asked his father, only mildly curious.

'We could get on with the inter-row hoeing much faster. Do four rows at a time!'

'It would still need two men, one to drive the tractor and one to steer the hoe!'

'Yes, but they'd be doing twice as much!'

'While the hosses were eating their heads off in the field!'

'We could do with fewer hosses then.'

'Don't keep on about that, Arthur! It's easy to over-mechanise and that'd be a waste of capital. Tractors cost a lot to buy, a lot to run and they wear out. Each one remains just one unit of power. The theorists say one tractor will replace four hosses. But four hosses can be used as one, two, three or four units if you've got the men to handle 'em, which we have.'

Arthur could not immediately counter this sound argument so he returned to the time factor and became emphatic.

'It's still a hell of a waste of time having one man and one horse doing a single row at a time. Even when we multiply it by three, it's still slower than four rows with a tractor!'

'Well, I'm not going to buy another tractor! We've got two already and that's more than any other farm round here.'

'We could sell one o' them and buy a row-crop model. Wouldn't be wasting any power then!'

'We'd be wasting money, 'cause it would still mean a big

outlay. The old tractor's not worth much!'

'I reckon it'd be a good investment!'

'Well I don't! We've got just the right set-up now, five hosses and two tractors and I'm not prepared to readjust at this stage. Your point about the slowness of single-row hoeing is valid and I'm doing something about it. In the eastern counties they use a four-row hoe – a skerry they call it – with wheels and a pole to which you can couple a pair o' hosses. One man sits on the seat and drives and the other walks behind steering the hoe. I'm going to order one, but it might not be in time to use for this season.'

'You'd far better put the money towards a new tractor,' Arthur said aggravatingly.

'We'd still have to buy a new hoe for the tractor, you fool! For God's sake, shut up, Arthur! It's about time you learned to take no for an answer.'

Meg frowned at her husband's harsh tone, but made no comment. She, too, sometimes became fed-up with her son's persistence.

Arthur flushed, bit his lip, then pushed back his chair and strode out of the kitchen. They saw no more of him that evening. The following morning he ate his breakfast silently as if deep in thought. He spoke to no one and did not appear to listen to the conversation. Towards the end of the meal he said suddenly, interrupting his father who was talking to the old man, 'I want to be off this afternoon. Is that all right?'

Robert Felton looked surprised, but said indifferently, 'Yes, of course. Where are you going?'

'Private business.'

'Ooh! How interesting! Can I come, please?' Edith said archly.

'No!'

'Thank you for that tactful, qualified refusal,' his sister said, colouring. 'What's the matter with you this morning? Got out of bed the wrong side?'

Her brother did not answer, but left the table quite expressionless.

'Oh dear! What was all that about?' Meg said to no one in particular. 'No good worrying, I suppose. We shall learn in due course.'

Arthur did not enlighten them at dinnertime either, eating his meal with quiet detachment. Afterwards he had a bath, put on casual clothes, got out his car – an SS he had recently acquired – and disappeared down the drive in a cloud of dust. He returned at teatime and joined his family at the table without offering an explanation.

'Aren't you going to tell us where you've been?' Edith asked indignantly.

'Sure I'll tell you! Went to see George Formby in *It's In The Air*.

'What, pictures in the afternoon?' his father said. 'That's unusual. A waste of daylight, surely?'

'My business didn't take as long as I thought it might.'

Nothing more was said during the meal. Afterwards Bob, feeling he had been too harsh with his son the previous day, and being concerned at Arthur's sulky silence, started discussing plans for the next year's crops, hoping to bring him to a happier frame of mind.

'I should've thought you'd 'a wanted to get the harvest out o' the way before you bothered about next year's plans,' Arnold Ratcliffe said. Then, seizing the opportunity to humour his grandson, added, 'Don't you think so, Arthur?'

'You can't start planning too soon,' the young man replied indifferently. 'You'll have to make some re-arrangements, anyway – certainly as far as the staff is concerned. I shan't be here!'

'What the devil are you talking about?' his father said crossly. 'What do you mean?'

'I mean that from now on you'll be farming without any suggestions from me. I've joined the army!'

'The devil you have. Whatever possessed you to do a stupid thing like that?'

'Were you stupid when you joined up, Dad?'

'That was different! The country was at war!'

'Yes, and it'll soon be at war again, if the politicians go on as they are. They seem bent on it. I may not agree with them, but I'm not going to be left out and I don't want to go up with a crowd of conscripts.'

'But farming's almost certain to be a reserved occupation! You won't be called up for the services!'

'Maybe not, but I'd go anyway. If I can get used to the life in peacetime, it'll be an advantage to me when war does come.'

'Well I think it's all bloody silly. You'd do more good here, where you're needed and where you're an expert.'

'Expert, am I? It didn't seem like that when you rejected every suggestion I made!'

'Oh come, Arthur,' his grandfather intervened, 'It's not been like that at all, as you very well know. You can't expect to run the farm all your own way just yet, can you?'

121

'I don't seem to have *any* say in running the farm, so I've become a soldier, and that's all there is to it. I go in a few days, when they notify me. I'll be away for five years, I'll see a bit of the world and then I'll come back to Derbyshire and settle down on a farm and run it my own way!'

Chapter 13

At first, the whole pattern of life at Oakleigh Farm seemed wrecked by Arthur's precipitate action. Of the farmhands only the retired Ernie's memory reached back to before Arthur's birth. The boy, then the man, had been there all the time for most of them. Edith was confused and frightened at the thought of life at home without her brother. A brother who teased, bossed and bullied her, it is true, but she knew he loved her fiercely with an elder brother's protective love, and she for her part adored this handsome, masterful young man who somehow seemed to be a modern edition of her father, mother and grandfather all in one.

Robert Felton was worried and disappointed for he had never visualised farming Oakleigh without his son and heir at his elbow. Arnold Ratcliffe did not seem to realise the import of the mealtime conversations. At times, applied thought seemed to be beyond the old man. Meg Felton was upset and showed it so clearly that Arthur felt guilty and ashamed every time he looked at his mother.

'Why did you have to do it, lad?' she said plaintively a couple of days later. 'We've been such a happy family, ever since Edith was born and I hoped we could go on like that – always.'

'Can't be helped now, Mum. It was bound to come sooner or later, anyway.'

'But there was no need to enlist secretly after an argument with your father. He'll be blaming himself now for everything that happens to you.'

'It won't do him any harm to think like that for a while. It isn't exactly the case, of course. I'd been thinking about it for a long time, and that little tiff with Dad just hammered the last nail in.'

'But couldn't you have joined the Territorials, Arthur? You could have lived at home then.'

'Week-end soldiering's no good, Mum! If war comes, say about Michaelmas, I'd have to go just the same and I'd only be half-trained. It's the fully-trained men who have the best chance of survival!'

'Well, I can't understand it,' Meg said sorrowfully. 'You've always hated war.'

'Yes, and I still do, Mum. War is bad, but to be beaten in war would be many times worse. I love this place Mum – every brick, every field of it, and the village and the dear old Trent. I should hate to think of a foreign army spreading over and desecrating it. So, no matter how much I hate war, once the politicians had caused it, it's up to me and everybody else to support it until we've won, and deal with the politicians afterwards.'

'Oh dear, it all seems a dreadful muddle! But you've had more education than any of us, so I suppose you must know. I thought we'd finished with war in 1918 when poor Sam was killed.'

'Yes, and perhaps we would have been if the politicians hadn't been such incompetent nitwits with minds warped with ideas of vengeance. The Germans were treated very badly at Versailles and it was quite justifiable for them to try and put things right, even by threatening force on a small scale. But this Hitler's going too far! We don't know where he'll stop, or if he'll stop. For my part I'd keep this country out of it until he attacks us, but I think the top men are not intelligent enough for that.'

'Isn't it going to be a bit hard for you to take orders, thinking the way you do?' his mother ventured.

'Well, no. It won't have to be, will it? The ordinary soldier can't expect to be told everything in the mind of the commander. He can only see his tiny part in the scheme and he must realise he is only one small unit in a world of men, mud and movement. Not only that, if I'm drawing army pay, then I'm the army's man and must carry out instructions, just the same as on a farm. I wouldn't allow any of my farm employees to argue about my instructions and the army won't allow it either. I'm certainly not going to test them! I'm going to be as good a soldier as I can, Mum, so that neither you, nor Dad, nor Edith, nor Grandad, nor Oakleigh Farm will ever be ashamed of me. Perhaps I'll be promoted, as Dad was. I'll certainly try for it!'

Meg Felton laid her head on her son's shoulder.

'Nobody will ever be ashamed of you in this house, lad! We'll be praying for the day when you can come back to us, take up your rightful place and, yes, argue with your father.' She smiled through her tears. 'It's your birthday next week, Arthur. We'll have a real big party for you!'

The War Office decreed otherwise and Arthur had to leave home early on the day that he became twenty-four. Farewells were said in the kitchen. Bob's silence matched Meg's reluctance. The old man raised himself to his feet, clapped his grandson on the shoulder and said huskily, 'If you make as good a sojer as your father, you'll do!'

Edith drove him to Willington station. She wanted to take Arthur's SS, but with a flash of his old manner, he said indignantly, 'No fear! I'm not having a blooming girl driving *that*. We'll take your car and if you ruin it on the way back, that's your affair.'

They took her Morris Eight. Edith was too sad to argue and too pre-occupied to resent the old bossiness.

'Look after the old people while I'm away, Sis,' was all Arthur had to say as the train barked out of the familiar little station.

'The house has never been so quiet,' grumbled Meg on the first night of Arthur's absence. 'At least, not since Betty's wedding, and that's nearly seventeen years ago. It's not only that Arthur's voice is missing. Nobody else is talking either.'

'There doesn't seem much to talk about, now the lad's gone,' Bob replied, 'and that's not surprising. For the last year or two practically all the talk has consisted of refuting his arguments. Well, we've got to get used to it! He's away for five years and the Lord knows what changes there'll be before he gets back. In the meantime, it's up to you women to make the conversation.'

'Thank Heaven we've got a daughter,' Meg said fervently. 'At least, she won't be joining the army!'

Edith got up and put her arms round her mother's shoulders.

'I won't leave you, Mummy, – ever,' she said with conviction.

'Mr Ratcliffe roused himself and made one of his increasingly rare excursions into speech. 'It's the old Derbyshire saying proving itself again. "A son's a son till he finds a wife, but a daughter's a daughter all the days of her life." Arthur hasn't found himself a wife yet, which is surprising, but he's gone to find himself a war, which is worse. I'll not see him working Oakleigh Farm again!'

'You're getting morbid again, Grandad,' Edith admonished him. She sat on his knee, put her arms round his neck and looked straight into his fading eyes. 'I shall be cross with you if you talk like that!'

'Yes, love,' the old man said, beginning to gasp for breath. He kissed her. 'Edie, I like fine to have you sitting on my knee, but don't press quite so tight on my diaphragm, I think it's called. You're a strapping girl – no light-weight any more and I can't breathe!'

With or without Arthur, the farm work had to go on. Shearing, hoeing, haymaking – all jobs in which the gaffer's son had played a great part – had now to be shared between Dick, Charlie and Len. Edith, who had learned to drive the tractor – once the engine had been started for her – sometimes drove it on simple jobs where the trailed implement needed no adjustment. She realised that if war came she might have to work long hours on the farm as her mother had done nearly thirty years before. She liked the company of the farm men, better in fact than that of her numerous suitors in whom she took little interest. One or two of her admirers had joined the Territorials, which Charlie was now planning to do, but on the whole she noticed a marked disinclination among farmers' sons to partake in defence activities on the grounds that the summer tasks on the farm were of over-riding importance. Edith felt very proud of Arthur then, although of course she knew that few farms were as large or so well staffed as Oakleigh.

The summer was not wet but rather cool and haymaking was protracted, lasting until the start of harvest in early August. There was a large acreage of corn to cut and Robert Felton bought a new binder, properly constructed to follow a tractor. This was allocated to Dick. Driving the tractor would be a simple job as the experienced Dick would be there to make mechanical responsibility, and it was offered to Edith who accepted it with alacrity. She was quite thrilled with her assigned task and in her youthful enthusiasm regretted that the rest of the farm staff were not there to see her. Bill and Gerald were cutting another field of oats with the horses and the rest of the men were fully extended trying to catch up with the stooking.

On its rubber tyres the tractor steered easily and all she had to do was to keep it on a straight course about two feet away from the standing corn. Behind her the brightly-coloured binder, under Dick's expert eye, was ejecting its sheaves with beautiful precision. Most of the time she looked ahead but now and again would show off her competence by stealing a glance behind her. On the corners she had to work hard and quickly, for the low-geared steering wheel needed rapid manipulation to complete the turn. At first she was distressed when she ran over a sheaf or two, but to avoid this she would have had to stop, climb down and remove the obstructing sheaves by hand. Then Dick showed her how, by steering the tractor gradually away from the crop and commencing to turn before the corner was reached, the change of direction could be accomplished without trespassing on the sheaf-rows. The binder would be running empty while turning, so no sheaves were ejected and the area remained clear for subsequent turns. This was more artistic too, Edith decided, for the uncut corn developed into the shape of a gigantic star with four elongated and sharp points.

The weather was hot and clear, the dew had dried off quickly, and they had been able to start at eleven o'clock. At dinnertime

126

Dick pulled out the draw-pin, lowered the binder-pole to the ground, and stood on the tractor behind Edith. Feeling even more important and slightly diffident, she jerked into top gear and raced out of the field at twelve miles an hour. She had never driven the tractor so fast and felt thrilled as the wind tore at her hair. She dropped Dick off at his home without stopping, waved to the surprised Mavis through the kitchen window, made a quick circle round the barn, pulled out the throttle again and roared home. Her grandfather observed her arrival and during the meal demanded an explanation.

'I'm driving the tractor for the new binder, Grandad,' the girl said proudly.

'Making a good job of it, too,' her father interposed, then added untruthfully: 'One side looked a bit scalloped, though!'

'Nothing of the sort!' Edith said indignantly. 'How dare you say that, Daddy? My driving is as straight as the drilling!'

'Don't get upset, love,' her mother said soothingly. 'You ought to know by now when your father's pulling your leg. I don't suppose he's been near your field this morning!'

'Well, *I'm* going near it this afternoon! I must see this!' Mr Ratcliffe said jocosely. 'A granddaughter of mine driving a tractor on the harvest field! Why, you'll soon be taking over Arthur's place in everything.'

'Will you ride on the tractor with me when I go back to the field, Grandad?' Edith asked innocently.

'No, thank you! I may be proud of your ability, but I'm not that proud and I don't want to test it! I'll just doddle down there on my two feet. I'm breathing quite well today and I think I can make it if I take my time.'

Edith left the table and moved towards the hall. Her father glanced at the clock.

'Where are you going?'

'I'm going upstairs to change into an old skirt. These jodhpurs are too hot for sitting on that tractor. I'm not going to be crawling about under machinery or anything. Dick can do that!'

'Well, buck up then. It's nearly time you went back. I don't want Dick kept waiting. He's a paid man, you know!'

Edith coloured at the reminder and tossed her head slightly but made no rejoinder. As a farmer's daughter she knew that one did not argue with the boss at harvest time!

Back in the field Dick held up the binder drawbar while Edith reversed her tractor up to it. She was pleased with his gesture for it meant that he had full confidence that she would not overrun him.

Then he connected the drive shaft and greased up the machine and they were off again, round the field endlessly under the baking sun. Dick was so pleased with the binder's performance that he must have been mesmerised by it, for he forgot to check on the supply of string and allowed it to run right out. Several untied sheaves were ejected.

'Damn!' he shouted, banging the metal cover of the elevators with his stick. At the sound, Edith instantly stood on the clutch, which was also the brake.

'What on earth's the matter?' she shrieked above the roar of the engine.

'Run clean out o' string. Must a' bin asleep! Stay right here while I fetch a couple o' balls!'

Edith slipped the gear lever into neutral, partially closed the throttle and swung down from the seat. She was stiff with sitting immovable and welcomed the chance to stretch her legs, away from the aura of fume-laden air which accompanied the tractor. She moved away a few yards and stood in the stubble, legs slightly apart, the slight breeze pulling gently at her hair. She seemed to be standing there in an empty world, for Alf and Charlie were stooking over the brow, out of sight. Not quite empty, she soon realised, for a tall man climbed over a rail-place in the distant hedge and walked towards her. In a few seconds she recognised him as Major Ratcliffe and wondered what he wanted. He had obviously seen her for he was making a beeline for her position.

'Good afternoon, Miss – er – Edith, isn't it? What a magnificent tableau you make, standing there in your beauty among the sheaves!'

Edith smiled. She knew she was attractive but, wearing a crumpled grey skirt, old shoes and no stockings, a once-white blouse which had one or two black smears where she had accidentally brushed against the binder, a perspiring face on which harvest dust had settled thickly, and unruly hair which wandered, she found it amusing to be called beautiful.

'Good afternoon, Major.' He was not too bad-looking a chap himself, she thought, although he must be nearing fifty, for she knew he was older than her parents. He was over six feet, perfectly upright with clean features and hair only just greying at the temples. The only noticeable imbalance was the slightly crooked left arm, and Edith now realised that this was her grandfather's handiwork. 'What brings you here in our cornfield, with a walking-stick instead of gun and dog?'

'I haven't been invited for the rabbits, as I'm sure you must know, young lady. I wanted to have a word with your father and as I heard the tractor when I paused in Beggar's Lane, I walked up by Red Coppice and over the Meads. Had I known such a pretty and charming girl such as yourself was operating here I would have risked your father's anger and brought my gun along to show off my prowess!'

Edith giggled at the extravagant compliment and looked up into Major Ratcliffe's smiling face.

'Your skill with a gun is so well known in Hartnall, you do not need to prove it, Major! My father isn't here. He's left the job in my charge.' Then she added archly, 'My man allowed the knotter to run out of string and he's gone to get some. Ah! Here he comes now.'

The Major looked down on her from his great height, and knowing that the girl must now feel quite safe with Dick in sight, he said with genuine admiration, 'My God, child, you're prettier even than your mother was in her teens! Both of you a glorious example of a Derbyshire country girl of your time. I wish I were a painter, so I could capture it for ever!'

Edith rippled with laughter again, then her expression changed for she heard an exclamation from her right. Turning, she saw her grandfather hurrying towards them, stick up-raised, his mouth working.

'You bloody villain!' The words came only faintly to them through the shimmering air, for the tractor was still ticking over at about the same distance away. 'By God, I'll finish it this time!'

'I appear to be *de trop*,' the Major murmured, but Edith did not hear him. She was horrified at the sight of the old man, for his face was purple and he stumbled. As they stared, he stumbled again, tottered, then crashed to the ground, falling in a crumpled heap in the stubble.

'Oh Grandad!' Edith gave a cry of anguish and ran to him. Dick, who had appeared beside the binder dropped the two balls of string and ran also. Major Ratcliffe came up with solemn strides.

'Young lady, I am very sorry to witness this . . .' but Dick interrupted him, boldly but without heat and without a trace of servility.

'Ah think you'd best go, Major Ratcliffe. It seems the owd gaffer passed out at the sight o' you. You'll not be popular when he comes round.'

'He won't come round, I'm afraid. Nevertheless, I can see that my presence may be an embarrassment. Goodbye Edith. I'm sorry our pleasant meeting should have had such a tragic ending.' He walked away quickly, weaving his long strides through the rows of sheaves.

Edith dropped on one knee beside her grandfather and Dick hovered near on the other side.

'Ah'm afraid he's gone, Edie. Poor owd lad, to drop down dead i' th' harvest field. Mebbe it's not so bad at that, though, endin' 'is life among the sheaves, on his own land that 'e's farmed for more'n fifty years! It's a rum do! Ah'll just straighten 'im up, like, so 'e's laying tidy,' and he did so, pulling down the eyelids at the same time.

'Have you got a clean hankie, Dick? Mine are so tiny.'

'There's one i' the top pocket o' my overalls. It's not bin used. If you'll tek it out – your 'ands are cleaner'n mine.' He pushed out his chest towards her and rather diffidently she unbuttoned the flap and drew out a clean folded white handkerchief with a coloured border. She opened it and laid it reverently over the still face, beginning to cry as she did so.

'What now, Dick? I don't think we should stop harvesting. It wouldn't seem right for a farmer.'

'No, but it wouldn't seem right either to leave the owd gaffer lyin' here alone like a dead rabbit. Ah think you should stay with'm Edie. Ah'll send Alf to th' farm on 'is bike and get on cuttin' wi' Len.'

'Dick, I'd rather you borrowed Alf's bike and went home to tell my mother. You've been here so much longer. I think Mummie will ring up for an ambulance. That's the most decent way to move him, and anyway there'll have to be an examination and an inquest, so he'd better go to the hospital.'

'All right! We'll let the binder stand for a bit, then. It wunna matter a lot – we'll finish in less than a couple hours.'

For fifteen minutes Edith kept her lonely vigil beside her grandfather's body. In that short time she re-lived her whole life; those incidents in which the dear old man had taken part stood out sharp, clear and pleasurable. Now he had passed out of her life forever. Forever? Surely not? Some faint thread must remain! Then the dreadful finality of it struck her and she felt overwhelmed and wept quietly.

Her mother arrived on her bicycle to comfort her. Then Dick returned, after having sought out the young gaffer, who drove into the field just behind him. Mercifully, the ambulance arrived almost at once. The body was loaded speedily but respectfully and the vehicle bumped away over the bonehard stubble. Edith insisted on driving the tractor to finish the field, although her father suggested she should go home with her mother. The girl replied that driving the tractor would stop her from thinking. There would be far too much time for that later.

The oat-field was finished and after tea all the sheaves were set up. To Edith, there seemed a solemn grandeur about the rows of close-set stooks, as if they were a conscious memorial to the late master of Oakleigh, who on this first night of the 1939 harvest, lay silent and sheeted in the mortuary of Derby Hospital.

Chapter 14

Arnold Ratcliffe's death in such dramatic circumstances cast a gloom over the harvesting operations. It was more of a gentle sadness than absolute grief for, as Meg Felton said, 'Dad was seventy-eight and hadn't been enjoying life too well just lately. It was heart-breaking to see him fighting for breath when the asthma got him. I wouldn't have wanted to see him get any worse. I loved him too much!'

Bob was silent and moody for days, for his mind would keep dwelling on the great debt he owed the dead man. When he had presented himself at Oakleigh as a runaway youth twenty-eight years before, Mr Ratcliffe had taken him on and given him a chance. Many farmers would have sent such a lad home with a flea in his ear. From the beginning, Bob had been treated as a son and consequently he mourned the old man as much, or more, than his own father.

Edith was inconsolable. This was the first death in the family she could remember and she found it difficult to believe or to accept. The farmhouse seemed so terribly empty so she spent as much time in the harvest field as she could, dreading the day when her grandfather would be put away for ever.

On the day of the funeral the harvest came to a full stop at Oakleigh and at other farms as well, for all the staff and their wives wanted to be there. The whole village was sufficient to fill the church to capacity and the addition of numerous farmers from further afield and relatives from distant homes caused overcrowding which was in itself mute testimony. Bob's sister Betty and her husband Edwin Salt came up from Stokenchurch the night before. There had been a bond as strong as father and daughter between Arnold Ratcliffe and Betty, who had charmed away his grief following the death in battle of his first-born, Sam. Betty had been married at Oakleigh – as one of the family.

The Salts stayed the night at the farmhouse and Edith remembered that she had hoped to question Aunt Betty about the alleged fight between the young Squire and the old farmer, but realised that in these melancholy circumstances it was quite impossible. The very thought of such probing seemed irreverent and Edith felt guilty of disloyalty for allowing it to enter her mind.

The Grand Old Man of Hartnall was placed in a grave beside

his wife, who lay next to their younger son, and after the funeral there was the usual meal at which Edith felt compelled to assist. Nearly all the guests had left their grief at the graveside, which the girl found difficult to understand. The jovial and complimentary remarks on the wonderful resemblance between mother and daughter were quite nauseating to Edith and she said as much to Arthur who had obtained compassionate leave. For some time she had been casting overt glances at her handsome brother, smarter than ever in his unfamiliar new uniform.

After the meal the will was read by the Burton solicitor whose firm had dealt with all the Oakleigh business since Arnold Ratcliffe had purchased the farm in 1911. The original Oakleigh farm of 200 acres, with house, buildings and tenant-right was left to his daughter Margaret, absolutely. The deceased's share of the remaining 200 acres, which he had purchased in conjunction with his son-in-law in 1921, was left to Robert Felton, as was Mr Ratcliffe's share in the live and dead stock. The result of this was that Meg and Bob were roughly joint owners of the property and business. All savings and investments were left in equal shares to his grandchildren, Arthur and Edith Felton. His watch – a gold hunter given as a wedding present by his wife – and his silver-mounted Sunday walking-stick were bequeathed to Betty Salt 'My comforter and friend for many years; and to Gladys Cook who 'has served me so well, my brass bedroom clock and fifty pounds'.

Betty was still sobbing as the crowd of guests departed. All that visually remained of Arnold Ratcliffe was a mound of Derbyshire soil, covered and surrounded by a multitude of flowers, rapidly fading in the harvest heat. Edwin Salt returned to his business but Betty remained at Oakleigh two more days to grieve with and console her sister-in-law and bosom friend. The two women reminisced so comprehensively and in such detail that Edith felt quite excluded. She was in no mood for chatter and the death of her grandfather made any other subject, even that of the secret encounters at Manor Farm, seem utterly trivial. Edith drove her aunt to Derby to catch the London express, but Meg went along too, so there could be no blurting out of embarrassing questions.

'We seem to be losing our family rather quickly,' Meg commented sadly on the way home. 'First Arthur, now Grandad. We three will have to snuggle in tighter, Edith.'

But the death of the old man, searching though it was, had soon to be relegated to the back of their minds by wider events. Rumours of war had become a near certainty. Britain, who had been discussing a mutual assistance pact with Russia for most of the summer, was stupefied by an announcement that the Soviet had signed a non-aggression pact with Germany. Our negotiators were left red-faced, speechless and groundless. Robert Felton expressed the opinion that this development made war less likely since it would be madness on our part to attack a Germany allied to Russia. He found this was not the general view. It was clear that Germany had made this arrangement to safeguard her flank while she invaded Poland, which was considered a certainty. Since we were pledged to assist Poland our involvement became automatic. And so it proved. Instead of attending church on the morning of the first September Sunday, the Feltons stayed at home and heard the Prime Minister's solemn announcement that we were at war from that moment.

Overnight, farming became all-important. Robert Felton, although believing to the last that hostilities would be avoided, had nevertheless bought two new tractors – one of them a rubber-tyred row-crop model so coveted by Arthur a few months earlier. Bob still remembered the shortages of the Great War. He smiled at the glib talk of the war being over by Christmas. If it was anything like the last – and no one could visualise it being different – fighting would go on for years. Tractors and other machinery would wear out and replacements might become unobtainable. He decided he has better prepare as much as was humanly possible.

Feeding-stuffs were going to be short, too, and he had foreseen this to some extent as far as the cattle were concerned. Recalling his experience of silage-making in the wet summers of 1930 and 1931, he had made several stacks early in the season when the grass was young and nutritious. If cake became short, his milking cows would be adequately provided for. As most of his own corn was grown for seed, he had bought oats and barley early in the harvest from other farmers for storing as pig and poultry food. Recalling the vast amount of food he had seen wasted in the army camps of his own war, he had increased his numbers of breeding pigs and determined to set up a pig-fattening unit at one of his outlying farms if a service camp materialised within collecting distance. Balloon barrages were going up between Hartnall and Derby, but the number of men involved was small.

Food rationing in the home was scarcely felt at first. As a matter of course Meg ordered several hundredweights of sugar every spring as her mother had done before her. Vast quantities of fruit were made into jam or bottled – possibly two years' supply at normal usage, and there was always lots of sugar left over. Butter could be obtained simply by keeping back a few gallons of milk once or twice a week and separating the cream. Meg had no previous experience of making butter, which is not normally done on milk-selling farms, but she soon learned, and so did Edith who also liked her share of butter. Eggs had always been plentiful on the farm and if butchers' meat was scarce there were plenty of wild rabbits and always a few cockerels around the yard. The killing and salting of pigs at home was a practice which had gone out of fashion long ago but it could be revived if not declared illegal. At this period orders and regulations were poured out daily by the Ministry of Food, and no doubt other Government departments as well, thought Bob. But as the months passed, the arrangements for the distribution of food and the issue of coupons settled down into a workable routine.

On paper, rationing of petrol was an obstacle to efficient farming. At first a basic ration was issued for every licenced motor vehicle and this was certainly adequate for Edith's little car, but less so for the family Ford. However, the milk was still taken to Willington by car and trailer, for which a fuel ration was issued. The four tractors were of the type which ran on paraffin, known as vaporising oil, but needed petrol for starting and coupons were allotted for this. Anticipating greater fuel difficulties later on, Felton bought a small lorry which could be used for milk or other produce and at a pinch for conveying small numbers of pigs or sheep to market and he obtained an adequate supply of petrol for this vehicle.

At the outbreak of war the staffing of the farm was disrupted by the call-up of Charlie into the Territorials, and of Len, who was a reservist, into the regular army. New farm men were not easy to get and a single man to live in the house and replace Charlie could not be found. Most such men were in the services or working in the booming factories. Len's family occupied a service cottage in the grounds of the old Hartnall Hall, now requisitioned by the military, and Meg insisted that they should remain there for the duration of the war. Bob did not disagree with this for he had no intention of attracting odium by dispossessing the dependants of a man on active service, but it meant that the cottage could not be used for a replacement. Fortunately Len's children were all of school age and his wife was free and willing to assist in the farmhouse during school hours.

In November Ernie died suddenly at the age of eighty-two. This was another upsetting event for the people of Oakleigh for he had been employed there for forty-two years – since Meg was three years of age. No one now could remember the farm without him. Once again on Meg's insistence, Mrs Wagstaff was given the cottage for the rest of her life. She was some years younger than her husband, but not young enough to return to helping in the farmhouse kitchen, which she had done for many years until Edith was old enough to assist.

Bob had been unenthusiastic about employing members of the Women's Land Army, and Meg was similarly unwilling to house them with domestic help likely to be a problem. Mrs Wagstaff sized up the position astutely, decided that she was young enough to tackle some extra work in her own home, and volunteered to board two girls. In retrospect, Bob found that he was glad to be able to accept this, for as one of the biggest farmers in the district he felt he had to give a lead in most things, including the use of makeshift wartime labour.

The total direction of farming throughout the country was applied through a War Agricultural Executive Committee for each county. Because of his reputation as a progressive and productive farmer Robert Felton was invited to be a member of the committee and, in addition, the representative for his own parish. He accepted, largely on the grounds that if he refused the positions might be filled by someone of less experience, understanding and tact. Major Mortimer Ratcliffe was also a member of the committee. As well as being a large-scale farmer he had acquired valuable experience of land ownership and estate management in his earlier years.

As the autumn progressed this committee work occupied more and more of Bob's time, for although discussions could take place at evening meetings, there were visits to farms which could only be made in the daylight. The general policy was to increase food production overall and one important basic step towards this was the ploughing up of unproductive grassland and converting it to productive arable. Although this could hardly fail to be profitable to the farmer, it was often strongly resisted, sometimes by farmers who opposed all change as a matter of principle, but more often because the farmer had not the equipment or the knowledge to grow arable crops. Several visits and much persuasion was needed and, sometimes, threats of legal proceedings.

These wide-ranging activities, covering the whole county, caused Bob to be absent from home frequently and Edith became an invaluable deputy. The very pressure of wartime farming with its shortages, its regulations and restrictions, its innumerable application forms and the need for maximum production, increased the office work many times over but Edith took this in her stride. More telephoning, more correspondence, more decisions fell to her. She maintained old contacts, made new ones and business callers became used to dealing with her instead of the boss. The farm men brought their problems to her, too, for although she was not competent to solve managerial difficulties in their entirety, at least she was capable of deciding between two alternatives which was the usual form in which the men presented their problems to her.

In the afternoons she would frequently take out a tractor to the fields. The farm was so well equipped there was always one available, and she would have a word with Bill or Dick Marshall at dinnertime, so they could tactfully suggest something for her to do. The men as a whole, although they continued to address her in the intimate but respectful way they used since her childhood – Edith – now spoke of her among themselves as Little Miss Gaffer. Her father was only too pleased to have some of the worries due to enforced absence taken from his shoulders, and Meg was proud of her daughter's competence and the easy way she had assumed responsibility.

The first winter of the war dragged on its undramatic way. The black-out, novel to begin with, became lethal when familiarity with its limitations bred contempt in their observance. Since many foods were still unrationed, people learned to make do with alternatives. The war news was uninspiring except when a naval encounter took place. Then all the paraphernalia of the propaganda machine was brought out, assembled and given a trial run. The Air Force made nightly raids into Germany, at first with leaflets, later replaced by bombs, which in those days of inferior technology sometimes fell on a neutral state. Germany replied with an occasional reconnaissance plane and, according to Robert Felton, this proved that Hitler was unwilling to come to blows with Britain.

On the Continent, the numerically impressive French army occupied the comfortable underground quarters of the extensive and expensive Maginot Line, guaranteed to repel all enemy attacks. Behind this fortification the British Expeditionary Force, which had been sent to France in September, settled down to prepare bases from which to launch, in due course, a war effort comparable with that of 1914-18. In variety programmes the BBC highlighted the British soldier in France at his leisure pursuits and the people at home felt comfortably involved.

Arthur Felton was a member of the BEF and sent chatty letters home stressing the placidity of army life. There were no difficulties apart from the intense cold, for Europe was shivering in the coldest winter for a century. In Scandinavia, Russia attacked Finland in temperatures so low that oil was reported to have frozen in the sumps of their war vehicles. In England, frosts of twenty degrees were of nightly occurrence. At Oakleigh, heavy snow blanketed the farm for weeks and continued heavy frosts prevented any work other than attention to stock and getting the milk away. Water became a problem, for any exposed to the air froze in a few minutes. Fortunately the extra tractors had enabled all the ploughing at Oakleigh to be completed in the autumn and the upturned ground benefited to the full from the deep frost which reduced the number of spring cultivations. Other farmers were less fortunate and Robert Felton, in spite of his own heavy sowing programme, felt obliged to offer them help with his own machines.

During this busy spring when there was more arable land in Britain than at any other time this century, the war machine throbbed into action. In April, there was naval fighting in the creeks of Norway. We were victorious but sustained heavy losses and failed to prevent the capture of a large part of our army in Norway. In May, the German armies in Europe moved forward. Disdaining the strongly-held Maginot Line, they simply rolled on through Holland and Belgium and entered France from the north-east. The Low Countries quickly capitulated and the resistance from the bemused French army was only patchy. The Germans surged on and our own army was in danger of being engulfed. Members of Parliament panicked at the dismal prospect and changed the Prime Minister for a man of more popular appeal.

It was evident that the war was to be long and bitter, for we had a lot of ground to recover from a position of near-defeat. The call went out for more men for the services, more women for the services; more men, more women for every branch of essential war work. Edith listened carefully to all the speeches, read all the announcements and the exhortations, dismissed them all from her mind, then the next day informed her mother that she wished to join the ATS.

Meg was dumbfounded and tearful as she groped with this new development.

'Edith, what are you saying? Surely we've enough to put up with, worrying about Arthur, without cracking jokes!'

'It's not a joke, Mum. I want to join the army!'

'But why, dear? You're doing such a good job at home! It's going to be awful for your father and me if both you and Arthur are away. Surely patriotism doesn't call for frivolous and pointless moves such as this! You're a farmer's daughter and can do more important things!'

'It's not really a question of patriotism, Mummy! Today's generation doesn't think like that. Well, perhaps they do, deep down, but they don't admit to it and probably don't even recognise such a feeling. No! The thing to do nowadays is to get into uniform like everyone else – one's brothers, cousins, boy-friends, girl-friends and so on. Everybody will be drafted into something before long. The men are already under conscription and it won't be long before the government conscript women!'

'But I'm sure they won't take girls from farming. It will be a "reserved occupation", I think I read somewhere. They're putting girls into farm jobs to release men, anyway.'

'That's true enough, Mum, and if I waited until all women are drafted I might not be allowed to go into the army. In a case of this sort the government know exactly what they want. *I* know that it would be a lot more patriotic of me and more use to the country if I stayed here and helped Daddy run this big farm than to join the army and type a lot of bumph for brass hats!'

'Don't be vulgar dear. You must have heard Arthur say something like that! You're a lady now, but I don't know long you will stay a lady when you get in the army!'

'The thing is, Mummy, I believe that everybody who doesn't get in this will regret it for the rest of their lives. It's the one big chance for most of us and we'll never get another.'

'Women going to war! It doesn't seem quite right to me!'

'We are equal with men now, Mummy, and we must make the most of it. The professions are open to women, why not the services? There must be millions of jobs in the Army, Navy and Air Force which can be done equally well by women, and release more men for fighting!'

'Hmm! I'm not at all sure that the men released for fighting will appreciate that!' Meg looked sorrowfully at her daughter. 'I suppose you will go, whatever I say!'

Edith put her arm round her mother's neck and kissed her on the cheek.

'I'd rather go with your blessing than without it!'

Meg put her arms on the table and sobbed into them.

'Oh Edith! My dear! I had so looked forward to our spending a few more years together! When you were little I used to say to myself, 'I shall be so glad when Edith grows up so that I'll have someone to talk to all the time. If you go now, I don't suppose we'll ever live together as a family again!'

'Oh Mum! You're only forty-five and I'm only nineteen! We've probably got over thirty years together yet!'

'Yes, you're nineteen. If the war goes on for three years, as your father thinks it might, you could come back married. You'll be old enough!'

'That's not very likely, Mummy. I haven't yet met the man who interests me!'

'Perhaps not, but you'll be meeting hundreds in the army – some of superior rank who might want to take advantage. Edith! You won't . . . er . . . er be too free and easy with the boys and let them get too familiar?'

Edith smiled and kissed her mother again.

'I know right from wrong, Mummy! I suppose I may join up, then?'

'My dear you've always got what you wanted, even when you were small. We may have refused you at first, but at the end usually gave in.'

'Seems to me I got a lot of things I didn't want as well, but I daresay I deserved them. Will Daddy agree, Mummy?'

'In this case your father will do as I say! But it will be a big blow to him. Over the last six months you've made yourself indispensable.'

'Nobody's indispensable, Mum! But it's not going to be easy for me either. I shall be sorry to lose my own office here – specially built for me and all that.'

'Well, you're doing it yourself! If you think like that, there's a hope that you'll change your mind, especially when your father hears about it!'

'I shan't change my mind and Daddy won't make me!'

Edith was not quite prepared for the violence of her father's reaction. If a thunderbolt had landed on the cow-shed at milking-time he could hardly have been more agitated.

'I can't possibly do without you, girl,' he stormed at her. 'You've taken over all the paper-work and some of the administration and done it well. The whole idea's ridiculous! What's behind it all?'

'I suppose I want to get into uniform like everybody else!'

'That's a stupid reason! The services can get thousands of girls to do their menial jobs, but there's not another girl in the Midlands who could do what you're doing here!'

'Nonsense, Daddy! But if that is the case, you'll just have to do it yourself!'

'Don't be so damned pert, child! I think I'm doing enough, what with running this sizeable farm, advising smaller farmers how to increase production, and giving half my time voluntarily to organising the county's farmings! On top of that, my only son – my right-hand man – is in the army and now you want to go. Is there no limit to the contribution one family must give to this damned war? You're a traitor to the farm, Edith! A rat leaving the sinking ship!'

'Sinking ship! Rubbish! A cat leaving a luxury liner to clear out the rats in the dockyard, more like! And when's the job's over, I'll be back!'

However much he might fume, Robert Felton had already accepted the inevitable. With every nerve he loved this bold and handsome daughter, but he understood her as well and knew that once she had made up her mind she was immoveable.

'I suppose you'll go, anyway,' he commented, more quietly. 'You're just as stubborn as your mother – in fact like all the Ratcliffes!'

'Hey! I like that, Bob Felton!' Meg said indignantly. 'Talk about the pot and the kettle!'

'Don't make this argument a threesome,' Edith intervened brightly, realising she had won her point.

'There's one thing, though,' her father continued, clutching at a straw. 'When you've got over the glamour of the uniform, which shouldn't take more than a few weeks, I can apply to have you discharged as being of more value here. In fact, I might do that, anyway!'

'Daddy! Don't you dare!' Edith's trepidation was mounting again. 'I'd never speak to you again, nor ever come home! If I join – I mean *when* I join the ATS, I stay in it until they throw me out!'

'Throw you out?' It was her father's turn to be indignant. 'I'd like to see the organisation that's got the nerve to throw out *my* daughter!'

'That's the spirit, Daddy,' Edith said and hugged him.

Chapter 15

Having made her point, Edith Felton lost no time in driving it home. After attending to the correspondence the next morning she got out her car and drove into Derby. At dinnertime she had not returned and Bob took the opportunity to air his misgivings to his wife, disregarding the presence of Gladys who had her meals with the family.

'I just don't know how I'm going to manage without the girl, Meg,' he said despairingly. 'I never envisaged anything like this. Edie's got all my business at her fingertips. I'll never get anybody else to take to it so well. It's not a full-time job for a proper secretary, of course, nor even half-time; about half-a-day a week for a professional. But I can't leave letters to be typed up only once a week!'

'Then you'll have to rely on me, Bob, won't you?'

'Don't be daft, Meg. You can't type!'

'That's all you know. I can't do it fast, of course, although it's not so different from piano-playing. When we set up the office for Edith I didn't see why I should be completely outshone by my own daughter, so I picked up all the office routine from her, where all the letters and papers go and all that. She showed me how to type, margins, headings, indents and so on and I've practised quite a bit in the afternoons when the office has been empty. So you see, I can do something towards keeping things running. It'll mean that Gladys will have to take over more of the cooking, but you won't mind that, will you Gladys? There will only be the three of us. Our family's been cut by half in less than a year!'

The stolid maid smiled nervously, which Meg took as an affirmative.

'Meg, it'll be a load off my mind if you can do some of it. I didn't expect that! But you're pretty competent, taken all round, and a grand wife for a chap to have.'

He reached across, put his arm across her waist and kissed her. Gladys blushed and turned her head away.

'Go on with you, Bob! Clear out and get on with your work. I know it's quite a change to have dinner in your own home these days but you don't have to act strange about it! Come on, Gladys, let's get this table cleared.'

Late in the afternoon Edith returned home, flushed and

triumphant, but her elation changed to a feeling of guilt when she found her mother checking things in the office.

'How did you get on, love?' Meg asked anxiously.

'Well, I didn't like the MO much. He's not half as nice as Doctor Whittaker. I passed A1 though, signed the pledge and now I just wait until I'm sent for.'

'Well, I hope that's a long time. You'll be able to show me more about this office work.'

'Oh Mum, you're not going to take that on, are you? Do you have to?'

'Your father's giving about half his time to the government, to the neglect of his own farm and business. Somebody's got to do some of this to help him when you're in uniform. Are you going to like it? I'm sure you'll look smart!'

'I don't go much on the khaki bloomers. Too baggy altogether, I think.'

'But do you have to wear them? Can't you use your own underclothes? You've got plenty.'

'That's what I've got to find out!'

The news from France was very bad – the Prime Minister's own words – and getting worse. Practically the whole of the British Expeditionary Force was being pushed relentlessly into a corner. Several fragments of the army forming pockets of resistance at various points along the French coast had already been captured. Evacuation was the topic of the hour. Of the earlier campaign in Norway, someone in the House of Commons had acidly reminded the government that 'wars were not won by masterly withdrawals'. This was even more applicable to the situation in France, but by commandeering every small boat within a hundred miles of Dover, and manning most of them with their volunteer owners, nearly 400,000 men were rescued from a few square miles round the port of Dunkirk. The German army, having swept victoriously for hundreds of miles across Western Europe, now apparently found itself unable to push forward the last five miles to prevent this withdrawal.

Robert Felton, although sharing with his family their deep concern over the fate of Arthur, suggested that this was another proof of Hitler's policy of not wishing to press Britain too hard in the hope that we should come to terms without risk of total defeat. Bob also pointed out that, although during the French campaign the RAF had deployed every available aircraft over Germany, bombing strategic targets and lines of communication, machine-gunning troops and tanks, there had been no retaliation in the air over Britain. Few people shared his views. Most were in too much of a panic to analyse the situation.

Early in June a letter from Arthur arrived, posted in Liverpool. He had been one of the last to be taken off from the sands of Dunkirk. 'What a hell of a way to spend my twenty-fifth birthday,' he wrote, 'crossing the Channel on a leaking pleasure-boat with planes scrapping overhead and sometimes having a go at us.'

A few days later he arrived home on leave in a disconsolate frame of mind.

'Thank God we're out of that lot,' he said moodily. 'But even now some of the fools in high places are talking of sending us back there! We've got a hell of a lot to do and a hell of a long way to go before we can meet the Jerries on equal terms!'

His father was sceptical that such a thought existed.

'Nobody can really think that, Arthur. We've been kicked off the Continent like a mongrel dog with its tail between its legs. We'd need an army on a continental scale before we could even attempt to return and it would take years to prepare. Is Germany going to keep static while we catch up? France has had it, and so might we if we weren't an island. That little strip of water makes us too tough a nut for anybody to crack. But we ought to accept our humiliation with dignity – not despair, mind you – and find a basis to talk terms.'

'That won't happen Dad, while Churchill is top man. If he can, he'll continue the war until every soldier on both sides is killed. It's the breath of life to him! But it's the sort of talk the people of the country want, so as we've got him and can't get rid of him, we must go along his way, and prepare for a struggle lasting years. I can't see Germany giving in. Why should she?'

'Especially now that Italy's declared war,' Edith chipped in.

'Fat lot of difference that'll make to anybody,' said father and son together. 'Except to Italy herself, maybe,' added Bob.

Arthur soon returned to his new base where his unit was to be refitted and presumably re-trained. Before he left home he vented his displeasure on his sister.

'Why the hell did you have to join up, Sis?' he demanded. 'I thought I told you to stay at home and look after the old people!'

'They're not old. They're in their mid-forties! And it's nothing to do with you. Why did you enlist, anyway? Why shouldn't I do the same?'

'It's different for men. I certainly wouldn't have if I'd known you were going to leave 'em in the lurch. Food production's going to be one of the most important angles of this war and it'll need all hands to the pump to keep the army marching on its stomach!'

'Dear me! Mixing your metaphors, aren't you?'

'Don't be cheeky. I'm worried about you, Ede. You don't know anything about the world. These army girls are not all angels, you know. They're not necessarily as tidy in their minds and morals as in their uniform.'

'Of course they aren't, you fool! They come from all classes, don't they? And the men are not all saints, either.'

'My God, how right you are! That's what worries me. In wartime the motto of the soldier is "Find 'em, love 'em and leave 'em" only they don't say "love 'em". It'd break the old people's hearts, and mine too, if you came home in a state of you-know-what.'

'How dare you! How dare you! How *dare* you?' Edith wept in her anger. 'Perhaps you'd like me to wear a chastity belt!'

'The army wouldn't allow it.' Arthur said this so cynically that Edith sobbed again in her chagrin.

He watched her for a few minutes, then, touched by her genuine distress, said ruefully, 'Oh, come on Ede! Pull yourself together. I didn't mean to hurt your feelings. But there are so many dangers facing a well-brought-up girl going into Service life.'

'Not so many dangers as there would be if the German armies landed here.'

'There you go again!' Arthur was angry that his sister had seized on a point which was unassailable, and he was not sure of the correct answer. 'We all think the world of you, Sis. We've put you on a pedestal and want you to stay there.'

Edith sniffed her tears away and held out her hand for her brother's handkerchief.

'Now that I've been well and truly put in my place by all three of you, I'll bear in mind what you've said. I must say, you've taken out all the fun of going, but I suppose I was wrong to look at it as fun in the first place. I'm sure Mum and Dad will be all right. They can afford to pay for all the help they'll need, and they're better off than most wartime parents.' She gripped her brother's arm affectionately. 'In years to come, we'll all laugh about this together.'

Two days after Arthur's departure, Edith was ordered to proceed to a collecting point to take up her duties. She was relieved and delighted when she was stationed at a camp on the far side of Derby, but within easy reach of Oakleigh. She sent a telegram home announcing this, and a day or two later presented herself at the farm, proud and smart in her new uniform.

'Funny thing, sending a wire, Edith,' her mother commented. 'Why not phone?'

'I don't like phoning from a public box, Mum. It's so noisy one can't hear, and there's always someone outside, pulling faces at the delay. A telegram's easier.'

'And do you like it as much as you thought you would?'

'Oh yes,' lied Edith who already hated the discipline. 'It's not very strenuous. I'm in a sort of typing pool and work something like ordinary hours. Finish at five o'clock and we're free for the evening then except for compulsory lectures. So I might be able to come home quite often. Not Mondays, though. We have to stay in barracks to do our sewing and things.'

'It's lovely you're so close. Pity you can't take your car. You'd be able to come home almost any time.'

'I might not be allowed to have it. I'd have to find somewhere to keep it, and a private's money won't run to that, Mum.'

'Don't be silly, dear. Of course, you'll still get your pocket money from home! You'll be able to put me right about the office work, so it might not be as bad as I thought, with you away from home. I must say you look the part of a girl soldier, doesn't she, Gladys?'

The maid did not reply, but the following morning which was Saturday, she shocked Meg by casually giving her a month's notice.

'Gladys! Whatever's the matter? What's happened to make you do this to us?'

'I'm going to join the ATS, Mrs Felton.'

'So that's it? Don't be foolish, Gladys. I'm sure you'll be happier with us. This is the same as your home! You've been with us ten years or more. We rely on you so much, now that Edith's gone.' Meg immediately wished she had not made the last remark.

'That's just it, Mrs Felton. If Edith can go, so can I. In fact, there was less need for Edith to go than me.'

'Whatever do you mean?'

'Well, if you don't mind me saying so, Mr Felton's not short of money, is he? And Edith won't be, either. She can have everything she wants and go anywhere she wants – in England, anyway. But ordinary working girls like me can't travel. We can't afford to! In the army I might be sent anywhere, and it's the only chance I'll have in my whole life. I'm twenty-six Mrs Felton, and I'll soon be past my best.'

'I should have thought you'd soon be getting married and settling down, perhaps in the village. What's happened to that chap Eric Rogers you were going out with?'

'That's sort of fading away, I'm afraid. He's due to register next month and he's bound to be called up, as he's not reserved. So I've no one to stay at home for! Besides, everybody's going! I hear that Phyl Cope's joining the WRAF!'

'I do wish you'd change your mind, Gladys. I'll give you a pound a week more to stay with us. That's a lot more than you'll get in the ATS. You'd be the best paid farmhouse girl in Derbyshire!'

'I've made up my mind, Mrs Felton.'

'But what am *I* going to do, Gladys? I must have *some* permanent help in the house.'

'I'm sure you'll be all right with the farm wives. They'll all buckle to and help. Mrs Long told me she was keen to earn a bit and Mrs Edwards, too. She's a good cook, by the way, and could take over the kitchen while you're in the office.'

'But why give me your notice so positively? It might be two or three months before they want you.'

'I want to do it according to the rules, Mrs Felton. You're entitled to notice so you can try for someone else. If I have to hang about for a few weeks before I'm called up, that's my funeral.'

'There's no need for that, Gladys. If you must join up, go for your medical and then carry on here until you get your papers. Of course I shan't stand in your way, but I'd like you to stay with us as long as possible.'

Mournfully, Meg told her husband the news.

'I thought the chance of keeping Gladys was too good to be true. Still, it could be worse, you know. If we weren't so near to a factory town which might be bombed, we'd have the house full of evacuee kids, and that *would* be a burden without plenty of help. All right if their mothers came too, I daresay. The authorities would never allow us two to keep this big house to ourselves.'

'We don't want it to ourselves – at least, I don't. But it's the way it happened.'

'True, but I wonder if we could do something with it. How about offering accommodation to a service couple, or perhaps two couples, preferably without children, of course. I'm sure there must be Army or Air Force wives who'd be glad to have a room here, help you a bit in the house and have their husbands join them when on leave.'

'That's an idea. How do we set about it?'

'Put an advert in the local papers – under a box number of course. And in the *Telegraph*, but in that case, state the county.'

'I'll do just that, Bob. Funny how there always seems to be a way round everything if you think hard enough.'

In the country as a whole invasion fever was running high. Block-houses were built at strategic points, tank barriers created and traps laid. Rivers were dredged and the sides revetted. Fearing an airborne landing, the authorities insisted that all large fields were obstructed by rows of implements which were later replaced by poles, cut down and dug in by local casual labour. If enemy aircraft or gliders landed, these obstructions were intended to cause them to crash, or at least to prevent them from taking off again for another load.

Daily the wireless broadcast a whole batch of new restrictions and regulations. Sadly, the ringing of church bells was prohibited, except as an alarm in the event of an invasion. Government ministers made frequent appeals for courage, fortitude, patience, economy and, of course, service. One of the most far-reaching of these was made by the immaculate Secretary for War, Anthony Eden, when he called for volunteers for a part-time force to be known as Local Defence Volunteers.

Meg told Bob of this one lunchtime, for in this dramatic period news bulletins were read every hour of the day. Bob was not very interested.

'Farmers have got plenty to do already,' he observed. 'Certainly I have; running this place and the War-Ag. work as well as overseeing the land which we're farming as a committee. It fills my time, so I don't want to be playing at soldiers. Might be a good thing for the men, though, and certainly the lads under military age – give 'em quite a grounding. They want weapons as well you say? We'll lend 'em our shotguns – two out of the three, anyway. I'd better keep one – we might not see 'em again.'

'Will you tell the chaps, if they volunteer they're to give their names to the village constable? They'll be notified when they're required.'

'Yes, I'll do that, Meg. I daresay a bit of morale-building will do no harm, although I don't think our chaps need it. They're all feeling pleased about this grand weather. I will say, Meg, this first summer of the war could hardly be better from a farming point of view. Hot and sunny with a wet day now and again; plenty of grass for silage and hay, and the right conditions to get it. Thank goodness the chaps don't mind working overtime.'

Later in the week Bob came home about ten o'clock, sticky and sweating after an evening at silage-making. Meg was laying the table for supper.

'Major Ratcliffe's been on the phone twice, asking for you. I told him you'd be in after ten, and he said he'd ring again. Don't bother to call him, Bob.'

'I'm not going to! Too hungry and thirsty! What have we got for supper?'

'There's cold fowl and ham, plenty of fresh salad, gooseberry pie and all the tea you can drink.'

'Lead me to it!'

'You'll miss these harvest meals when you're in the army, Glad,' the farmer said conversationally as he attacked his heaped plate.

The young woman's lip trembled and she coloured slightly as she answered, 'If I make my bed uncomfortable, I've got to lie on it and put up with it, Mr Felton.'

Before Bob could reply the phone rang and he left the table with a sigh of disgust.

'Good evening, Felton. I've caught you at last!'

'Yes, I have a farm to run, Major, and this is a busy time.'

'Of course, it is so for all of us.'

'I'm just in the middle of my supper, Major, and it's nearly ten-thirty. What can I do for you?'

'You can help me form a company of LDVs.'

'The hell you say! Good God, Major Ratcliffe, don't you know I'm fully extended already? Four-hundred-acre farm, the committee's land to oversee, and the War-Ag. meetings. How can I take over any more duties? I'm sure the government doesn't expect working farmers to steal time from their farms to do weekend soldiering!'

'Ordinary farmers, no! But you're not an ordinary farmer, Felton.'

'What do you mean, man?'

'Felton, you're a man with military experience. You distinguished yourself as an officer in the last war. You cannot withhold that experience when your country needs it!'

'Country be damned! My country's had enough out of me and is doing! My son and daughter have shown a misplaced sense of loyalty in joining the colours and left me . . .'

'Come, Felton, I'm sure you have as much admiration for Arthur and Edith as everyone else has in the village. The recruiting position in this district was noticeably improved when they enlisted.'

'Maybe, but in this I can't help you, Major. I'm lame from an old wound and couldn't stand it physically.'

'Nonsense! You're as tough as ever you were. What about me? I've only one good arm!'

'Serve you right too,' Bob thought, but said aloud, 'You've got a bailiff to look after your farm. Burns is quite capable of managing the place in your absence.'

'Damn it, Felton, you've got good men too. That old Marshall has been with you since the last war, and his son has never worked anywhere else, I believe. Your farm is in good hands whether you are there or not!'

With a sense of frustration Felton found himself running out of arguments. He tried the political angle.

'The whole thing is a lot of damned nonsense, Major Ratcliffe. There's not going to be an invasion! This is just a confidence trick, dreamed up by Churchill, no doubt, to make the people think that things are worse than they are. Germany's held off attacking us over the last nine months for a reason – she thinks there is a chance of getting us to talk terms. She's not going to ruin her chances by launching a full-scale invasion which could not succeed as long as we have a navy. And if there was an attack on our coasts, do the authorities think a few armed civilians could make any impression on the crack assault troops of the German army? They'd die like rabbits in the harvest field!'

'Hell, I'm not arguing politics with you, Felton. Of course what you say is correct, but it is unwise to say it too forcefully. I must say it comes strange from you, who have done so much for your country, past and present. I agree the LDV would be insignificant if it came to real action, but they can replace fully trained troops for guard duties. As you say, it is largely morale-boosting, but the powers have decided to use this method and it's up to everyone with special knowledge to ensure its success. You and I have that knowledge.'

'What exactly do you want of me?'

'I want you to be platoon officer for Hartnall, at least until things are running smoothly. You have a gift for organisation, Felton.'

'Running smoothly? Fat chance of getting away from this sort of spider's web! What's your place in this?'

'I shall be Company Commander.'

'My God, I never thought I'd live to take orders from you, Major Ratcliffe.'

'In emergencies personal differences must be put aside. You won't be the only man in the Forces who dislikes his superior officer. There are many others – about a couple of million, I should say.'

'Very well, if I can't get out of it.'

'Good man! Now, I want you to be at my house, in uniform, at 7.30 - 19.30hrs – rather tomorrow night – to meet the other platoon officers and draw up a schedule of action. I want this company to be the finest in the division, perhaps the . . .'

'Do you mind if I go back to my salad, Major,' Bob said and put down the receiver.

Chapter 16

The following evening Robert Felton dutifully retrieved his 1919 uniform from the moth-ball wrappings and attended the conference at Home Farm. He said little to Meg when he returned, brushing off her enquiries with irritation. Thereafter he attended parades at the Commemoration Hall on Sunday mornings and two evenings of each week, lecturing, supervising basic training and planning programmes of more intensive training at other centres, all in co-operation with his Company Commander. He was invited to conferences of senior officers, contriving the strategy for local defence, selecting provisional sites for block-houses and tank barriers. All the Oakleigh men joined the unit and chortled among themselves to see the gaffer in his narrow, antiquated uniform 'like somebody out of a bloomin' owd film'.

Within a few weeks the first uniforms arrived and were accepted with hilarity. The outfit resembled a voluminous boiler-suit which the LDV was expected to slip on over his ordinary working clothes if called out during the day-time. The effect was so ridiculous that Bob refused to wear his own, preferring to stick to his quaint-looking breeches and tunic of the Great War. Later, it transpired that the bulky denims were merely provisional issue designed in haste to enable the civilian army to fulfil the requirements of the Geneva Convention.

At the end of the summer proper serge battle-dress was issued, and Bob felt a mild thrill when he saw Meg sewing on his official status symbols. From then on his replies to her enquiries became less irritable but he always complained bitterly about the waste of farming-time. Meg began to take this with scepticism.

'Go on with you, Bob, you like it really only you won't admit it. Taking you back to old times on the Western Front, isn't it?'

'I don't like it at all, Meg. You make me cross when you say that! It's just that if I'm doing a job – any job – I like to do it as well as I can, and this lark's no exception.'

'You've always been like that, haven't you? I remember Dad saying it of you when you'd only been here a few days. But it seems to me you're putting your heart and soul into this.'

'If a thing's worth doing at all, it's worth doing well! The reason I seem to be putting my heart and soul into it, as you say, is this damned Mortimer Ratcliffe. He pushes me into everything, hauls me off to every conference whether I want to go or not, asks my advice on everything and frequently accepts it. I wonder the other platoon commanders don't get jealous.'

'He must think a lot of you. I'm sure his respect for you dates back to the time when you knocked him flying in Vestry Field in 1911.'

'Whenever our eyes meet I ask myself if he is thinking about that scrimmage. I always thought he bore me a grudge about that and about later happenings.'

'I'm sure he did Bob, but there's a war on now and I suppose he thinks he is setting a good example by forgetting all old scores. People of his class regard duty to their country as sacred, don't they?'

'It's a sort of feudal attitude Meg, and I should be sorry to see it die out completely. In wartime farmers have to struggle with conflicting loyalties, to their profession and to the state. This has been a grand summer, Meg, and often we've left the harvesting to keep to LDV arrangements. If the weather had been changeable I just wouldn't have done it! The war would have had to take second place.'

'What do you really think of the war prospects, Bob?'

'We can't possibly win, Meg. I should have thought that was obvious. How can a small island muster a large enough army and build up sufficient war material, which has to be brought by sea, to defeat a whole continent. It's just ludicrous! But being an island, we can't lose either. Our forces are good enough to ward off any attack by land, sea and air. So you see it's bound to end in stalemate, when we'll have to talk terms. So why not start talking now?'

'You say we can't lose, Bob? What about the submarines?'

'They can make it very difficult, I agree. But we shall simply keep building or buying more merchant ships in such numbers that the U-boats just can't sink 'em all. And if the ships sail in convoy, that is, huge groups surrounded by destroyers, they're relatively safe. A U-boat which attacks a convoy rarely escapes, I understand.'

'But if what you say is right, Bob, surely the government must know it.'

'Of course they do. But the government is led by Churchill who's doing his damnedest to get America in on our side. He is half American, you know. He'll use every trick, fair or foul, to get them in. You know the LDV is to be named the Home Guard?'

'I think I remember reading it in the paper.'

'That's another of Churchill's ploys to ingratiate himself with American sentiment. There was a Home Guard in the American Civil War, you know, when all the crippled old men and the bigger schoolboys on the Southern side turned out to defend their homes against the Yankee invaders.'

'What will happen if America does come in?'

'I don't know! Certainly the two sides would be more evenly balanced so it might go on for ever, or until the present leaders of all the countries are dead. Of course, America has more resources than Germany really, but they would have to be brought across thousands of miles of ocean which cancels out some of their superiority.'

'You make it sound dreary and hopeless, Bob. Perhaps Russia could chip in and help us.'

'Not very likely. Hitler's seen to that with his friendship pact of last year. Not that we want help from Communists. They're worse than the Nazis!'

'What about those underground movements in the conquered countries? Mightn't they help enough to tip the balance in our favour?'

'I don't think so, Meg. It's a horrible way of making war anyway – stabbing some poor soldier in the back who's just doing his duty as ordered. These fanatics are only bringing misery and death to themselves and harsher conditions for everyone round about, without making much impact on the war as a whole. Of course, our authorities are encouraging them as much as they can, as it's not our people's lives that are involved.'

'It would be hateful if we had that sort of thing here.'

'Don't think of it, Meg. But I hope we'd have more sense. If a country's defeated in war it's much better to accept the position with dignity, at first anyway, than to take part in murder, sabotage and destruction, which can only harm one's friends. I'm against all that.'

'I hope it's not treason to talk like this,' Meg said in belated alarm.

Bob grinned.

'Not in this house, love. But one can be diligent in one's duty in fighting a war without swallowing all the rubbish they put out. Truth is war's first casualty!'

'I'm not sure what that means. But what a good thing it is that the best way we can help is by producing as much food as we can. It's what we like doing anyway, and in wartime most people are doing things they don't like.'

'As always, you've hit the nail on the head, my dear, and I'm sorry that my LDV – sorry, Home Guard – duties prevent me from devoting even more time to food production.'

'You're doing well enough at both, seems to me.'

'Maybe, but one's make-believe and the other's real work, and profitable. Everything we can produce can be sold at a fair price which is quite a change from some years. We've had good crops too, so the Almighty's on our side.'

'How do you know the crops in Europe have not been good too. Perhaps the Almighty is neutral in this.'

'Now who's talking treason?'

Oakleigh Farm had certainly never been so productive as in 1940. The same number of cows had been maintained on a reduced acreage of grass for some of the permanent pasture had been ploughed for grain crops, while more of the older arable had been planted with extra acres of potatoes, carrots and onions for which there was an insatiable demand. An extra field of sugar-beet, for which the farm staff showed their lack of enthusiasm by referring to it caustically as 'bugger-beet', was also included in the drive for more food.

By judicious grazing of winter corn, sugar-beet tops and other residues, the flock of ewes had been maintained at its normal number and the lambs fed to heavier weights. The pig unit at Clayfields, under the control of a new man, Ron Bailey, assisted by two land girls, May and Julia, had now grown to a forty-sow unit producing about 700 heavy porkers a year. Half of the food requirements were met with kitchen waste from Service camps, collected by Ron who was allotted an old lorry for the job, and the other half with home-grown vegetables and grain screenings.

According to the regulations, the kitchen swill had to be steamed or boiled for a set time and for this Felton had installed the most modern equipment he could get. The smell was not pleasant unless you lived with it as did Ron and his two girls. It was offensive and cloying and its very heat caused the fumes to penetrate deeply into one's system. Bob and Meg kept away from Clayhills as much as possible and so did the other farm men unless work demanded their presence. It was said that at feeding-time the noise could be heard at Hartnall, two miles away and Meg remarked that it was a pity Oakleigh was only halfway to the village. Bob replied, 'Keeping hundreds of pigs on swill is not my idea of pleasant farming, but it's a necessary wartime chore and it pays well. But when the war finishes, the pigs finish too, I promise.'

Because of his proven standing as a modern and successful farmer, Robert Felton was expected by the War Agricultural Committee to act as host to experiments and demonstrations, designed to educate backward farmers into adopting new methods to increase production. Silage-making, at which Bob was now an acknowledged expert, was followed by the effect of deep and shallow ploughing on the same crop; fields of grass and grain were dressed with fertiliser in strips of heavy and light application; row-widths and plant-count per acre of root-crops; the pig farm was inspected and applauded and other innovations of management were analysed and discussed. At first, when these meetings attracted only a handful of onlookers, Meg supplied them with afternoon tea, but when the attendance swelled to over a hundred she reluctantly gave it up. 'The tea and sugar ration won't run to supplying half the farmers of Derbyshire,' she commented.

In addition, as a member of the committee, Bob was expected to take over and farm various parcels of land from which the owner had been dispossessed because of failure to comply with notices served on him. Plots of land acquired by speculators for future building development, untouched for a year or two, were in such a state of dereliction as to be a reproach to a country at war. Since they could not be farmed by an absentee owner with no farming interests, they were usually handed over to the nearest committee-member. Oakleigh Farm absorbed several of these as did Major Ratcliffe's Home Farm.

Robert Felton's biggest prize, or worry, according to the point of view, was the acquisition of two hundred acres of parkland about three miles from Oakleigh on the higher ground. This belonged to a retired business man named Lowe who lived in a splendid house known as Hankley Hall, at the top of the park. For years the grassland had been used only for the summer grazing of a few dozen ornamental cattle.

This large area of under-grazed amenity land attracted the attention of the committee in the first autumn of the war and the owner was ordered to plough it up and sow to corn for the 1940 harvest. Mr Lowe emphatically declined and suggested a tenant be found who would deal with the land as the war effort demanded. The lease was offered to Robert Felton who accepted it, reluctantly at first as he considered himself already fully extended. However his staff and his tractors proved equal to the task and by working long hours each evening and on Sundays, the whole area was ploughed, cultivated and sown by the end of April.

Bob said to Meg, 'I never expected to do field work with tractors on Sundays. I wonder what your father would think of it.'

'I think he would have said, "Better the day, better the deed". He was always ready to adapt, Bob. Of course, we didn't work on Sundays in the last war. We only used horses then and they needed their day of rest. These tractors don't recognise Sunday and they don't get tired.'

Mr Lowe regarded the long avenues of tiny green spears with mixed feelings.

'It looks very smart now, Mr Felton, I must agree. But what about these large areas which you've had to leave round each tree, unploughable I take it, because of roots and shading. By the time the corn is harvested these patches of grass will be long and rank and the whole effect will be deplorable. Can't you do something about it?'

Bob thought for a moment. He was always willing to co-operate if possible.

'All I can do, Mr Lowe, is this. When the corn is carried and in stack, I will fence off the ricks and turn in some cattle to graze off the stubble, the corners and under the trees. They can stay there until nearly all the Park is ploughed again. That will tidy the place up for you.'

'If you do that, Mr Felton, I'll be delighted and I won't charge you any rent. I'd love to see cattle here, if only for a short time.'

Bob decided it would be good business to fall in with the wishes of his rich landlord.

With such a large acreage of cereals, Felton decided he would need his own threshing machine. There would be a total of forty or fifty days' threshing and to rely on a contractor who had many other customers was altogether too tenuous. Normal farming operations were multiplied many times by the war and new machinery was difficult to obtain. Although the demand was great, manufacturers were concentrating, no doubt by government decree, on armaments and their components. The small number of new tractors and heavy implements coming forward were allocated by the War-Ag. Machinery Committee to the farmer most likely to make the fullest use of each machine.

Felton, as an important member of the Committee, had no doubt that the new thresher would be allocated to him if he applied for it. He declined to do this, for string-pulling did not appeal to him. He planned to visit farm sales in arable districts to search for the right machine. The need for implements of any kind was so great that the auction prices soared much higher than the cost of new articles. The government quickly issued an order controlling the price of secondhand machinery at the current level of new equipment. At an auction there would often be a dozen clamouring bidders when the controlled price was reached. Expectant buyers were then asked by the auctioneer to enter a raffle, the prize being the privilege of buying the article at the maximum price allowed. The proceeds from the sale of the tickets were given to the Red Cross and everyone involved was relatively happy.

Robert Felton was lucky at his third attempt and thus purchased a twenty-year-old thresher for the price of a new one. He was also fortunate enough to secure another rubber-tyred tractor at the same sale and by the same means. He had them despatched by rail to Willington station where they arrived a week later. Dick and Len accompanied him to the station and inspected the new acquisitions with dubious interest. Dick remarked dolefully, 'It's all very well having our own drum, Gaffer, but when you hire one from a contractor he comes in the yard with three or four men. I don't see how we're going to have men enough to work this and do all the other jobs as well.'

He reckoned without the organising ability of his employer. August and September were hot and sunny throughout and once started, the harvest went through with scarcely a halt. The three miles to Hankley Park was too long a journey for the horses every day, so Felton concentrated all his tractor power on that land. He decided to thresh the whole crop direct from the stook, so the new machine and the old iron-wheeled tractor to drive it was sent over in advance. Dick and Len, with two land girls who were passable drivers, took tractors and trailers. These had been constructed at odd times, when no overtime nor LDV duties clashed, by Dick, Len and sometimes Gerald, using old lorry chassis as a base. At Hankley, Bob arranged through the Committee Labour Office for a continuing daily supply of volunteer soldiers. Half-a-dozen of them helped Dick and Len operate the thresher, and four others went out with each of two trailers, which were wider, longer and lower than the mophreys. On these they built a semblance of loads which were brought in alternately by the girl drivers. Every day, merchants' lorries arrived for the threshed grain. Occasionally the whole outfit paused for a day while a later plot was cut with the binder. The work took five weeks to complete. There were no Home Guard hindrances, for Bob had told his senior officers very forcibly that the unprecedented harvest must take priority.

At Oakleigh Farm, Bill and Gerald, with a team of six land girls from the hostel and the part-time help of Alf and Ron, secured another two hundred acres of corn with the horses, stacking the sheaves in barns and ricks, Bill Marshall reluctantly acting as stacker when Bob was not there. Pearson, a local thatcher, made the stacks weather proof almost as soon as they were built, as he had done since Ernie Wagstaff had grown too old for ladderwork.

The harvest seemed endless. The dirt, the heat and the magnitude of the task affected everybody and tempers were short. Two or three times Arthur, now a corporal, and Edith appeared and pitched in to help, rather shamefacedly. Meg supplied drinks and refreshments ad lib for the Oakleigh gang who frequently worked near the farmstead. This caused resentment among the people working at Hankley. Meg would have been prepared to cycle there every afternoon with drink and food, but with fourteen soldiers and four members of the farm staff, the load would have been impossibly heavy. Mrs Long and Mrs Edwards worked valiantly cutting sandwiches and making pastry and cakes. Meg now had Sylvia Howard living in the house – the result of an advertisement for a Forces wife. Sylvia was twenty-seven and had recently married a captain in a tank regiment, since despatched to the Middle East. They had no home of their own and Sylvia did not wish to remain with her own family or with her crowded in-laws so she was delighted to accept the offer of a room of her own – a double bedroom which could be shared by her husband when on leave – in a rich farmhouse. She attempted all the farm activities enthusiastically and could drive a car although she did not possess one. When the non-provision of harvest meals at Hankley approached a crisis, Mrs Howard reminded Meg of her driving ability. Every afternoon for the rest of the harvest, she drove Meg over in Edith's car, loaded with cans of tea, bottles of lemonade, bread, butter, jam, lettuce, eggs and tomatoes, apple tarts and fruit cakes. By this time, extra harvest rations on a set scale were issued to farmers for their employees, otherwise Meg could not have catered for such a large number of helpers.

By the middle of September, when in the south-east the Battle of Britain was at a crucial stage, the cereal harvest was finished. At Oakleigh, all the barns were full and numerous stacks had been thatched for winter threshing, while at Hankley the straw ricks were covered in and fenced round for possible use or sale later. To the delight of Mr Lowe, forty handsome Scottish-bred bullocks were acting as scavengers in his beloved park. The farm staff had earned much larger sums of overtime than ever before and the Oakleigh Farm bank balance had never looked so healthy.

'I suppose we can resume Home Guard attendance now,' Felton told his men complacently on the last day when all the equipment was brought home. 'Mind you, there's still plenty to be done. Next week we start on the potatoes and sugar-beet, then later the carrots, mangolds and swedes, but we shan't need to work evenings, so it will be all right for you to attend parades. In fact, I shall expect you to.'

The men were too well-mannered to voice their real thoughts but Meg who was present had no such inhibitions. However, she forebore to comment until they went into the kitchen.

'That's a nice way to talk to your men, Bob Felton. They limp in here, sweating and grimy and nearly out on their feet after six of the most gruelling weeks of their lives and you calmly tell them to start Home Guarding again at once. If I'd been one of them, you'd have had the length of my tongue!'

Bob grinned.

'They're too well-mannered to do that. In any case, privates are not allowed to answer back their superior officers. It's an offence.'

'On parade, perhaps. But not on the farm!'

'Oh, yes. The regulations clearly state that a Home Guard officer retains his rank even at his civilian job. Otherwise the rankers would be taking the mickey out of their officer as soon as he was out of uniform.'

'Well, I don't know! You officers and bosses have it all your own way in wartime don't you? Good thing the chaps don't take you too seriously. Still, I think jokes are out of place when they've worked so hard and kept it up through such a long harvest. They deserve a bonus, Bob.'

'I daresay they'll get one when we have the harvest supper. What do you suggest we give them? Two weeks wages?'

'What are they getting now? Forty-eight bob a week, isn't it?'

'It is, plus their overtime of course which is one-and-three an hour. By gum! Farm chaps'll soon be paying income tax!'

'Twice forty-eight is ninety-six shillings. Make it up to a fiver for them.'

'If you say so, Meg. Nobody gives us a bonus though!'

He was wrong. After the Home Guard parade a few evenings later, he returned to Oakleigh with a resigned smile on his face.

'Why are you looking like that, Bob?' Meg said as he strode in. 'Have they given you an honourable discharge?'

'No such luck! They've promoted me to Captain, damn them, and made me Company Commander. That means more work, more application, more time away from the farm!'

'Oh dear. Why on earth have they done that to you?'

'That blasted Mortimer's behind it. He just won't leave me alone. All the time pushing me to the forefront, where I don't want to be.'

'I'm sorry Bob, when you've got so much to do,' Meg said formally.

'For goodness' sake, Mrs Felton, don't humour him,' burst out Mrs Howard who was having supper with them. 'He ought to be downright pleased he's been promoted! Anybody else would be. You farmers seem to do things by opposites!'

Chapter 17

As the harvest ended the Feltons were surprised and disappointed to hear from Arthur, now a sergeant, that he was on his way by sea to an unknown destination.

'The Middle East for a certainty,' Bob muttered when they received the flimsy air mail letter-card. 'That's where the next flare-up's going to be. We can't get at the Jerries but we may pick up some easy successes among the Italians in North Africa. But I'm afraid we shan't see Arthur again until the end of the war.'

'Don't be so blooming pessimistic, Mr Felton,' Sylvia Howard said. 'My husband's out there too you know, and I certainly hope I'll see him!'

'Not very likely, Mrs Howard. They don't run cheap holiday return tickets in wartime, especially halfway round the world.'

'We must just grin and bear it,' Meg said sadly.

'Don't be too down-hearted, Mrs Felton. If we can't see them we can wish them well. Arthur's a sergeant now, isn't he? Perhaps he'll get more promotion and come back an officer. Perhaps Reg'll get promotion too. I hope so, it'll mean more money at this end. I wonder if they'll run into each other? Splendid if they did, wouldn't it?' She rattled on, refusing to be depressed by Robert's tactless remark.

A few days later Edith paid one of her evening calls. She also was subdued about Arthur's departure for it clashed with her own bad news. She announced it as casually as she could.

'No more of these snatched visits, I'm afraid, Mum. At least, not for a while.'

Her mother's heart felt very heavy inside her and she did not reply.

'I'm being posted to Ripon tomorrow, so this is good-bye for a while.'

'Keep in touch, dear,' was all her mother could say. 'Write every day if you feel like it. We shan't mind.'

'That's the understatement of the whole war,' grumbled Bob, who had just come downstairs in his Home Guard uniform. 'First Arthur and now you. Your mother and I will be Darby and Joan while we're still young enough to be Jack and Jill.'

'It was bound to happen, sooner or later,' protested Edith. 'You didn't think I'd spend the war within ten miles of Derby, surely?'

'I hoped you would, dear,' admitted Meg.

'Oh, Mummy!' Edith kissed her. 'Ripon's not so far away, really. I'll be able to come home whenever I get forty-eight hours' leave. But I must be off now. I only came to let you know and to say good-bye. I'll send you a wire as soon as I arrive.'

Meg smiled in spite of her disappointment.

'I don't know why you don't phone. I'm getting quite used to the sight of the telegraph boy.'

Bob drove off to his Home Guard parade, taking Edith with him to catch the bus. Mrs Howard alighted from the same bus and returned to find Meg crying softly to herself in the kitchen.

'Don't upset yourself Mrs Felton. I saw Edith as I got off the bus and she told me the news. She was quite excited. Don't you think you're spoiling it for her if you take on so? I'm sorry you're losing her, but I'll try and make up for both of them.'

'It's kind of you to say that, Sylvia. I suppose it is selfish of me to cry, really. It's young wives like you, separated from their husbands, who have the most to put up with. Although when I come to think of it, I suffered that, too, in the last war.'

'One can get used to anything it seems,' Sylvia Howard said resignedly.

Robert Felton's Home Guard promotion did not in any way reduce his obligations to the County War-Ag. The committee meetings seemed to make heavier demands on his time, for agriculture was being regulated and regimented as never before in its history. The war had entered a new phase. It was now generally accepted that the struggle must go on for a long time – perhaps three or four years. Plans which had been rapidly improvised in the early months were now being properly shaped and consolidated. Every wartime innovation had a feeling of permanency. What had begun as hastily thought-out ideas for increased production became firm rules and any deviations might earn black marks from the committee which was becoming more and more powerful. Although labour was not plentiful, farmers were expected to employ a full staff, carefully worked out by the Labour Committee according to the number of cows or other stock, acres of grass or acres of arable, so that standards should not fall. Farms and farmers were graded as to condition, fertility and management ability. Those in the top grade giving maximum production were invariably farmed by such men as Robert Felton who, in addition to giving their time to committee work, were setting an example to their less able contemporaries.

There were several intermediate grades. Those second from the lowest grade were generally small farmers who, through lack of knowledge, equipment or capital were not farming productively. They were placed under supervision, given a plan to work to and were visited frequently by selected members of the War-Ag. to see that the programme was carried out. The lowest grade of all consisted of those unfortunate members of the profession who, through old age, infirmity, lack of money, lack of knowledge or just stubbornness, were considered to be beyond redemption and ultimately dispossessed of their land so that an abler farmer could take over.

Such drastic action was not taken without long and earnest discussions by the full committee. There was much heart-searching among the older members who were uneasy at the thought of taking away a fellow-farmer's living. All the committee members were mature men, but Robert Felton and Mortimer Ratcliffe were at the younger end of the scale and were sometimes looked on as juniors. In fact, as experienced and progressive farmers they were more inclined to take a detached view of each case than the older members.

One old man was proving particularly recalcitrant. For forty years he had rented an eighty-acre grass farm but latterly, recently widowed and with both his daughters living in their own distant homes, he had allowed his farm to become so dilapidated as to be an eyesore to the district and a reproach to the efforts of the War-Ag. Robert Felton, putting sentiment out of his mind, was for taking the farm over without further delay. The older members were more cautious.

'It's all very well for you, Mr Felton,' said one senior member. 'You've been right on the ball all your life as far as I can hear. Allus full of new ideas and wi' the skill and energy to carry 'em out . . .'

'Here, here,' interrupted Major Ratcliffe.

'. . . but you're a bit impatient wi' owder men who think and act more slowly. Owd Woodcock now he's had a fair bit o' bad luck – his wife had such a long illness before she died. It's left him a bit muddled and we ought to sympathise with him a bit more.'

'Sure, sympathy's all right in its place,' agreed Bob who had made several visits to the farm over the previous few months, 'but he's not going to improve is he? He kept half-a-dozen cows last summer, gave away most of his hay crop to the man who got the rest of it in for him. How old is he? Seventy five? Too old to start again. He's going to get worse instead of better.'

'And in the meantime young Taylor is waiting to move in

164

there.' Major Ratcliffe pointed out. 'We've let him the farm and must see that he's able to take over, however distasteful it may be.'

'No problem about the land surely?' another elderly member said hesitantly. 'Taylor just goes in and farms it, takes over Woodcock's cows at valuation, or keeps 'em for payment until the old man takes 'em elsewhere.'

'It's the house,' someone else said. 'It wouldn't be pleasant for Taylor, working the land and using the buildings while the dispossessed tenant is still in the house which is next door to the cowshed and controls the cooling-place.'

'He's been told times enough he must give up the house,' Bob insisted. 'Taylor is getting married and needs it. After all, we let him the farm complete with farmhouse and must comply with our side of the bargain, even if it means eviction!'

Some of the farmers stirred uneasily at this forthright statement. There was silence for a minute until Major Ratcliffe spoke.

'We cannot let this matter hover, gentlemen. I suggest we write to Woodcock giving him a further fourteen days to vacate the house. If he still refuses, we put in motion the eviction procedures.'

The chairman proposed this as an official motion and it was agreed by a small majority on a show of hands.

Robert Felton was worried about his involvement in the unsavoury affair and confided his fears to Meg as they walked back from church Sunday evening a little later. This was their most relaxed period each week, for unless harvest work was particularly pressing, they attended evensong and strolled back at a leisurely pace.

'What's it all about, Bob? Who is this farmer?'

'An old man – seventy-five, they say he is – of White Hill Farm, Broughton. You wouldn't know it. We've never had occasion to go out that way. It's about ten miles from here on the road to nowhere. His wife was very ill for a long time and he let the place go to rack and ruin while he looked after her.'

'That's not unusual, surely, and it's not a crime!'

'It's not acceptable in wartime, Meg. He should have arranged for somebody else to look after things. Now there's a new tenant due to go in and Woodcock won't give up the house, so he's got to be evicted.'

'Oh no Bob! Surely not! Can't they leave him there to finish his life out?'

'There's a war on Meg, and everybody's got to obey the rules.

We can't make exceptions!'

'You're not personally involved, though, only as a member of the committee?'

'I am involved, damn them! The committee decided that one of our members should be present, just to show that we don't shirk our duties, I suppose. Then I'm hanged if one member didn't propose that either Major Ratcliffe or Captain Felton – that was a smirk – should undertake it as we were the youngest and most progressive men on the committee. Of course, when it was put to the vote it was carried unanimously. They were all anxious to get out of it.'

'Well, of all the nerve!'

'Yes, Ratcliffe and I tossed and he won!'

'Does that mean you've got to oversee this disgraceful affair?'

'If it comes to that, I'm afraid it does.'

'Don't go, Bob. Let them do their own dirty work!'

'One can't flinch from duty just like that, Meg. I'd look an awful coward.' Bob dared not tell his wife that he was one of the main instigators of this ultimate sanction.

A few weeks later a letter was received from the secretary of the War Agricultural Committee, informing him that the police were ready to evict the aged Mr Woodcock and would Mr Felton be on the spot by 10 am on a certain date.

Silently Bob showed it to his wife.

'I'm coming too,' Meg said at once.

'The devil you are!'

'I most certainly am! It needs somebody to look after that poor old man's interests.'

On the appointed day they set off together after breakfast. They crossed over the A38 at Willington, then later over the A50 into the deep villages near the Staffordshire border. A hard cinder-track between the two high hedges led to the farmyard, on the far side of which stood the ivy-covered small house. Two police cars blocked half the width of the lane and Bob pulled in behind them. A police inspector walked up to them, before they had time to alight.

'Good morning sir. May I have your name?'

'I'm Robert Felton. This is my wife.'

The inspector touched his cap.

'Good morning, madam. I was informed you were coming sir, but I wasn't expecting any ladies. I'm Inspector Ball, and this is Sergeant Haines. We have four constables as you can see.'

'Quite a show of force. Are you expecting any trouble?'

166

'Well sir, our information is that Woodcock might be a little queer in the head. We don't want to take any chances.'

'Have you seen anything of him?'

'There have been movements in the house and he's there alone. The three windows facing us are, from right to left, scullery, kitchen, sitting-room, and I fancy he's prowling from one to the other.'

'He's not dangerous, is he?'

'I don't know sir. He's almost certainly got a gun. A great man for rabbiting until the last year or two, so the local constable says.'

As he spoke, the unmistakable roar of a Bentley could be heard coming along the road, dropping to a healthy mutter as it pulled in behind the Felton's car. Major Ratcliffe, complete in Home Guard uniform, got out.

Meg bristled.

'Good morning, Major Ratcliffe. Have you dropped in to see the fun?'

'Good morning, Margaret. That is not very kind. Good morning, Felton, Inspector. Has anything happened?'

'Not yet sir. We're just going to hail him.'

A constable brought him a loud-hailer. Meg thought its effect disappointing. Any normal farmer could shout as loudly with his natural voice.

'Mr Woodcock! Mr Woodcock! Can you hear me?'

'Go to hell,' replied a quavering voice from the kitchen window.

'Mr Woodcock! We are police officers as you can see, and I must ask you to leave these premises as required by law.'

'Go to hell! Ah'm not leaving my home for nobody.'

'We don't want to use force, Mr Woodcock, but we shall have to do so if you don't come out peacefully.'

'Use force, will you? That's a game anybody can play. Ah've got me gun 'ere and Ah'll use it if you don't leave me alone.'

The twin barrels of a shotgun appeared over the window-sill.

The constables withdrew rapidly, the sergeant did so with less haste, but the inspector maintained his ground with the loud-hailer.

'Threatening police with firearms is a serious offence, Mr Woodcock. I advise you to put the gun down at once and come out. We don't want any bloodshed.'

'Well, you'll get it if you don't go. Ah'll blast anybody to bits as comes near this winder!'

'This is a pretty kettle of fish,' muttered Bob. 'I certainly didn't expect this!'

'Could I go and talk to him, Bob?' Meg whispered. 'I'm sure he won't shoot a woman!'

'Certainly not!' Bob and the Major said together, and Ratcliffe added, 'This is no time for heroics, Mrs Felton.'

The inspector joined them.

'Well, gentlemen, it seems we're in for a siege, possibly a long one. That is the policy. We're not going to risk lives by rushing him. Just wear him down until he falls asleep or gives up. Confound the fellow! He's brandishing that gun again.'

Major Ratcliffe raised his field glasses and gazed intently at the kitchen window.

Robert Felton groaned at the inspector's statement.

'If this goes on for more than half-an-hour, somebody from the village is bound to come along. It'll spread all over the village, the Press will soon be here and the story will be read over the whole country. That's exactly what we don't want!'

'That gun almost certainly is not loaded,' Major Ratcliffe said as he lowered his glasses after a prolonged examination. 'The barrels are filthy. Hasn't been used for some time – months, I would say. Probably hasn't any cartridges.'

'An interesting surmise, Major but who's to prove it? The fact that it hasn't been fired for some time doesn't necessarily mean that it's not loaded now. I can't allow any of my men to take the risk.'

There was a silence for a minute or two, then the Major said quietly, 'Felton, it's up to you and me!'

'What?'

'I suggest you and I walk straight up to him. If he has cartridges he can't shoot both of us.'

'By God, he can, though, if he's got one up each barrel! It'd be the riskiest thing since I was at Thiepval.'

'Bob! No! No! You mustn't!' Meg clutched her husband by the arm.

'It's our reponsibility, Felton,' pursued the Major. 'We voted for eviction and we're here to see it put into operation. I suggest we walk boldly side by side and separate when we're about thirty feet away. I'm sure he'll talk to us. We're not uniformed policemen or complete strangers.'

'Who's talking heroics now?' Meg sobbed. 'It's too dangerous! Oh Bob, please don't go! Major, you shouldn't try to persuade him!'

'My estimate of the position is that he will not shoot, and I'm prepared to back my judgement. I'm not doing this rashly. I have

168

a young family at home, as you well know.'

'I cannot allow this, gentlemen,' said the Inspector fussily. It was just the nudge that Bob needed.

'We are not under your command, Inspector. I'll go with you, Major.'

The Inspector bit his lip and remained silent. Two wealthy farmers, and one of them a Major, over-awed him slightly.

'Bob, *please!*' Meg sobbed.

Her husband ignored her, took his walking stick out of the car and moved off in the direction of the cottage.

'Coming along Major?' he said as casually as he could.

They walked abreast across the grass-tufted stone yard.

'Mr Woodcock!' Bob called grimly. 'We're farmers, not policemen and we want to talk to you, but not with a twelve-bore pointing at us.'

'Don't come no closer then. Ah know who you are. Ah've sin you both i' Derby market and Ah seen one on this farm a few times but Ah conna remember the name. But stay wheer you are. Ah dunna want to 'urt nobody.'

The two farmers kept walking, slowly but calmly. Felton went to the left of the window, Ratcliffe to the right.

'Steady on, Woodcock,' said the Major. 'We're not going to rush you. We merely want to talk!'

They reached the wall of the house. The shotgun still wavered between them. Major Ratcliffe started speaking again, soothing the old man who turned his head towards the speaker. Felton's hand darted across, seized the barrel well down near the stock and wrenched it from Woodcock's bony fingers. He heard the trigger click, but there was no resulting explosion. Bob broke the gun open and showed the empty barrel to his companion.

'I told you so,' grinned the Major. 'Now, Mr Woodcock, come outside and we'll talk about things.'

The old man shuffled away from the window and emerged through the cooling shed at the end of the house, moving very slowly. He was unshaven, thin and bent and his hands trembled.

Meg ran across to him.

'I'm afraid you've had a rough time, old fellow. Come and sit in the car awhile.'

She led him away and put him in the back seat. The inspector came up.

'Madam, I'm afraid I must arrest this man and charge him with obstructing the police in the execution of their duty and threatening them with firearms.'

'Nonsense, Inspector. I'm taking him home with me so he can have a clean-up, a meal and a good rest. You can come and see him tomorrow morning if you like, or the day after at Oakleigh Farm, Hartnall. The gun wasn't loaded, you know!'

'It's very irregular, Mrs Felton. I agree he is very shaky and I am sure you will look after him. I don't know what my super will say!'

'What is the position about his household furniture?'

'The court bailiff will be here shortly with a couple of furniture porters. They will remove all the things and place them outside. Their duty ends there!'

'What, leave them out here in the yard with no one to keep an eye on them. Mr Woodcock hasn't any relations near. What if it rains?'

'Well, that is the usual procedure. Generally the neighbours turn to and help. Here there are none.' He paused a moment. 'I daresay in this case the stuff could be stacked in the outbuildings. Here in this shed, which has been used as a garage at some time. Ah, here is the bailiff.'

A stout elderly man wearing a trilby hat manoeuvred himself out of the driving seat of his small car, followed by two lesser men carrying aprons. The large man raised his hat to Meg who said rather haughtily, 'You are in charge of the proceedings now, I take it?'

'That's so, ma'am.'

'I would like Mr Woodcock's furniture loaded straight into a removal van and delivered to my farm at Hartnall. It's ridiculous to leave it outside at the mercy of the weather, and thieves too, I daresay. Can you do that?'

'*I* can't, madam, my instructions are to clear the premises. But my assistants are removal men from a Derby firm. Perhaps they can get a vehicle. What about it, Jack? Can you get a van here to pick up this stuff at once?'

'Not likely,' said the senior of the two porters who had now removed their jackets and put on their aprons. 'We're pretty busy. All the vans are out to-day. To-morrow, mebbe. I dunno. We may be booked up.'

'We must clear the premises,' said the bailiff and looked to the inspector for confirmation.

'Dunna bother yoursen, Missis,' called the old man from the car. 'It's wuth nowt, so it'll 'a to take its chance.'

'Nothing of the sort!' said Meg sharply.

A youngish man appeared from nowhere. Hatless and

170

jacketless, wearing cord breeches and hob-nailed boots.

'Can I be of any help?' he asked, addressing the group.

Robert Felton recognised him as the new tenant of White Hill Farm.

'Who are you?' Meg asked. 'Another of the vultures?'

'Vultures be damned, Mrs Whoever-you-are,' the man said, colouring deeply. 'My name's Taylor and Ah'm the incoming tenant. I applied for this tenancy when it were advertised, and got it, all genuine and above board. Th' outgoing tenant's nowt to do wi' me really, but Ah'm willin' to help in ony way Ah can.'

Meg gave him one of her charming smiles.

'When do you propose to move in, Mr Taylor?'

'Not for a wik at least. My young lady wants to clean it all through.'

'Can Mr Woodcock's things stay there until a van can bring them to my home?'

'Surely, Missis. It won't be more than a day or two, I reckon.'

The bailiff and the inspector huddled together for a few minutes and then announced that the position was that Mr Taylor had taken possession and was storing Mr Woodcock's furniture until it could be removed. The law was satisfied and the court bailiff was satisfied.

'We seem to have been eclipsed by your wife, Felton,' said Major Ratcliffe when the police and the others had left the farm.

'It's always as well to let the women have their way in these things, Major.' Bob said with a grin as he got in his car. Meg was about to voice her indignation when Mr Woodcock's quavering voice broke in.

'You folks is bein' reight good to me. Ah dunt know why. Ah've done nowt for you.'

Arriving at Oakleigh, Mrs Felton showed her protégé into the bathroom. The old farmer seemed confused.

'Well, Ah don't know! We niver 'ad a bathroom at White Hill . . .'

'That's all right Mr Woodcock. I'm sure you haven't forgotten how to have a bath, but first I'll show you to a bedroom you can use and give you some of my husband's or son's clothes to wear while yours are laundered. You haven't been looking after yourself much lately, have you? Then you can come down and have a good dinner with us and this afternoon I'll telephone your daughters if you'll give me their numbers.'

'Could I . . . could I borrow a razor, Missis?'

'Of course. There's an old one of Arthur's on the top shelf of the bathroom cupboard.'

Later, washed, shaved, in clean clothes and having eaten an enormous and tasty lunch, Stanley Woodcock became contrite.

'Ah'm sorry for causing all the trouble Ah did . . .' he began slowly but Meg interrupted him.

'That's enough of that, Mr Woodcock. That's all over, except perhaps for some formalities with the police. You're a guest in this house and you don't have to make excuses for yourself. This afternoon you can go to bed and sleep if you like – the bed is aired – or you can wander around the farm. I'll try and get in touch with your daughters.'

Mrs Felton spent some of the afternoon and part of the evening trying to contact her guest's two married daughters, one in Lancashire and the other in Suffolk. She succeeded at last but to her utter indignation neither of them wanted to accept any responsibility for their father.

'We went to Mum's funeral and spent some time there, squaring things up for him. He should have been all right from then on and would have been if he'd pulled himself together. I certainly can't have him up here. Get the Council to give him an almshouse or something. Thanks for what you've done, but you didn't have to, you know.'

Later, the other daughter who had obviously been advised of the situation by her sister, reacted in exactly the same way. Meg was sick with anger and disgust, but worried as to her next move.

During the evening Major Ratcliffe telephoned. Meg explained her problem to him and asked him to use his influence to get Mr Woodcock the tenancy of the next available almshouse. The next morning the Major rang again.

'Ah, Margaret! I think I have the solution to this problem.'

'Thank God, Major. Of course he's all right here for a week or two . . .'

'I don't think that will be necessary. There will be an almshouse shortly – No 5, which is occupied by a widower with a terminal illness. But those cottages, standing in that narrow alley and overshadowed by taller buildings, are not ideal for a retired farmer who's spent all his life in his own farmyard.

'I have a cottage at Dower Farm – practically in the yard itself, occupied by a widow of a former stockman, Baldock – you may remember him. She has the cottage rent free as a sort of pension from the estate, and she is willing, in fact anxious, to take this old chap as a lodger, both for the company and the cash. He will draw the old age pension of course, and I have no doubt that when he has disposed of his cows and horse, his implements and furniture, he will have a few hundred in addition to any cash he may have saved. I think he should be able to pay Mrs Baldock the twenty-five shillings a week I have arranged, and he can live there and enjoy all the activity of the farm around him.'

'Thank you, Major. You're an angel – in this case,' she added hastily.

'Thanks for the afterthought,' he said and rang off.

Chapter 18

'Are you pleased with yourself?' Bob asked Meg a few days later when Woodcock had left for his new home. They lent him the pony and float to take his essential belongings which he had rummaged out from his furniture which was now stored in the Oakleigh barn. He looked proud and happy as he drove the lively horse away, for it was a much smarter outfit than he had ever possessed on his own farm.

'I did what I thought I had to,' she said shortly. 'We couldn't leave him stranded there looking like a ship-wrecked Robinson Crusoe!'

'Just one more casualty of the war, Meg. We can't avoid some of them you know.'

'No need to treat them with brutality, though.'

'Nobody could accuse you of being brutal, Meg. At least, not in this village. Why, you spend half your time carting stuff to the sick and the drop-outs.'

'Well Bob, we've got so much and they've got so little.'

'We shan't have so much if you give it all away.'

'Oh, shut up, Bob! I can't see you ever being poor.'

'Farmers always do well in wartime, Meg, as you should know from the last war. It can't be otherwise with everybody needing food which can't be shipped from abroad any more.'

'Damn the war, I say. How's it going, Bob? You were right about the Italians in North Africa. We seem to be wiping the floor with 'em. Is it the beginning of the end?'

'It certainly isn't that. The Italians don't count for much. But Germany's getting stronger.'

'That's why they're able to do all this bombing, I suppose?'

'Yes, but plenty of places have had it worse than Derby!'

'I know that, Bob. Look at Coventry! I heard yesterday that Phyl Cope's hotel had been utterly wrecked and she and all the staff and guests – over seventy of 'em – had to be dug out of the cellars from the back end!'

'She's not on the stage now, then?'

'Oh no! She gave that up at the start of the war. Going in for a career in the hotel business and is – or was – a trainee waitress.'

'I daresay she'll soon be a trainee something else!'

'Funny you should say that! Phyl's so mad at being bombed

she's told her mother she's going to join the WRAF to get her own back on Hitler.'

'Good for her! They'll need all the volunteers they can get!'

'There's no end in sight yet, then?'

'No, Meg! At the War-Ag. we are told to assume the war will go on indefinitely. All we can do is to keep on farming at full throttle.'

More milk, more meat, more grain, more vegetables, more flax for parachutes, more sugar-beet, more wheat for bread, more barley for beer, that was the continuing pattern and it all added up to more work. No slacking, no time off, for newer techniques were producing heavier crops which took longer to gather. The Women's Land Army was now well organised for supplying gang labour, but there seemed fewer soldiers available. Possibly they were training for a more important and dangerous task.

The early summer of 1941 brought the surprising and not unwelcome news that Germany had invaded Russia and the harvest started with a background of daily reports of the German armies pushing deeper and deeper into Russia, but further and further away from Britain. Most people took a little comfort from this, but it meant that the war might go on even longer because of it.

The 1941 harvest was a re-run of the previous year in quantity but, lacking the genial weather of 1940, it was tiresome and frustrating. There were frequent stops for rain and the sun was never very hot. Sheaves frequently had to be turned and re-stooked for the rain was persistent enough to soak well into the straw. Felton followed the same plan as before – hired gangs harvested Hankley Park with tractor power while the regular staff cleared the sheaves of the Oakleigh fields with horses.

It was a long drawn-out process lasting until the second week in October, which meant a late start to the potatoes and sugar-beet. This was no longer contemptuously referred to as 'bugger-beet' for this muddy and arduous job had been assigned to visiting Irishmen, rough in appearance but rapid in execution. They took on both fields at a fixed sum, leaving the farm staff free to concentrate carting the crop off the field and to harvest the potatoes. November was well advanced before all the root crops were cleared and the last days were muddy and unpleasant. The sowing of winter wheat took them into December. The war news took a dramatic turn. America and Japan joined the struggle as antagonists. The war, like a hideous octopus was spreading its tentacles over the whole world and the initial Japanese successes were frightening. The end of the war looked further off than ever.

Robert Felton was worried about his inability to get his harvest in within a reasonable time and confided his problem to Meg who was already aware of it.

'I don't like this late finish Meg. It looks incompetent. We're badly overstretched.'

'It's been a bad year, Bob. Isn't everybody late – some with far less to do than us.'

'True enough, but I don't reckon to class myself with the tail-enders. I prefer to set an example of efficiency.'

'You can't do it all in the same time if they keep pushing more land on to you. Well over six hundred acres, now isn't it?'

'Yes, but one can't refuse it. Would be a negation of responsibility.'

'You'll think of something, Bob! If you can't, then no one in the country can.'

'Well, I'm certainly not likely to lose faith in myself while you're around. We make a good team, Meg.'

He reached over, gripped her hand and pulled her towards him.

'If you two are going to play lovebirds, I'm going out,' Sylvia Howard said firmly. 'That is, when I've cleared the table.'

They all smiled but Bob's soon faded and he continued, 'We've got to think out a new system, Meg. Stream-line operations a bit. Things are changing – the whole concept of farming is becoming different.'

'Where are you going to start then?' Meg prompted, hoping to stimulate his imagination.

'To begin with, I don't think we can do any more binder harvesting at Hankley Park. It's too slow at that distance and the absence of some of my best men for weeks makes harvesting slower still at home, here. So next harvest I think I'll hire a combine-harvester for Hankley, arrange for the merchants to collect the grain every day, and if it needs drying, they'll have to provide the facilities. There are a few grain-drying plants around. Not very near to us, though.'

'What about the straw? Loose straw'll take some handling, won't it?'

'That is a problem. We don't need it ourselves – there's enough here at Oakleigh for our requirements. We've always got a bit of the previous year's still left when we start harvesting.'

'I suppose you can't burn it in the swath?'

'Too risky with the blackout restrictions. I'd look a right mug to my fellow-members of the committee if I got prosecuted for having fires at night. Besides, it'd seem like waste to the public, and

176

there'd be too much to plough in.'

'Couldn't you give some of it away?'

'That's an idea. As soon as the combine starts I'll offer it to any local farmer who likes to take it. That'd get rid of some of it. Then send a couple of hay sweeps, an elevator and a stacking gang and make ricks of it. That'll be the tidiest way, even if they don't get used.'

'Couldn't you hire one of those big wire balers the thresher man used to bring sometimes? Sweep the straw to it and bale it. You might be able to sell the bales.'

'Possibly, but hiring the baler, the engine and two men would cost as much as the bales would fetch. I s'pose I could buy an old baler, but I wouldn't have much use for it – unless I put it behind our threshing drum and baled everything. That's another idea worth considering.'

'Things are changing too fast, Bob. This isn't the sort of farming we grew up with.'

'Machinery is taking over and must do to keep up with the pace of today. Horses and waggons are finished I'm afraid, or soon will be. The rubber-tyred tractor and trailer is so much quicker. We shall still use the binder here at Oakleigh for several years yet – we get better straw that way and its easier to handle. But we'll pick up the sheaves with trailers. The old mophreys won't be needed any more and as I hate to see old wrecks about, I'll have 'em broken up. The front carriages, that is. Of course, the carts will come in handy, for years yet, for tipping work.'

'Oh no Bob, please!'

'What on earth's wrong, Meg?'

'The mophreys – don't break them up. Not all of them anyway. Whenever I see one rumbling by I think of those lovely endless summers when I was a little girl. We always used to climb in the empty mophreys when they went back to the field. Happy, happy days! Besides, Arthur and Edith did the same when they were small, you remember?'

'I didn't know you were so sentimental, Meg.'

'How about you then? Arthur told me how you blew him up when he wanted to grub out the willow copse.'

'You're not supposed to remember what happened there!'

'Well, I do!'

'I only did it to please you!'

'That's a good 'un,' Meg dug him sharply in the ribs. 'But there is another thing you can do to please me.'

'And what's that, pray?'

'Just keep one mophrey intact, Bob. Put it in the shed round the back so I can go and look at it now and again and think back to the time when you first came here!'

'You wouldn't like me to build a glass case round it?'

He fended her off as she tried to dig him in the ribs again.

Bob was thinking ahead and another summer went by. It was the summer of 1942 when the fortunes of Britain seemed at their lowest ebb. A small German force sent to North Africa to prop up the toppling Italians proved so effective that the Eighth Army was chased back to the Egyptian border. The harvesting weather was marginally better than the previous year and due to Bob's reorganisation the corn harvest was completed in September, the potatoes in October and the sugar-beet lifting was well-advanced. The British armies in the Middle East also advanced, rolling the enemy away from the frontiers of Egypt, an operation which went on, slowly but remorselessly, across the whole of North Africa.

At Oakleigh, the wheat was all drilled and the beet carted off the field by the end of November, and there was a break in the urgency of the farm work for a few days. Bob told Meg of his intention to complete a few tidying-up operations. After breakfast she was surprised to see Gerald drive Prince out of the yard, hitched to one of the mophreys. He was away all the morning and brought the horse back without the vehicle. She supposed that Bob was putting his mechanisation-of-transport idea into effect at last and he had sold this conveyance. She remembered her request of last year and shrugged. There were three more mophreys in the rickyard; she must remind him of her girlish whim. However, more pressing things than fantasies occupy the mind of a busy farmer's wife, even on a December afternoon, and the subject passed from her thoughts.

On the last Friday before Christmas when she and Bob returned from their usual weekly visit to Derby, her husband said casually as he drove into the yard, 'There's something I want to show you before we go in.'

'Can't we have a cup of tea first?'

'Better not. I might forget.'

They walked to the far end of the rickyard, round behind the barn to the shed where all the out-of-season implements were kept. In the most distant bay, among the permanent cobwebs, a mophrey glistened, newly painted in its original colours. The cart-body had been painted in the usual beige or stone colour, the wheels, undercarriage, shafts and raves were a bright farm-yard red. On the offside front corner of the cart-body, a square black metal plate bore, in bold white lettering, the legend 'A.S.A. Ratcliffe, Oakleigh Farm, Hartnall, Derby'.

'Oh Bob, what have you done?'

'Well, you said you wanted me to keep back a mophrey and I wouldn't want my sheds desecrated with a wreck, so I had the old thing repaired and repainted. She's good for another forty years.'

'Longer than us, I daresay. And you've had Dad's name put on in the old way. Bob, it was sweet of you and I'm so touched. What a lovely Christmas present!'

'It isn't quite Christmas yet. I may have something else for you next week. This is just an extra. I know you'll like it, but don't go making love to it, because there's a little trapdoor up there which opens from the stable, and I wouldn't want the waggoners to see you making a fool of yourself!'

'I knew that little door there years before you did my lad! Pity we can't have it round the front,' Meg said thoughtfully as they walked away.

Bob smacked her bottom playfully.

'I wish all our problems could be solved as easily,' he said.

1943 was a better year altogether; a dry spring for sowing, a warm, damp growing season and adequate weather for the increasingly large harvest. The war news was now coloured by dramatic events daily. From North Africa, then Sicily, Italy, Burma, the Pacific islands, and of course Russia, came stories of victories or defeats according to the way the reader interpreted the facts. The propagandists firmly believed that exaggerating victories and minimising defeats was necessary for morale. But even allowing for that, it was obvious that the enemy was being hit hard and at last the tide had turned in favour of Britain and her American and Russian allies. But the greater the pressure on shipping and materials to prosecute the ever-extending war, the greater the need to produce more from our own soil. The pressure on farmers never slackened. Although the newspapers could work themselves into hysterics about victories, real, possible and unlikely, and hint that the end of the war was not too distant, farmers were bombarded by directives and exhortations urging them to use less fuel, less labour and grow more food. It was now suggested that the shortage of imported food would continue, even after hostilities had ceased, possibly for years. Stocks were low and would get lower still, for ships were needed to move the vast armies which were in preparation. They could not be spared to import luxuries, or even necessities. The Home Guard were still needed to protect vital points against possible saboteurs, for even fewer regular troops could be spared for this humdrum task. The word invasion was never mentioned now – not of England. But talk of the invasion of the continent was beginning and communists daubed idiotic slogans untidily on walls and bridges: 'Second Front Now' as if it were only a case of a few soldiers each packing a kit-bag.

Meg read the papers without discrimination.

'When's it going to end Bob?' she would ask after reading a journalist's account of a particularly thrilling victory, in which the size, scope and impact were cleverly masked.

'This year, next year, sometime, never!' Bob replied grimly.

Meg was sadder than she allowed even her husband to know. The absence of her children gnawed at her like a cancerous pain. Edith was now serving in the Middle East – they thought Cyprus. She had been promoted to Sergeant, which delighted her parents. She still sent her weekly cablegram and Meg was always mystified by it, as letters also arrived regularly. Edith had perfected a miniature style of writing to get as much as possible on the single square sheet of the airgraph letter which seemed to Meg to have been photographed and reduced in size.

When Edith had been posted abroad, she and her parents fondly hoped that she would meet her brother. But by the time she reached her destination Arthur was in the Far East. He had now been commissioned and was proud of it. So was his mother.

'He's catching you up, Bob,' she said proudly when the news arrived, swallowing her feeling of sadness at the thought of the enormous distances which now separated them.

Arthur's letters were filled with enquiries about the farm, plans for the future and comparisions between Oakleigh and the peasant-type agriculture in the lands where he fought. War-weary and occasionally homesick, he referred to 'the green-and-gold fields beside the Trent, the rippling corn crops on the fertile arable, the straight potato-ridges bursting open with tubers, the friendly shorthorns cudding in the Rickyard Close on Sunday afternoon, and the farm horses, standing with calm dignity in the shade of the trees on their day of rest'. 'Not so many of those now,' Meg said to herself. It was easy to see where Arthur's heart lay. How long before he could see the English countryside again? How long before his mother could see him?

After receiving a letter from one of her children Meg liked to steal away and shed a few private tears, but Sylvia Howard discovered her and roundly condemned such a luxury.

'As long as I'm here you're not going to give way like that, Mrs

Felton. *I* don't and you're not going to. You must forget about Edith and Arthur being away and concentrate on those who are still here.'

Sylvia meant well, but that remark was unfair, for Meg Felton spent all her spare time helping others with advice, comfort and materials. She frequently took gifts of food to the wives of the Oakleigh men and to any service wives she knew of, for she felt it strengthened her ties with her own children.

1943 moved into 1944 and the huge build-up of troops and war material was obvious to anybody in the southern half of England and even further afield. At Oakleigh, the spring crops were sown and the sugar-beet showed strong and green in the drills, when the invasion of Normandy – the long-heralded D-Day – actually took place.

The popular papers displayed massive headlines, huge military maps plastered with curved black arrows, purporting to show the depth and direction of the Allied thrusts. To add to the general confusion, other American armies landed at various points in the south of France.

Throughout the rest of the summer, in spite of the optimistic and confusing maps and the conflicting reports of victories and set-backs (there were no defeats to refer to any more) it was clear that the German armies were being forced back, slowly, stubbornly, but relentlessly, clear of the soil of France, back to the defences of their own country. In December the enemy made a lightning advance in the region of the Ardennes. The conditions were dark and snowy, the Allies were not expecting a battle in such weather and their total air supremacy could not be exploited. A few days of panic among the Allied armies, then the weather cleared, the advancing Germans ran out of fuel, Allied aircraft took to the air in their thousands and the last German push of the 1939-45 war was over. There were other set-backs and delaying actions here and there where, as Bob said to Meg, our local commanders became too ambitious or too impatient, but the tide of war rolled relentlessly to and over the Rhine. On 8 May, when the mangolds were being drilled at Oakleigh and the last row of potatoes was planted, the remnants of the German army surrendered to General Montgomery and the war in Europe was over.

Much to Robert Felton's relief, the Home Guard had been disbanded the previous December. Although diligent in its services, he had always begrudged the time involved as he begrudged any time spent away from farming. Now he hoped to be at home more, perhaps take things easier, although the War-

Ag. Committee work showed no signs of slackening.

Meg seldom left the village other than on the weekly market day, but many afternoons she trudged round Hartnall distributing her gifts. Less often she drove the pony and trap, for some of the calls resulted in lengthy conversations and the pony could become restive. Hitching-places were not common in village streets in 1945. Meg took a maternal interest in the wives and families of the farm men and expected, sometimes demanded, that all domestic problems be brought to her for solution.

She had heartily wished that her son and daughter had been engaged in the European theatre of war, for the German surrender might then have heralded their early return home, at least on leave. But Arthur, now a Major, was deeply involved in the Far East (Burma, Bob feared) and Edith, now happy in her new rank as Captain, had been posted to India. So Meg kept a brave face on her village tours and publicly showed natural pride in the achievements of her family. Inwardly, she was sad and uneasy that many more months must pass before she could touch them again. She took care not to harp on this, for although she knew her husband was fully sympathetic, she was unwilling to face the sharp remonstrance of her outspoken housekeeper.

The summer of 1945 dripped on its dismal way. The root crops and the weeds grew rapidly and so did the hay fields. The hot sunny periods were few and far between and the thick rows had to be moved many times before they could be finally ricked, often brown or grey in colour. There was little green hay made that year, but somehow it did not seem to matter so much for, although the Japanese were still fighting tenaciously, the war in Europe was over and somehow even farming seemed temporarily less important.

Chapter 19

The sunless summer delayed the start of the harvest and August arrived before any corn had been cut. The combine harvester was always later in starting, of course, as the grain needed to be fully ripe when cut, but at Oakleigh Bob still persisted with the binder and thresher as the handiest methods of handling both grain and straw. The first few days of August were dry and bright but very little of the corn was ready.

Most of the staff was busily engaged in carting manure from the yards on to the leys due for ploughing, while some of the land girls were hoeing through the mangolds for the last time. Both groups were discussing the terrible effects of the first atom bomb which had been dropped on a Japanese city. Bob decided that he would cut the first field of oats the following day, using two binders. He would ride Dick's machine. For the first time for years he felt able to allow himself to do a light, almost a leisurely job.

The next morning was bright and improved Bob's spirits. He went in to dinner in a happier frame of mind. The oats in Squarelands were just dry enough and he had left orders that the binders should be ready for an immediate afternoon start. His mind dwelt again on the possibility of buying his own combine harvester and using it for the whole of his cereal acreage. The weather was not very settled, and if it was wet his countless thousands of sheaves would need an army of helpers. If he combined everything, he would need his own drying plant, for some of the corn was bound to be damp. There was the collecting of the straw too, an untidy and time-consuming job. But it had to be done. In Derbyshire the dairy cow still reigned supreme, in spite of the reduced acreage of grassland, and straw was essential. But the cost of collecting it must not be greater than its value. He had bought a huge stationary baler which produced wire-tied bales, and the straw at Hankley Park was now swept up to this machine. But it was a slow job and the bales were very heavy. He would have to use the same method at Oakleigh. If he combined everything, he would need storage bins too. Oh dear! There seemed no end to the ramifications. He sighed a little as he entered the kitchen, thinking wistfully of the leisurely, uncomplicated harvests of pre-war years.

As usual Meg had the meal on the table, steaming hot. They

were to eat alone, for Mrs Howard had gone to spend the day in Derby, visiting her husband's relatives. Bob sat down at the table gazing at his wife with the admiration which had not diminished in over thirty years. Her golden hair had faded slightly but there was not a streak of grey visible. She wore it in a roll, modern and very becoming. Her eyes were still the same bold blue, the rosiness of her cheeks unaltered. Bob suddenly realised that with the war three parts over he would have more time to appraise his wife, to make a fuss of her and take her places.

Meg was proud of her husband too, more so than she admitted to him, but she took his admiration of herself for granted as she had done since she was sixteen. As a farmer's daughter and a farmer's wife she had always taken a keen interest in the farm and this was an asset to be added to her personal charm. She was not thinking of farming on this day, however. There had been a special announcement on the wireless since Bob had been in to breakfast and she was bursting to get the news out.

'It's all over, Bob!'

'What is?' he asked as he cut a portion of the smoking bacon.

'The war, silly. It's finished! The Japs have surrendered.'

If she expected him to jump for joy she was mistaken.

'Not much else they could do with atom bombs droppin' on 'em. A couple o' dozen would ha' wiped out the whole nation.'

'I know it's a terrible weapon, but the war itself was terrible and anything that brings it to an end must be accepted. Don't pretend you're not pleased, Bob.'

'I'm more relieved than pleased, Meg, and the relief is only just sinking in. There are wider and more frightening issues, you know. If this discovery of using atoms gets out of hand it will mean the end of civilisation.'

'Oh Bob, don't lose yourself in these obscure and far-off chances of disaster. I'm only going to think of the happiness the end of the war will bring to millions, including us. We can expect Edith and Arthur home now, you know. Don't tell me you're not excited about that!'

'Of course I am! Like to see 'em home and settled down. I want Arthur to take over the management here, or some of it.'

'And then we must decide what we can do for Edith.'

'*We* must decide? What ever we want, Edith will go her own way, the stubborn madam.'

'She can stay home as long as she likes, Bob. She's a good girl at heart, and thinks the world of us. Look how she's sent a telegram home every week since she joined the army. I'd have been quite content just to have had regular letters, but she insisted on sending wires as well. I've never known why.'

Bob knew, but had never told his wife, by Edith's expressed wish. The girl realised that in country districts in time of war, the arrival of a telegram invariably meant disaster and bereavement. By sending innocuous telegrams regularly, Edith made sure that her mother would be spared the first shock if the uniformed boy ever brought a message of death. Not many girls would have thought of it, Bob told himself, but he said aloud, 'Of course she can stay. This is her home. She doesn't have to do anything really, except find a husband. We're not poor, Meg. We've done well these last few years.'

'Out of the war, you mean?'

'Not exactly out o' the war, but mainly because of it. For the last six years it's been possible, compulsory in fact, to grow as much as we could and be certain of selling it at a fair price, and it hasn't always been so while I've been at Oakleigh. Not since the last war, in fact.'

'Well, it's grand to farm such a big place, farm it well, and to know we own so much of it. Otherwise I don't see what good all this money's going to be to us. The kids might not think that way, though.'

'We could afford a good holiday, Meg. Anywhere in the world in fact.' Bob surprised himself by the suggestion. 'Next year perhaps, when things have settled down and Arthur's back home to take over.'

'You're talking daft, Bob! What do farming people want with all that travel? Far better stay at home and look after the farm. That's all I want.'

'Oh come, Meg! We've got twenty-five or thirty years of life left to us yet and we can spend all of it on the farm if we choose. But why not a real spectacular trip first. Say, to New York or California, or a cruise to the West Indies or a visit to Capetown. Arthur and Edith have both been there you know, on the way to India. They've been to Egypt, too. We could call there, travel up the Nile and see the pyramids, call in at the Holy Land and the other biblical places. Anything you can think of, we can do.'

Meg laughed again, but not so derisively.

'You're a persuasive chap, Bob. I'm beginning to think it's not impossible. Just a once-for-all grand tour, as the Americans used to say. Like a second honeymoon!'

'A second honeymoon? When did we have the first? I left for France the day after we were married, as you should remember, and that was no honeymoon, believe me. Since then we've always been busy farming.'

'We went to see Betty several times,' she reminded him.

'That's true and it seemed quite enough at the time. But now it's different! We're rich and we don't have to keep to the same old grind.'

'The old grind hasn't been too bad, has it, Bob?'

'Our life generally, you mean?' He sat up straighter, pushed his plate away and looked full at his wife with a deep, glowing tenderness. 'No Meg, it's been as near perfect as it could be, I reckon. How could a man be otherwise than happy with a wife like you?'

Meg made a deprecating gesture, but was not displeased.

'Shut up, you old spoofer! Is there something you want from me? All right, don't grab me now, I want to get the pie out of the oven. It's the first plum pie this year, and I hope you'll enjoy it.'

'I shall enjoy it, if it's made by you.' Bob was determined to be gallant.

'Well, you've never grumbled yet, I must say. Better get on with it. I want to get cleared away and go down to the village this afternoon.'

'I'll run you down.'

'No you won't. You get on with your harvesting. It'll do me good to walk. When I saw the doctor last week he told me I should get out and about even more. It's staying in the kitchen so much that's making me put on too much weight.'

'You're just right. I like you the way you are. But if you're worried about the kitchen work, why not employ somebody to do the cooking?'

'What, somebody else running my kitchen. Not likely! Sylvia helps with some of it, of course and so does Mrs Edwards. They'd like to do more of it I daresay, but I'd rather keep it in my own hands. Where would I get anybody else, anyway?'

'What have you got on in the village this afternoon?'

'I want to see Bill Marshall's wife. She's not at all well, and might be going right down. I know the doctor's worried about her. It's a good thing Bill is fully retired now. At least he's there to look after her. And then I want to see Dick's wife, too. She's having this baby at thirty-nine after a ten-year gap and I'm a bit worried . . .'

'Why do you worry over 'em so much. You can't carry the problems of the whole village on your shoulders. It isn't necessary these days. They earn enough to look after themselves and buy anything they want!'

'Maybe, but the Ratcliffes of Oakleigh have always helped the village folk – especially our own employees – and I'm not going to be the first to stop it.'

'Well, don't overdo it.' Bob sighed for he knew the stubborn side of her character too well. 'I suppose I'd better go over to Squarelands and see how the harvesting's going.'

He walked over to his wife and kissed her fondly as he always did every time he left the house. She hugged him a little, for despite her show of nonchalance she was touched and excited at the prospect of a holiday in glamorous places.

Bob drove to the field in the Commer pick-up. Dick Marshall had already made three circuits and the long, heavy-headed sheaves lay straight and neat and close in their rows. The land girls had just arrived from the root field for the stooking. He sent Len and Frank to get the other binder going, for he intended to see that the girls were kept fully occupied, and mounted the seat of the big binder himself. It was a new seven-foot machine, driven by a power-shaft from the tractor's transmission, and travelled faster than the horse-drawn machines of his early years. It did not get tired in the evenings either, keeping up its five or six miles an hour until the last minute of a long day. Grease-points replenished twice daily eliminated oil-can stops, which were frequently used to breathe the horses. He watched the sheaves being flung out, rapidly and monotonously, round and round the field. It almost sent him to sleep. In such a level clean crop and the binder working well, it was not really necessary for him to ride the machine at all. But it was pleasant, and from his high seat he could see all that went on in the field, the other binder and the land girls setting up the sheaves – rather too leisurely, he thought. Might have to jog them up later on. With two machines they should have the whole field cut by five o'clock and the tractor-drivers could help with the stooking.

Dick swept round the corner by the field gate, the powerful tractor running smoothly and pulling the machine without noticeable effort, set into the corn again and coursed down the long field. Half-way down, some sixth sense made the farmer turn round in his seat and look back. A school-girl was running down towards them, trying to catch up, waving and shouting as she ran. A pin-point of sound must have pricked his subconscious. It was Dick's youngest girl. Her mother must be in trouble. He struck heavily with his stick on the metal shield of the binder deck. The dull clang momentarily drowned the even beat of the engine. Dick stood on his clutch instantly and Bob nearly pitched headfirst on to the binder-reel.

'What's up, Gaffer?'

'Your girl, Dick. Mavis must've come to her time.'

Dick paled and frowned, then scrambled out of the tractor seat and ran with long springy strides up the field, past the binder, to meet his daughter.

'What's up, Shirley? Is your mother . . .?'

She ran past him.

'It's not you, Dad. It's the Gaffer. Mr Felton, Mr Felton!'

She reached the machine and stood with heaving breast and flushed face, her long dark curls settling down over her shoulders. Surprised, Bob jumped to the ground as the girl recovered her breath.

'What is it, Shirley? Why . . .?'

'It's Mrs Felton, sir. 'Er's took bad and fell down in our garden!'

'Well, it's nice of you to come running so hard to tell me, Shirley. But it can't be serious. Mrs Felton was as right as rain at dinnertime.'

'Mum sent me to the Post Office for 'em to phone the doctor and the amb'lance, and said I was to come on and tell you.' She burst into tears. ''Er's real bad, 'er is. Real bad!'

'All right, Shirley. Don't cry. I'll get along and see your mother. Will you ride back with me?'

'Mum said I was to stay i' the field, Mr Felton.'

'Very well, but keep with the other girls and don't go near the tractors when they're moving. Carry on, Dick. I don't suppose I'll be back.'

'Mrs Felton's real bad,' the girl sobbed again as he turned away.

The farmer walked to the top of the field as fast as his lameness would allow. He was concerned at Shirley Marshall's genuine distress. Of course, there could be nothing wrong with Meg – she was as strong and healthy as a cart mare. Just a fainting fit, he supposed, but he would go and see Dick's wife first and find out exactly what had happened.

He stopped the pick-up outside the cottage gate, and Mrs Marshall, heavily pregnant, appeared at once, framed in the front doorway. As he walked down the brick path Bob noticed the devastation in the flower-bed – the crushed montbretia, flattened michaelmas daisies and deep footprints in the soft red earth.

The woman had obviously been crying. He looked at her with sympathy and friendliness, recalling that as a school-leaver she had come to Oakleigh to be nursemaid to Edith, then housemaid to them all until she had left to marry Dick and make a home with him in this new cottage he had built for them at Hilltop Farm.

'Tell me what happened, Mavis.'

'The Missis come to see me about an hour since, to talk about me new baby – kind as 'er allus were, as 'er allus has been, to us and to iverybody i' the village. We talked and 'er made suggestions, like, and told me about the things 'er'd help with. 'Er said as 'er'd see if Dick could bring the pick-up 'ome ivery night, so it'd be there if 'e'd to go for the doctor, sudden like. 'Er sat there 'alf-an-hour chatting, then when 'er got up to go, 'er said, "Don't worry, Mavis. We'll see that you're all right." 'Er stepped outside the door, sir, put 'er 'and up to 'er 'ead, swayed once, then just dropped down on the garden. I couldn't move 'er, Mr Felton, so I put a cushion under 'er 'ead, covered 'er with a quilt and sent Shirley to the 'phone. Then the amb'lance come, but there were no movement, sir! God 'elp us, Mr Felton, I think the missis 'as gone!'

She started sobbing, brokenly, her huge form trembling with emotion. Bob was shaken, but tried hard not to show it.

'Keep calm, Mavis. Don't upset yourself. It can't be as bad as you think. Mrs Felton was full of life at dinnertime. We were talking of having a long holiday!'

'Ar – 'er towd me that, sir. 'Er seemed to be getting a bit excited about it. P'raps it was too much for 'er. Maybe it's not as bad as I thought, but they've taken 'er to the Uttoxeter Road Hospital. Let me know, please Gaffer, as soon as you can find out!'

Felton thought quickly. The hospital was eight or nine miles away; it covered a large area, and he was unfamiliar with the lay-out. It would be better to go home and telephone. He drove to Oakleigh, more disturbed than he was prepared to admit, even to himself. Disdaining the office, he strode through Meg's silent kitchen, through to the hall and the telephone. He asked the girl at the exchange to get him the hospital, for he was too impatient to look for the number himself.

'Can I help you?' said a considerate female voice.

'I am enquiring about a Mrs Felton, who has probably just arrived at Casualty. How is she, please?'

'Who is making the enquiry?' asked the telephone.

'This is her husband, Robert Felton.'

'Hold on, please.'

He sat there, drumming with his right hand on the little oak table. His mind was blank until he realised he was trembling violently. He shook himself back to normal. This wouldn't do! Then he heard, over the wire, the clip-clip of approaching shoes, the scraping sound as the telephone was picked up from the desk.

'Are you there, Mr Felton?' The voice was formal, but full of calculated sympathy. 'I'm sorry to have to tell you that Mrs Felton died before reaching hospital.'

Chapter 20

The terrible finality did not strike Bob immediately, and in a detached way he started on the essentials. First of all, he rang Betty at her home in Stokenchurch. Her husband and twin sons were away at the war, that he knew, but there was a daughter, Caroline. Fortunately she was staying with school friends and Betty was free at once. Yes, of course she would come early and organise the social arrangements for him. He telephoned the local undertaker and late the following evening Meg Felton rested in her oak coffin in her own parlour as her little brother, her mother and her father had done before her.

Bob cabled Edith in India and Arthur in Burma, but knew they could not attend. The war was over but its exigencies and disciplines remained. He gave general instructions about the harvesting, walking or driving absentmindedly from field to field. Dick Marshall was his senior hand – a sort of foreman – and would not let the farm down, for all his working life had been spent at Oakleigh and he served the Feltons as loyally as he had served the Ratcliffes.

The loquacious Sylvia Howard was struck silent by the news. She prepared all the meals adequately and, with the daily woman, kept the house clean, otherwise she kept right out of Mr Felton's way. For all her outspokenness, she knew better than to intrude on private grief.

On the evening that Meg was brought home Bob was hovering between the kitchen and the sitting-room, for he could not keep away from the loveliness of his wife in repose, when Bill Marshall passed the window and knocked at the kitchen door. He removed his cap politely as he entered at the farmer's invitation.

'Ah see the Missis 'as come 'ome, Gaffer. Could I – could I just see 'er a minute?'

Bob hesitated. He felt somehow that he wanted to keep Meg to himself for the short time remaining.

'It's more'n twenty-eight year sin' Ah come 'ere, Gaffer. 'Er were the finest young woman in all the world, and Ah were reight fond on 'er. 'Er's bin that good to me and mine, Ah wish Ah could say good-bye, like.'

His employer led the way into the front room. The old man looked down at the dead woman, then turned away, head down and shoulders twitching.

'It's not reight,' he muttered brokenly. ''Er's more'n twenty years younger'n me – in the prime o' life.' He swallowed a lump in his throat and shuffled slowly out of the room. 'There's another thing, Gaffer,' he continued uneasily as they paused on the way to the kitchen door. 'The other farm lads asked me to put it to you. All o' the same mind, we were. Could we – could we tek the' missis to church oursens?'

Bob's eyes softened.

'You mean a waggon funeral? That's a tender thought, Bill, and I'm touched by it. Well, why not? Meg would have liked the idea.'

'Ar, Gaffer. Ah thowt we'd tek 'er on th' last mophrey. Th' missis was pleased as a nipper wi' a new toy when you had that painted up and set away for 'er. 'Er used to come down there, now and then, and admire it, 'er eyes shinin' that soft . . .'

'Don't Bill, please!'

'It'd be fittin' to use it, Gaffer. We'll put boards across the cart-body so 'er'll ride level. And can Ah drive the 'osses, Gaffer?'

'No, Bill. Gerald's the waggoner now, and he'll have to drive. It's his job.' Marshall's face fell. 'Tell you what, Bill. Put old Boxer on in front o' the other two and you can lead him. We'll go the long way round, through the village.'

'Can I 'elp carry 'er then, Gaffer?'

'No, Bill. You're over seventy and Mrs Felton's become a heavyweight just lately. It's a job for the younger men. Dick and Len, Gerald and Alf will be the bearers – if they're willing. You do the organising – I don't feel able to tackle it. Go and see Mountford, tell him what we want to do and he can arrange his part o' the supervision. Two-thirty on Saturday is the time.'

The following evening there was a great cleaning-up of harness in the Oakleigh stable, with metal polish, saddle-soap and neatsfoot oil. Gerald commented on it.

'Niver sin so much activity i' this stable i' my time, an' Ah wish we 'adn't to do it now.'

'These 'osses've niver pulled such a valuable load afore,' remarked Bill who had come in to help with the sombre preparations. 'Ah reckon Meg Felton were just about the kindest woman that iver lived.'

Betty Salt had arrived the day after Meg's death. She came prepared to sympathise with and comfort her brother but when she felt the emptiness of the kitchen and recalled the happy years they had all shared in that homely room she was herself crushed by a deep sense of melancholy.

'Oh, Bob dear,' she whispered to her brother. 'It's cruel, it's just too cruel. How can you take it so calmly?'

Bob could only shake his head. So far, Meg's absence struck him only when he entered the kitchen, for in his thirty-four years at the farm she had never been out of that room for more than a few hours at a time. As long as she lay in the next room he still felt her presence.

'I'll leave it all to you, Betty. Everyone who comes will want a meal of course, but I don't want 'em here or even to make conversation with 'em. What do you suggest? The cost doesn't matter.'

'That's all right, Bob. Leave it to me. I'll have a meal laid on in the Commemoration Hall. None of them will want to stay the night, anyway. They'll all want to get back to their harvesting.'

'How about yours?'

'The foreman has it all in hand. I don't play much part in the day-to-day organisation now. The horses and my committee work keep me occupied.'

On Saturday morning, Robert Felton watched as if in a dream as Mountford and his assistant vigorously screwed down the coffin lid. It was just a job to them, he thought. Flowers had arrived as if from nowhere – great and small wreaths and crosses with little messages, some tender, some pathetic, some distressing, some comforting, but all touching a chord in someone. The smart mophrey, resplendent in its unblemished paint, was drawn by the three nonchalant horses to the garden gate in the Front Croft. The four stalwart farm workers, in their Sunday suits and black shoes, shuffled uneasily into the drawing-room and shouldered the heavy coffin under the instructions of the undertaker. Their faces were white and grim. Dick in particular bit his lip hard to choke back his emotion, for he had worked for Meg's family since the age of fourteen and memories threatened to drown him.

Walking slowly with their unfamiliar burden they edged out of the front door of the house where Meg had been born. She passed, unknowing, through her garden for the last time. Wreaths were placed neatly on the coffin and stacked on the front platform of the vehicle. Then the three horses in single file paced a wide circle as they turned their load to head for the drive. The mophrey rocked slightly as the iron-tyred wheels left the grass and grated on the hard surface of the drive, angling the shallow ruts until falling into line behind the extended horses. In the lead, Bill Marshall's thin white hair bent to the gentle breeze which stirred the flowers on

193

the jolting vehicle.

Robert Felton thought of the many times he had passed along that rutted drive, starting as a boy of sixteen with the milk float. Every time Meg had been there, at the end of the homeward run. Now he was taking her away, away from Oakleigh forever. This time he would return without her. Could he bear it? The very thought unnerved him and he stumbled. Betty gripped him firmly and put out her other hand to grasp the hay-raves on the rear of the mophrey. Behind the brother and sister followed an unending line of relatives from far and wide, employees and their families, parish officials, villagers and farmers, each and all paying homage to the beloved mistress of Oakleigh.

The cortège reached the high road and turned right towards the village. The wheels rolled more easily on the gritty surface and the flowers settled down to a steady tremble. On the edge of the road a tall spare figure was waiting, a major's crown on his Home Guard uniform. He saluted smartly, then fell in behind the relatives. The village mourners respectfully made way for Mortimer Ratcliffe, the son of their former squire. Bob was not surprised to see him, though he had fought this man for Meg's honour while both were still in their teens.

On their left, the cattle in the River Fields, surprised and curious, raced alongside the hedge. At the corner of the field, when they could follow no longer, they put their heads over the hedge and bawled in frustrated wonder.

The horses plodded on, steadily, indifferently, nearer and nearer to the point of final farewell. They reached the outlying cottages where women and small children stood at their front gates, sadly attentive. Behind them, drawn curtains mutely honoured the dead. One little girl held up a tiny bunch of wild flowers – late honeysuckle and poppies – as if wondering how to present them. She broke away from her mother's restraining arm, trotted alongside the mophrey for a few yards, then threw her posy high in the air towards the coffin. Her aim was true, for it ledged momentarily on the outside of a wreath, then dropped off gently to disappear in the body of the cart. The child stood still and waved her hand high.

'Good-bye, Mrs Felton,' she shrilled.

Her mother ran up to her and shook her in admonition.

'But she was such a lovely lady, Mummy, every time she came to see us at school,' protested the child.

At the lychgate Bob stood and shivered as his workmen lifted their mistress' coffin from the hay-wain. Betty tried to comfort him, for had he not comforted her when he had led her through here to her wedding, twenty-three years before? The bearers plodded slowly towards the church, cautiously, deliberately, for there must be no error, no stumble, nothing to mar Meg Felton's last visit to her church. The sad crowds filed in after them, knelt, prayed, sang the dead woman's favourite hymns and filed out again into the sun-bathed graveyard.

Meg's was the fourth in the row beside the stile. Her young brother Arthur, died 1913; Her mother, 1920 – Sam's name was on this stone, too; her father, 1939; and now Meg herself, only six years later. Bob stood among the packed silence, entirely alone with his thoughts. Incredulously, he saw his wife's coffin disappear into the depths of the rich red earth, heard the crumbs rattle on the oaken lid. 'Earth to earth, ashes to ashes, dust to dust,' the vicar intoned. Bob added to himself, 'Meg to her family.'

He could stand the well-meant, wordless but oppressive sympathy no longer. Gripping Betty's arm in farewell, he turned away from the scene, stepped over the stile and strode away across Oakleigh fields to Oakleigh Farm.

His footsteps sounded too loud in the empty kitchen, for it was silent except for the ghostly movement of the tall clock, which had ticked Meg's life away, or so it seemed. There should have been another sound – the gentle stir of burning coal in the cooking-range, but the fire was out. Apart from the occasional sweeping, he had never seen the grate dead before – not in the daytime. Already the absence of the mistress' hand was being felt. Bob sat down in the Windsor armchair, so long used by Mr Ratcliffe who had sat in it when he, Bob, had first applied for a job on that February evening in 1911. He could see them all, clearly; the burly, forthright, irascible farmer; the kind, motherly, velvet-gloved Mrs Ratcliffe; Sam the stalwart, the loyal dedicated land-lover; the affectionate exuberant young Arthur and the lovely, bossy Meg. Now all had gone and he was left alone. He, who had been a casual interloper among that tight family circle had outlived them all, and the farm, now doubled in size, was all his own. He, who had come to the farm as a runaway newspaper boy, was among the biggest farmers in South Derbyshire. But he didn't want it, he told himself. All he wanted was his Meg, his Meg, his Meg! This was her house, her kitchen. She must come back, she must! How could they part after thirty-four years without a single word of farewell?

He was only fifty. How could he face twenty, twenty-five or

even thirty years of life without Meg beside him? They had been born in the same month. Why could they not die similarly? He had no wish to struggle on. The farm, about which he had been so grandly proud was now as meaningless as a late cuckoo. There would be no joy in it, no peace, no pleasantries, no relaxation. He would simply be filling his mind and his days with routine thoughts and decisions, to keep himself from brooding over his grief, which threatened to suffocate him like an overturned load of sheaves. He just didn't want to farm any more. He didn't want to farm Oakleigh or any of the other properties. He wanted to be with his wife, his partner, his own Meg, lying together in the cool damp earth – the fertile soil which they had worked on and for during the whole of their lives together. Why couldn't this be so?

He let his gaze stray upwards to the ceiling. But of course it could be so! He had the means to hand. Two shot-guns lived permanently above the mantelpiece – Mr Ratcliffe's and Sam's. Both were superb weapons but had been little used of late, for Bob was not a keen sportsman, although an adequate shot, and of recent years Arthur had been shooting at bigger game than rabbits.

Bob toyed with this new idea, liking it more and more as he turned it over in his mind. One faint touch on the trigger and his misery, his grief and his intolerable loneliness would be over and he would be with Meg again. It would be fitting to carry it out right here in the kitchen where he and Meg had spent so many thousands of hours and which held so many other sweet memories – Arthur and Edith lisping at his knees. For a moment his mind clouded, then cleared again. His son and daughter would understand, for they knew just how much he had loved their mother.

He took down Mr Ratcliffe's gun, blew off the dust, broke open the well-oiled lock, squinted down the barrels. A little dust at the end, perhaps, but it was immaterial to his project. He reached for the cartridges from the top shelf of the cupboard, kept there from time immemorial, out of the reach of his own children, and before that, of Meg and her brothers. The thought of Sam came into his mind and he paused. Sam dying in the trenches, shot to pieces. His thoughts went back to the carnage of the Western Front, the broken bodies of his own companions swamped in their own blood. Who would be the first to find him on the kitchen floor, his head blown open and his life-blood soaking into the spaces between the shining tiles? Would it be Sylvia Howard or his own sister Betty? Could Betty stand the shock so soon after the loss of

Meg, to whom she had been closer than a sister? No! He couldn't subject either of them to such a gruesome sight. Another thought struck him. If it were obvious that he had died by his own hand they might not bury him beside his loved one. His knowledge of these matters was hazy and he would need to think again.

Robert Felton sat immoveable in the silent kitchen, staring into the empty grate, concentrating. He knew the answer would come, sooner or later. The seed of an idea germinated in his brain, grew and flowered in seconds. The Trent! The shaded, swirling waters of the river would be ideal for his plan, and fitting, too. There, in the clump of willows where he and Meg had first declared their love and where Arthur had been illicitly but so joyously conceived. He would poise himself on the very brink, lean his body over the water, grasp a willow branch with one hand and discharge his gun with the other. His body would splash into the deep water which would wash away the blood and the horror and when he was found there would be nothing which would positively prove that he had taken his own life. They would bring him back and place him beside Meg, and they would lie together, locked firmly in the Derbyshire soil for eternity.

It was a good plan and now was the time. He got up, slipped two cartridges into the breech, took one last look round the room which seemed to contain the whole of his life and turned to go, then stood petrified. As clear as a bell, piercing the prison of his subconscious, he heard Meg's voice in the old imperious tones of her younger days.

'Pull your socks up, Bob Felton! You've harvesting to do! *And* two children coming home!'

Abstractedly he unloaded the gun and returned it to its place. He could do no other, for he had always obeyed Meg in the kitchen. If she said he must stay around for their children's sake and the farm, that was what he must do. Dear, lovely, efficient, bossy Meg! Perhaps he hadn't lost her after all!

Automatically he walked over to the window, stared blankly at the familiar yard. It was the hub of the farm, the kingpin of his existence for more than two-thirds of his life. Every door, every window, every brick, every square inch of concrete could and would remind him of some incident in which Meg had taken part and he could not escape from it.

The cows slouched into the yard followed by Alf, still wearing his clean shirt and black tie. The mistress of the farm might be dead and buried, but still the cows had to be milked as though nothing had happened. Then Bob heard the flat clopping of many hooves, and the three stately Shires, with Bill and Gerald in melancholy attendance filed past the window with natural dignity. Behind them the last mophrey creaked woodenly by, rolling slowly to its final resting place.